JUSTICE REDEEMED

SCOTT PRATT

THOMAS & MERCER

Text copyright © 2015 by Scott Pratt

Published by Thomas & Mercer, Seattle

www.apub.com

Amazon, the Amazon logo, and Thomas & Mercer are trademarks of Amazon.com, Inc., or its affiliates.

ISBN-13: 9781503950542

ISBN-10: 1503950549

Cover design by Brian Zimmerman

Printed in the United States of America

JUSTICE
REDEEMED

ALSO BY SCOTT PRATT

This book, along with every book I've written and every book I'll write, is dedicated to my darling Kristy, to her unconquerable spirit and to her inspirational courage. I loved her before I was born, and I'll love her after I'm long gone.

Justice is like an abandoned child in a dark forest. She meanders slowly, in search of the light. One must hope she will eventually find her way.

PROLOGUE

I felt a surge of anger as my uncle Tommy, who would be dead in fewer than six months, shuffled in and sat down next to me in the crowded courtroom. He looked frail and pale, a shadow of the man I knew when I was very young. He'd been diagnosed with colon cancer eighteen months earlier, and the disease, along with the treatment, had taken its toll. His brown hair was thin, fine and now liberally sprinkled with gray. The fact that he was handcuffed, shackled, and wearing a gray-and-white-striped jailhouse jumpsuit was simply one final insult from the district attorney, the man who had been so instrumental in falsely convicting and imprisoning him for the past nineteen years. Ben Clancy, the district attorney, and Joe DuBose, the sheriff of Knox County, Tennessee, had accused Tommy Royston of murdering his wife—my aunt Linda—and had conned a jury into agreeing with them. Tommy had then been sentenced to life without the possibility of parole.

I looked up as Judge Clinton Waycaster began to speak. Waycaster was in his midforties, relatively young for a criminal court judge. His hair was dark brown and thinning, and a pair of reading glasses was perched on the end of his nose. He had recently replaced Judge Billy

Ray Jaworski, the man who had overseen Tommy's sham of a murder trial nearly two decades earlier. Jaworski, who had made the appellate process as difficult as possible by ruling against our legal team and for the prosecution dozens of times, had fallen ill and had retired, and Waycaster had been appointed by the governor of Tennessee to finish out his term. Waycaster was an unusual choice in the sense that he'd never served as a prosecutor. Nearly every judge I'd ever known had put in at least a couple of years at the district attorney's office, but Waycaster had spent his career handling complex civil litigation and high-profile criminal defense cases. He knew the law and he applied it equally. He showed no favoritism to the district attorney's office, which was also unusual, at least in my limited experience.

"I've never read anything quite like this from an appellate court," Judge Waycaster said as he held up a copy of the fifty-page opinion. "It is a truly extraordinary document, and one that troubles me deeply."

Ben Clancy, the prosecutor who had put Tommy in jail and had done everything in his power to keep him there, was sitting at the prosecution table to my right, along with two of his assistants. Clancy was in his early fifties, redheaded and chubby. I loathed him. Just being in the same room with him made me nauseous. He cleared his throat and stood.

"Your Honor, if I may," Clancy said.

"You may not," the judge said. "Take your seat."

"But Your Honor, I—"

"Utter another syllable without being asked to do so and I'll have you arrested for contempt," Judge Waycaster said.

Clancy melted back into his seat as I suppressed a smile. I'd waited for this moment for a long, long time, and even though my senses were telling me it was happening, I was having some difficulty believing it.

"Mr. Street," Judge Waycaster said, and I stood. I was surprised when my thighs began to twitch slightly.

"Yes, Your Honor?"

"As you know, I've only been on this bench for two months," he said, "but I've spent a good deal of those two months going back over this case. You've done some extraordinary work here."

"Thank you, Judge," I said.

"How many hours would you estimate you've put in since Mr. King first alerted you to the problems with this case?"

The "Mr. King" he was referring to was the late Ralph King, a bourbon-guzzling assistant district attorney who had died of liver disease. Just before he died, however, he'd summoned me to his bedside and made a conscience-clearing confession about how Ben Clancy had railroaded my uncle Tommy. King knew everything about the case because he'd helped Clancy put Tommy away. I was twenty-six years old at the time, only a year out of law school, so I had convinced a veteran lawyer named Richie Fels—one of the most respected criminal defense attorneys in the state—to help me with the appeal.

"We've been fighting them for four years to get to this point," I said, "but I have no idea how many hours I've put into it. I knew I wasn't going to get paid, so I didn't keep track."

"What's your best guess?" the judge said.

"Probably between twenty-five hundred and three thousand hours," I said.

Judge Waycaster shook his head and looked over at Ben Clancy.

"Three thousand hours, just on Mr. Street's part," he said. "Then there's all the time Mr. Fels put in, plus his investigators, plus all the time you, Mr. Clancy, and your assistants and investigators have put in, plus the time spent by judges and clerks and everyone else who's been involved. And all of it for what? To falsely accuse and imprison this man for a crime he obviously did not commit. This is one of the most expensive and most egregious miscarriages of justice I've ever seen. As a matter of fact, I'm of the opinion that this case crosses the line from prosecutorial misconduct to criminal behavior. The record is replete with examples of incompetence, malfeasance, mishandling of evidence, obstruction of justice, and even perjury."

"That's enough!" Clancy bellowed from fifteen feet to my right.

I saw him spring to his feet, walk around the prosecution table, and stop ten feet in front of the judge. He stuck his chin out like a fighter at a weigh-in.

"You want to put me in jail?" he continued. "Go ahead, but I'll be damned if I'm going to sit here and listen to a man who has been on the bench for a grand total of sixty days impugn my reputation and the reputations of those in my office who serve the people of Tennessee. I'm the district attorney general. I've been elected by the people of this district twice and fully expect to be elected again next year. You're a temporary appointment with limited experience who obviously has some sort of political agenda. I've been personally involved in this case since the beginning. I knew the evidence. I tried the case in front of a jury. I secured a conviction and a life sentence and have been fighting these never-ending appeals because it is my duty to do so."

"You secured a conviction because you withheld from the defense blood evidence that was found at the scene," the judge said. "You withheld fingerprint evidence and footprint evidence. You withheld witness statements. Nothing you did in this case showed an ounce of integrity, and because of your actions, not only did this man serve nineteen years in prison for a crime he didn't commit but the real killer committed two more murders before he was finally arrested and put behind bars."

"I don't know that I care to have my integrity questioned by a man who was, until very recently, a glorified ambulance chaser," Clancy said.

Judge Waycaster had handled a lot of medical malpractice cases prior to being appointed to the bench, and Clancy was calling him an ambulance chaser. I looked over at Richie Fels and rolled my eyes. "Unbelievable," I whispered.

"I can't help but wonder how many other cases you've handled in a similar fashion," Judge Waycaster said. "But for now, since you've chosen to confront the court in such a disrespectful manner, you've earned yourself a contempt charge. Bailiffs, take Mr. Clancy to a holding cell until I can find the time to formally charge him and set his bail."

I watched in disbelief as two bailiffs approached Clancy and took him by the elbows.

"Cuff him," the judge said. "I think he should know what it feels like."

"You'll pay for this," Clancy said as the cuffs snapped shut on him and they led him out of the courtroom. "You have no idea what you're doing."

I suppressed a strong urge to applaud the judge after the door closed behind Clancy. I looked around the crowded courtroom, and it was as though everyone was in shock. Judge Waycaster picked up his gavel and made a motion like he was going to pound the table with it, but he quickly realized that nobody in the room was making a sound and gingerly set it back down. He had to have been as shocked as everyone else by what had happened.

"Mr. Royston, will you please rise?" Judge Waycaster said.

Tommy stood next to Richie and me.

"It being the judgment of the Tennessee Court of Criminal Appeals that you have been wrongly convicted and are, in fact, innocent of the charges filed against you, this court hereby honors the judgment and declares you not guilty of murder. For my part, I offer my apologies on behalf of the state of Tennessee and wish you the best in the future. Bailiff, remove Mr. Royston's handcuffs and shackles. Mr. Royston, you are free to go. You can pick up any personal belongings you have remaining at the jail at your convenience."

The judge disappeared immediately. I looked over at the prosecution table. The two young assistants who had been sitting with Clancy were hurrying through a side door. A uniformed bailiff removed Tommy's restraints and quickly walked out of the room. Suddenly, the place turned into a small carnival. Our legal team was slapping each other on the back. My mother, who had been sitting right behind us throughout the proceeding, was crying. Tommy was trying to thank me, but I couldn't concentrate on what he was saying. Reporters were pointing cameras and shouting questions.

"In the lobby," I heard Richie say over the din. "We'll take your questions in the lobby."

As the herd of people slowly made its way out of the courtroom and spilled into the large lobby, Richie moved close to me.

"Watch what you say," he said. "I know you're angry and you have a right to be, but don't let them bait you. Don't say anything that will come back later and bite you on the ass."

An impromptu press conference ensued with Richie taking the lead. There were somewhere in the neighborhood of two dozen reporters, eight or ten cameras. The story had gained a lot of traction within Tennessee and had gotten some regional recognition, but with ongoing problems in the Middle East and racial tensions flaring in the United States, Tommy's release after nineteen years in prison hadn't gained a lot of national attention.

Richie was restrained in his criticism of Clancy and the late Sheriff Joe DuBose, choosing instead to focus on Tommy and his future. Tommy answered a few questions, but he was reserved by nature and I could tell he didn't feel well. As the questioning slowed and the enthusiasm waned, a reporter from the *Knoxville News-Sentinel*, an older guy named George Brighton who I'd seen around court a few times, said, "What about you, Mr. Street? You're the one who got this process started. How do you feel about your uncle being released from prison after all these years, and more importantly, how do you feel about Ben Clancy?"

I felt Richie tense as he stepped back and I moved forward. "Easy," he said under his breath. I looked at the crowd, then I looked at Tommy, and I noticed my vision had tunneled slightly.

"Ben Clancy is a criminal," I said. "He should be held accountable for what he did to my uncle. He should be disbarred and he should be prosecuted. That's my opinion, but I realize my opinion isn't worth the breath I just used to express it. I also realize that we have absolutely no recourse when it comes to Mr. Clancy, no remedy at law."

At that point I reached in my front pocket and pulled out a red bandana, one exactly like the stained red bandana that Ralph King had told me about on his deathbed. Clancy and Sheriff DuBose had hidden the bandana from Tommy's trial lawyers. We found it in a box tucked away in a corner of the evidence room at the sheriff's department, had it tested for blood and DNA, and it eventually led to Linda Royston's real killer, a drifter named Henry Pulanski.

"But there *is* a remedy at the polls," I said. "Ben Clancy is up for reelection in eleven months, and I guarantee you his arrogance will not allow him to step back voluntarily and let someone else take over the district attorney's office. I also guarantee you that I, as insignificant as I may be, will do everything in my power to see to it that he is defeated next August."

I held the red bandana above my head and waved it at the crowd. "I'm going to encourage whoever opposes Mr. Clancy in the election— and I'm sure there will be opposition—to make this bandana a symbol of the kind of evil that results from the misuse of power in the district attorney's office. I'm going to encourage them to hang one of these bandanas from every campaign sign they put on the street. Hell, maybe I'll encourage them to hang one from every sign *Clancy* puts on the street. I will work my fingers to the bone; I will donate what little money I can; I will do anything, *anything* in my power to see to it that Ben Clancy never gets the opportunity to railroad another defendant."

I stepped back as an awkward silence filled the space. It was broken by Richie's gruff whisper.

"Beautiful," he said. "Clancy and his assistants will step on every client you represent from this day forward."

"Fuck Ben Clancy," I said loud enough for everyone to hear. "He isn't going to be around much longer," and with that I turned and stalked out of the building.

PART I

CHAPTER ONE

TWO YEARS LATER

I'd never laid eyes on Jalen Jordan before he and his mother came into my office for an appointment. They called early that morning and told my secretary it was urgent that they see me. Jalen had been arrested two nights earlier and needed an attorney immediately. I was still a young lawyer, a thirty-two-year-old specialist in criminal defense, with an office in downtown Knoxville I was in my seventh year of solo practice, and I'd worked hard to gain a reputation in the local legal community as someone who was smart and hard-nosed. I could spot a constitutional violation a mile away, and if I couldn't find one, I'd try to create one. I was a tough negotiator in plea bargaining and an effective trial lawyer who could take even the worst set of facts and give the prosecution a run for their money in front of a jury. The other defense lawyers around town and some of the prosecutors had started calling me Brawler.

Jalen Jordan was a creepy mixture of goth, cowboy, and metro. He was twenty-five, tall, and lanky with jet-black hair that was parted in the middle and crawled down over his shoulders to the middle of his back. His skin was pale and scaly, his eyes like flat, black stones. He had three small rings in his left eyebrow, another in his left nostril, and a goatee that oozed from his chin like dark sap. He was wearing glasses with black frames, brown leather pants, brown chaps, cowboy boots, and a white button-down shirt with an open collar that revealed a pentagram hanging from a beaded chain.

He and his mother, Marion Jordan, walked in, and we introduced ourselves and traded a little small talk before we got around to his case. I read the police report that Jalen handed me and initially thought the case consisted of misdemeanor traffic violations plus a felony resisting arrest and assault on a police officer, but I quickly found out it would involve much, much more.

"Run me through what happened," I said to Jalen.

"The police stopped me for no reason," he said with just a hint of a lisp and an unusual accent for East Tennessee. He sounded intelligent, almost highbrow British. It had to be something he had practiced for a long time. "I was just driving through town, minding my own business."

"The report says you were driving around and around a public park in a residential area," I said. "It says you had a broken taillight."

"That isn't true. I wasn't speeding, wasn't swerving, wasn't drinking or high, and there wasn't a thing wrong with my taillight. It isn't against the law to drive through residential neighborhoods, is it?"

"It was midnight," I said. "What were you doing in that neighborhood?"

"I'm afraid that's none of your business," he said. "The last I heard this is still a free country. I can drive where I want when I want on a public road."

"Don't give me attitude," I said. "I don't need it. You're more than welcome to walk on out of here and find yourself another lawyer."

"I think not," he said. "I've read about you, Mr. Street. I read about what you did to the district attorney a couple of years ago, getting that man off on the murder case after they'd locked him up for twenty years. Wasn't he related to you? Your cousin or something?"

"Uncle," I said.

"Ah, yes, uncle," Jalen said. "And then you started that red bandana campaign and got the district attorney beaten in the next election. That was impressive. And besides that I started asking around as soon as I got arrested. I don't have many friends, but I was able to speak with some of the people who were in the holding cell with me. Everyone says you're young and hungry and that you have good connections with the new district attorney."

"It's nice to know I'm so highly regarded in the criminal community," I said, "but if I'm going to defend you, you're going to answer the questions I ask you. If you don't want to tell me the truth, then lie, but keep in mind there will be consequences if you lie to me and I find out about it later on. So what were you doing in that neighborhood at midnight?"

He blinked a couple of times, looked over at his mother, and said, "Give him the money."

Marion, whose red hair color had to have come straight out of a box and who had the jowls of a bulldog, reached into a large handbag and started pulling out bundles of cash and setting them on top of my desk. Each bundle had a band around it that said it contained $10,000. By the time she was finished, she'd stacked five of them in front of me.

"That's fifty thousand in cash," Jalen said.

"A little steep for a couple of traffic violations and a low-grade felony, don't you think?" I said.

"It'll be worth it if you can get me out of this . . . situation," he said.

"Where did you get that kind of money?"

"It's my money," Marion said, "but Jalen needs it, and I'm more than happy to help."

I looked at her and smiled, but I was thinking she was pitiful, like so many other mothers I ran across in the past half-dozen years. It was probably all she had to her name, but anything for momma's baby, even if momma had raised a piece of shit.

The cash was tempting. My wife, my six-year-old son, and I had recently moved into a house Katie desperately wanted but we couldn't afford. Katie and I were married seven years earlier and things weren't going well. We rarely saw each other, talked to each other only when necessary, and hadn't touched each other in months. I hired a private investigator to follow her, and my suspicions had been confirmed. She was having an affair. I was probably on my way to a divorce, and $50,000 in cash—which Katie would know nothing about—could at least give me some breathing room, if only for a short while.

"It's nonrefundable," I said to Jalen. "Agreed?"

Jalen nodded while I buzzed Rachel, my secretary and paralegal.

"Bring me a fee contract," I said. "Felony case, fifty thousand, non-refundable. Jalen Jordan is the client."

It took Rachel less than five minutes to print a contract and bring it to me. I signed it and handed it to Jalen, who also signed it. I picked up the contract and the money and handed them both to Rachel. She took them and walked quickly out of the room.

As soon as Rachel was gone, Jalen said, "You're my lawyer now, correct?"

"I suppose so."

"Everything I say to you is confidential?"

"Your mother's in the room. The privilege is waived when a third party is present."

Jalen looked at his mother, a woman who had just forked over $50,000 for his sorry ass, and said simply, "Get out." Marion got up and padded slowly out the door.

"I was checking out a playground," he said when the door closed.

"Why would you do that?"

"Because a friend told me to."

"You're not making any sense."

"Would you like me to tell you about this stop or not?"

I leaned back in my chair, folded my arms across my chest, and said, "Go ahead."

"I was driving down Delaware Avenue, doing about five miles an hour below the speed limit. I admit it was the third time I'd been around that particular block, but I hadn't had anything to drink in two days, hadn't smoked any dope since the night before. I was straight, okay? Stone sober. I wasn't speeding or swerving, and everything on the van was working. All the lights were fine. All of a sudden this cruiser rolled up on me from out of nowhere the blue lights flashing, the siren blasting. So I pulled over. I looked in the side views and I saw there were two of them; a man got out of the driver's side and a woman got out of the passenger side, and they both walked up on either side of my van. The man asked for my license and registration and insurance card, and I asked him why he'd stopped me. He said, 'License, registration, and insurance card.' I said, 'This is outrageous. You don't have a reason to stop me.' So he walked to the back of my van and broke out the driver's side taillight with this big flashlight he was carrying. Then he walked back up and said, 'You've got a broken taillight. Step out of the car.' I told him there was no way I was getting out of the car after what I just saw. The next thing I knew he had the door open and he had his forearm up under my chin and he was pushing my head backward. He unlatched my seat belt and jerked me out of the van. I managed to get loose for a second, and when he came in to grab me again, I took a wild swing at him and I caught him square in the mouth. Not five seconds after I hit him I saw this flash and I went down. The woman had hit me in the back of the head with her flashlight. The man dropped on my back and got me in a choke hold. He choked me until I lost consciousness, and when I came to, I was cuffed and they had those plastic wraps around my ankles."

"There's going to be video," I said. "They all have video in their cruisers."

Jalen shook his head. "There won't be a video. I promise you there won't be a video."

"What makes you say that?"

"Because of what I'm sure they found when they searched the van."

"What did they find?"

"Two pairs of underwear in a bag in the glove compartment."

"And this underwear belongs to . . . to you?"

"Not exactly. It's too small for me."

"Then how did it get into a bag in the glove compartment of your van?"

"I'm not sure how much I should say about that."

I felt myself growing uneasy. Everything about this guy—the clothes, the hair, the dead eyes, the smug accent—all of it made me want to get away from him as quickly as possible. But I'd just taken $50,000 of his mother's money.

"Are these two pairs of underwear that were in a bag in the glove compartment of your van significant to the police in some way?" I said.

"They could be," Jalen said. "They might be. Yes, I suppose they are."

"In what way might these pairs of underwear that were in a bag in the glove compartment of your van be significant to the police?"

"They could possibly be evidence in two murders. They might have found other evidence, too, maybe hairs or prints or something. They impounded my van."

I unfolded my arms, leaned forward, and placed my arms on my desk. I laced my fingers and thumbs and closely looked at Jalen. He had just a hint of a smile on his lips, but his eyes were still as lifeless as cardboard. He wasn't perspiring and his voice had remained steady, almost defiant. It was as though he was playing a game, and he was enjoying himself quite thoroughly.

"Okay, Jalen," I said. "We seem to be getting into a dangerous area. If you sit here and tell me you committed a couple of murders and you wind up getting charged with them, I can't put you on a witness stand later during a trial and knowingly let you sit up there and lie in front of a jury. So be careful what you say from this point forward."

"I have this friend," he said without the least bit of hesitation. "I'm with him all the time, constantly, as a matter of fact. This friend, as he's gotten older, has started having some pretty lurid fantasies. They're of a sexual nature, I guess you would say. He's told me all about them. They involve little boys around six seven years old. My friend knows he isn't supposed to indulge these fantasies, but he can't help it. He thinks about these boys all the time, thinks about all the things he'd like to do to them. It has become an obsession that probably runs to psychosis. He realizes there's something wrong with him, but these urges, these impulses, are so powerful that he can't resist them. What this friend told me was that about eleven months ago he got so caught up in these fantasies that he went ahead and kidnapped a little boy. My friend's very intelligent—you might even describe him as cunning—so he was able to capture this little boy in such a way that nobody really saw him do it and he took the boy up into the Great Smoky Mountains National Park and acted out some of his fantasies. Then about six months later—"

"Hang on," I said, holding up my hand. Images of newspaper headlines were running through my mind, flashbacks about murdered boys. I noticed my hand was trembling so I lowered it quickly, but Jalen had noticed it, too. "Are you about to tell me this friend of yours is the person who kidnapped, sexually assaulted, strangled, and tossed two boys into the river out near Gatlinburg?"

"Sometimes it's difficult to be friends with him," Jalen said. "He does some pretty terrible things; he really does. But like I said, he simply can't help it. So anyway, back to this underwear. My friend might have moved out of his mother's place into his own place recently so he could have more privacy to do these things he wants and needs to do, and the last two things he was moving were these two pairs of underwear that he had kept as a sort of memento, and he had perhaps forgotten they were in the glove compartment. Or maybe he found some unusual sense of satisfaction in carrying them around with him. I don't know. What I do know is that if the police test these two pairs of underwear for DNA, then they're probably going to try to lock my friend up forever or maybe even send him to death row. So I need you to do what lawyers do and beat this."

I reached for the phone and buzzed Rachel again. This time I didn't care about my hands shaking. I could barely control my voice. "Bring that contract and the money back in here," I said to Rachel. "And do it in a hurry. I won't be representing Mr. Jordan after all."

Jalen Jordan and I had a tense staring contest for the next few minutes while Rachel retrieved the money and the contract from the office safe. After she'd gone back out, I ripped the contract in half in front of him and tossed it into the trash can.

"Take your money and go," I said. "Our conversation is privileged. I won't say a word to anyone."

He looked over my shoulder to an old filing cabinet that sat just behind me.

"That's your son, isn't it?" he said, pointing to the top of the cabinet. "That's your little Sean?"

My throat tightened and I felt my heart speed up.

"How do you know his name?" I said.

"You'd be surprised how much you can learn about somebody in a short time on the Internet," he said. "I probably know his age, his address, where he goes to school. Probably know quite a bit about his mother, too. Katie, isn't it?"

"Get out," I said, standing. "Take the money."

Jalen got up and started walking toward the door.

"You keep that money, Counselor," he said over his shoulder, "and you do the right thing by me. It'd be a terrible shame if my friend was to throw little Sean off a cliff."

At that moment, I decided Jalen Jordan would have to die. I just wasn't sure when or how.

CHAPTER TWO

I probably should have killed Jalen Jordan right then and there. I had a pistol in my desk drawer because I dealt with scumbags on a daily basis. I should have pulled the gun out, run out into the street after him, and just started shooting. I could have pleaded temporary insanity or extreme provocation and maybe gotten away with it. But I didn't kill him. Instead, I called my wife. She worked part-time as a personal trainer and part-time at a women's designer clothing boutique. She was at the boutique that day.

"Is something wrong?" Katie said when she answered the phone.

"I need you to pick Sean up from school right now," I said, "and I need you to take him to Mom's and wait there until I call."

"What? Why? I'm working."

"I know you're working, but this is important. There was a guy in the office just a few minutes ago. I think he's the guy who killed those two little boys they found out in the national park. He wanted me to represent him, and when I refused, he threatened Sean."

"Killed who? Threatened Sean? What did he say?"

"He recognized the picture of Sean on the filing cabinet in my office. He knew Sean's name and said he knows how old he is and our address and where he goes to school, and he said he knows some things about you, too. Just go pick him up, please Katie? Do it now. Take him to Mom's and hang out until I get there. I'm going to the police station. I have to find a couple of officers and talk to them. I'll call you as soon as I'm finished, and we'll figure out what to do from there. Okay?"

"I can't just leave, Darren. I'm working the floor."

"Katie," I said as I felt my blood pressure surge, "I swear to God if you don't walk out the door right now and go pick up Sean, I'm going to come down there and strangle you with my bare hands."

"Don't threaten me, Darren."

"Did you hear what I told you?" My voice was full force now. "The guy threatened Sean! I think he's already killed two little boys and he threatened Sean! He said, and I quote, 'It'd be a terrible shame if my friend was to throw little Sean off a cliff!' Now please, for once in your life, think about someone besides yourself and do what I ask."

"Stop yelling at me, Darren. You know I hate it when you yell at me."

"Are you going to pick up Sean?"

"I already told you, I'm working the floor. We're having a sale. I can't just leave. Besides, I think you're overreacting."

She hung up on me. I swore under my breath and dialed my mother's number. I explained the situation to her, and she agreed immediately to leave the beauty salon she'd owned and managed for twenty-five years and to go pick up Sean. I got up, walked into the reception area, and told Rachel to cancel the rest of my appointments for the day. I walked back through my office and went into the bathroom. I ran some cold water into my cupped hands and splashed it onto my face. I took a deep breath and looked at myself in the mirror. At thirty-two, I still had a bit of a boyish face. I suppose I was handsome enough—I had smooth, dark skin, a full head of black hair, green eyes, and dimples in both cheeks. My nose was crooked because it had been broken a couple of times during wrestling matches and mixed martial arts fights, but it wasn't too bad. I wasn't tall—five feet nine inches—and I wasn't a bruiser, but I ran six miles five days a week, could do a hundred push-ups in less than three minutes and could do twenty pull-ups without breaking a sweat.

"Calm down," I said to myself in the mirror. "Breathe. Think."

I walked back out of the bathroom. Rachel was standing in the doorway between my office and the reception area.

"Did you hear what he said?" I asked her.

She nodded and said, "What are you going to do?"

"Before or after I kill him?"

"I'm serious," Rachel said. "What are you going to do?"

"I have no idea. I'll talk to you later."

I picked up the $50,000 Jalen left sitting on my desk, stuffed it in my briefcase, and headed out to my car. Police headquarters was on Howard Baker Jr. Avenue, less than ten minutes from my office on West Hill Avenue. As I walked toward the parking garage, I dialed Bob Ridge's number. Bob was my age and was one of the members of the Knoxville Police Department I knew best. We'd both graduated from Farragut High School and had played football together. We'd also both attended the University of Tennessee, where Bob, who was six feet six and weighed nearly three hundred pounds as a freshman, played four years of football. We'd remained pretty close over the years—we drank a beer together every couple of months and played golf on the same team in a charity event every year. Our families had had dinner together twice, but my wife and Bob's wife didn't seem to like each other very much, so we kept the friendship between him and me. I kept up with his daughter and his son, though, and he always asked about Sean. Bob had joined the Knoxville Police Department right out of college, had been with them for ten years, and was already a captain in the patrol division.

"I need to know if a couple of your patrol officers are working," I said when Bob answered his cell.

"Well, hello, Darren," he said. "I'm good. You?"

"Their names are Olivia Denton and Terrance Casey. They're part-ners. They made a stop two nights ago on Delaware Avenue and arrested the driver."

"What's wrong?" Bob said.

"I'll explain in a minute. Are they working?"

"Hold on." I could hear him tapping keys on a computer. "They're off," he said when he came back. "Came off shift this morning at seven and won't be back for four days."

"Where can I find them?"

"How the hell should I know?"

"It's important, Bob. Give me addresses, cell phone numbers, what-ever you have. Please. Sean's life could be in danger."

"Hold on, now," Bob said. "You sound a little uptight there, buddy. What's this about Sean?"

I took a deep breath and filled Bob in—what little I could ethically tell him—on my encounter with Jalen Jordan. When I was finished, he reluctantly provided me with the cell phone numbers of the two officers.

"I'd try Olivia first if I were you," Bob said. "Terrance won't care much for you."

"He doesn't like lawyers?"

"He doesn't like anybody."

I dialed Olivia Denton's cell number, and to my relief, she answered after the third ring.

"Officer Denton, my name is Darren Street and I'm a lawyer here in Knoxville. I need to speak with you about something you found during a stop you and your partner made two nights ago."

"How did you get my cell number?" she said in a cold, distant voice.

"That isn't important. What is *extremely* important is that I speak with you immediately. Today. Within the hour if possible."

"We gave the bag to the feds," she said. "Talk to them."

The cell phone went silent. I called her back, but the phone went to voice mail. I called again. Same result, so I left her a message: "Officer

Denton, this is Darren Street again. I have a six-year-old son who has been threatened, and it relates to the bag you found in that van the other night. I'm sure you know there have been two young boys murdered in the past year. Please, please call me back."

My phone rang in less than two minutes.

"Do you know the botanical gardens by the veterinary college on the UT campus?" Officer Denton said.

"Yeah, I've been there a couple of times."

"Meet me in fifteen minutes."

CHAPTER THREE

Officer Olivia Denton had short, shiny, brown hair and a frame that was a bit on the rotund side. She looked to be a couple of years younger than me; she also looked exhausted. Her face was puffy and her brown eyes had dark circles beneath them. She was wearing a white University of Tennessee hoodie and blue jeans. It was early April and the temperature was near sixty. Billowy white clouds moved briskly across a high, blue sky. The only people in the gardens besides us were two agricultural students who were spreading mulch.

"Thank you for meeting me," I said. I reached out to shake her hand and felt a small sense of relief when she took it. "I hope I didn't wake you. I know you just came off graveyard this morning."

"Haven't been to bed yet," she said. "I'll stay up until around nine tonight and then pass out, try to get on a regular schedule tomorrow for a few days until I have to go back. I've heard of you, you know. You actually have a decent reputation in the police department."

"Good to hear."

"But they say nobody wants to be cross-examined by you."

"I'll take that as a compliment."

"So what's this about your son?"

"Let me ask you a question first, if you don't mind," I said. "Is there a video of the stop you made on Jalen Jordan Sunday night?"

Her eyebrows raised slightly as if I'd surprised her; then she crossed her arms, looked down, and pawed the ground with her right foot.

"I think the camera was malfunctioning," she said. "I don't think there's a video."

"Shit," I said. "He was telling the truth."

"Who?"

"Jordan. He came to see me and wanted to hire me. Said you guys stopped him without a valid reason and then your partner broke his taillight out. I was hoping he was lying and that it was a good stop."

She shrugged. "I'm not quite sure how to respond to that."

"You don't have to," I said. "The look on your face tells me pretty much what I need to know."

"He's a good guy most of the time," Officer Denton said. "He just goes a little crazy every once in a while."

"I assume you're talking about your partner, Officer Casey?"

She nodded. "We were on the fourth straight night of twelve-hour shifts, seven p.m. to seven a.m., so we were both pretty tired and maybe a little stressed out. There had been a bunch of burglaries in the area around Delaware Avenue over the past few weeks, and we were watching it pretty close. We passed this van that just screamed 'I'm a burglar,' so Terrance drove back around the block and parked in a cul-de-sac. We saw the guy pass again in about ten minutes and then maybe five minutes later we saw him again. It was really strange because he kept circling Sam Hill Park. So Terrance decided to stop him. I told him he should follow the guy until he committed some kind of traffic violation, but Terrance gets impatient when he thinks his gut is telling him something. So we stopped him and the rest, I suppose, will be hotly contested in court."

"You thought he might be a burglar?" I said.

"That was the original suspicion," she said.

"Who found the bag with the underwear in it?"

"I did. After the guy punched Terrance in the mouth—he got him pretty good, split his lip—we subdued him and secured him, and then I called for backup. Scotty Slagle and Jeremy Deakins rolled up a couple of minutes later, and they ended up hauling Mr. Jordan to jail for us. I got the first aid kit out of our cruiser and managed to get Terrance's lip to stop bleeding, and then we searched the van. I thought for sure we'd find drugs after I got a look at Mr. Jordan, but we didn't find a thing besides that brown paper bag in the glove compartment. When I first took them out of the bag I thought it was gross, you know? This guy carrying his underwear around in his glove compartment, but then I looked a little closer and they were both just so small. One pair was blue and the other had *Toy Story* characters on it, and I said to Terrance, 'Why do you think he's got kids' underwear in his glove compartment?' And I thought about those two little boys that had been found murdered and I thought, 'No way.' But I bagged it up anyway and I called my supervisor and told him what we'd found. He told me to call the FBI office since the murders were committed on federal land and it's their case. I called, but it was after midnight and there wasn't anybody there. I left them a message and got a call back the next afternoon, but by that time your man Jordan had bonded out so they didn't talk to him. An agent named Freeman came by late yesterday evening and picked up the bag. It was right before I went in to work, so I met him at the evidence locker. He said he was going to send the underwear off to Quantico for DNA testing, but it would be a minimum of six weeks before they got anything back."

"Who has the van?"

"Freeman said they'd pick it up and have their forensics guys go through it. They probably have it by now."

"Was he planning to talk to Jordan?" I asked.

"Didn't say. I mean, you'd think he would, right? But he didn't say."

"It doesn't matter," I said. "Even if Jordan confesses, which he won't, they're not going to be able to do anything to him. At least not until he kills another kid."

"Why do you say that?" she said.

"I think you know why. Any good lawyer will destroy you and your partner on that stop. Anything you found in the van will be suppressed."

"Maybe not," she said.

"You're going to go into court and commit perjury?"

"If it means catching a child killer, you're damn right I will, but you didn't hear me say that. You haven't told me about your son. Did Jordan threaten him?"

"As a matter of fact, he did," I said. "And because of you and your partner, it looks like I'm going to have to find a way to deal with him outside the system."

CHAPTER FOUR

Ben Clancy had lost an election, but he was still in the same line of work. Within a month of being beaten, Clancy was hired by an old friend and fraternity brother, Stephen Blackburn, who happened to be the United States Attorney for East Tennessee. Clancy had been deeply wounded by the election defeat, but he was glad to have been presented with so prestigious an opportunity so quickly. Blackburn assigned him to violent felonies and serious drug cases, which meant he was in the thick of it.

At that moment, Clancy was meeting with Special Agent in Charge Dan Reid of the FBI along with Special Agent Paul Freeman. All three men were in a conference room across the hall from Clancy's office in downtown Knoxville.

"I think this is the break we've been hoping for," Freeman said.

Freeman, a forty-year-old, ten-year veteran of the bureau, along with dozens of other law enforcers, had been working the case of the two murdered six-year-olds for nearly a year, but thus far, the killer had eluded them. The boys had been kidnapped from public playgrounds in low-income neighborhoods, and their naked bodies had been found in the Little River near sheer rock cliffs in a desolate part of the Great

Smoky Mountains National Park known as The Sinks. Not a trace of physical evidence had been left behind. The only information the FBI had developed was a rough sketch of the kidnapper drawn from a description provided by a nine-year-old girl who might have seen the first victim being led away from a public park in Maryville and two reports that the kidnapper may have been driving a white van.

"Have you talked to the boys' parents?" Clancy said.

Adrenaline had surged through Clancy when he'd received the news about the photographs. A case like this could go a long way toward restoring his reputation—not to mention his self-esteem—after his bitter defeat at the polls. He needed something to help him refocus, to help him regain his sharpness.

Freeman slid four photographs he'd taken of the underwear that was found in Jalen Jordan's van across the circular table to Clancy.

"I talked to all four parents, and I showed them these," Freeman said. "Timothy Grigsby was wearing Hanes underwear with a *Toy Story* design, and Ronald Baines was wearing light-blue Fruit of the Looms. The sizes match, too."

"You've already sent them to the lab?" Clancy said as he stared down at the photos.

"Went out this morning," Freeman said.

"What do we know about this Jalen Jordan?" Clancy said.

"Not a lot, but I'm working on it. I have booking photos from old arrests and the booking photo from the other night. He has one arrest and conviction for indecent exposure four years ago in Knox County. Probation and behavioral therapy. He had a misdemeanor drug arrest last year in Knox County, possession of less than a half ounce of marijuana. Diverted to drug court. I've reached out to his probation officers and have asked for his files."

"What about the van?" Clancy said.

"We have it," Freeman said. "Our guys are going through it as we speak."

"Where is Jordan now?" Clancy said.

"I'm not sure."

"What?" Clancy said, his pale-blue eyes fixing on the FBI agent. "Why don't you know where he is?"

"Because I just got some of this information. He bonded out of jail before I even knew he was in jail, before I learned any of what I'm telling you. We have a couple of guys watching the address he provided during the stop, but they haven't seen him. When I plug the address into the Internet, his mother's name comes up, too, so I'm not even sure if he's living there. But it's the address on the license he gave the cops and it's the address he gave the booking guys at the jail. We're in the early stages, right on the front end. We're here because we think this is our killer, and we want to know how far we can go."

"You can go as far as you need to," Clancy said. "I want a black bag team in that house or apartment or whatever the hell it is, and I want bugs in there immediately. I want tracking devices on any vehicle he has access to. I want electronic and physical surveillance around the clock. I want his cell phone tapped. I want his mother's cell phone tapped. I want their cell phone records."

"We don't have warrants for any of that, Ben," Freeman said.

"I'll take care of the warrants. You get everything else set up. Top priority. If the guy spits, I want you to know. Did you make a priority request to the lab at Quantico?"

"I did, but you know how it goes. They're swamped."

"I'll call them myself, and if that doesn't work, I'll get the politicians on it. Are you talking to Jordan's friends, acquaintances, relatives, all that?"

"We're taking take care of it."

"All right, get to it," Clancy said. "By this time tomorrow, I want to know everything there is to know about Jalen Jordan, and I want him bottled up tight."

"Right," Freeman said, and the agents stood and began walking toward the door.

"Agent Freeman," Clancy said as the men reached the door. Freeman and Reid stopped and turned. "And this goes for both of you. Keep me in the loop at all times. If this . . . this . . . *thing* kills another child in my district, you'll answer for it. I may be from Knoxville, but don't mistake me for a hick. I have plenty of friends in Washington, and if you guys screw this up, your careers will be over."

CHAPTER FIVE

My next stop was at Richie Fels's office downtown. Richie was a sixty-four-year-old, barrel-chested, thirty-seven-year veteran of the local criminal court scene who ran what was perhaps the most highly respected criminal defense firm in the state. He had taken an interest in me because I'd told him the first time we met that I wanted to be just like him—I wanted to practice criminal defense law exclusively and I didn't give a damn if I went hungry while I was learning to do it. Once he saw that I was serious, he took me under his wing and had been an invaluable source of information and advice for me during the seven years I'd practiced. He'd even gone so far as to help me get my uncle released from prison, and he didn't receive a dime for it. But Richie had become distant over the past two or three years. He was drinking a lot—I knew because I drank with him occasionally—and he seemed to be getting caught up in his own legend. I couldn't ever get him on the phone, and when I managed to get an audience he would inevitably regale me with the same stories of glorious victories of which he'd been a part.

"I have a client in the waiting room," Richie said as I walked into the disaster area he called an office. There were files piled everywhere and the place was dusty. The off-white walls were bare except for an old diploma and a law license hanging directly behind him.

"You always have a client waiting," I said, "just like you always have a judge waiting on the phone and three prosecutors downtown cursing the day you were born."

His cobalt-blue eyes—which reminded me of images I'd seen of Santa Claus—twinkled and his smile revealed slightly crooked, yellowing teeth. I'd peeled a hundred-dollar bill off one of the stacks in my briefcase before I walked into Richie's office. I took it out of my pocket and laid it on the desk in front of him.

"Retainer?" Richie said.

"Call it whatever you think you have to call it," I said. "I need to talk some business."

"What's so important that you had to piss off my secretary?" he said.

"Let me give you a little background first," I said, and I told him about my meeting with Jalen Jordan earlier, Jordan's threat regarding my son, and my subsequent conversation with Officer Olivia Denton.

"Good God, Darren, this sounds like the criminal defense lawyer's ultimate nightmare," Richie said when I was finished. "Let's see if I have this straight. First of all, you could tell the police what this Jordan fellow told you about his friend's sexual fantasies and his friend kidnapping a couple of children, but if you do, you could be disbarred or suspended for a long time for violating the ethical rules regarding privilege. What's worse is that if the police act upon the information you provide to them in violation of your ethical obligations, there's a chance that a judge would rule any evidence they gathered inadmissible and this Mr. Jordan would walk away scot-free.

"But if you don't tell the police and you live up to your ethical obligation to zealously represent your client you could wind up being an unwilling facilitator—if not an outright accessory—to another child murder since Mr. Jordan has indicated to you that he's just getting started. It seems to me the chances of him killing again are extremely high if you get him out of this.

Scott Pratt

"And finally, if you live up to your ethical obligation yet your client doesn't like something about the way you're handling the problem with the two overly enthusiastic police officers, your own child could be kidnapped and killed. Is that a fairly accurate summation of your problem?"

I took a long, deep breath and let it out slowly, trying to control myself. I'd been struggling internally with the situation, but having someone actually spell it out like that caused a near panic.

"What the hell am I going to do, Richie?" I said.

Richie laid his right arm across his substantial belly and began tugging at his left earlobe with the fingers of his left hand. I'd seen him do it many times before. It meant he was perplexed.

"I have to tell you, Darren, in my nearly forty years of lawyering I've never run across anything like this. I don't really know how to advise you."

"Between you and me and the wall over there," I said, "I've given some thought to killing him."

When I'd mentioned killing Jordan to Rachel earlier, it had been an off-the-cuff remark. But the more I'd thought about what Jordan had said, the more I thought about the eerie way he looked and spoke, the more frightened I'd become for Sean. During the drive to Richie's office, I'd even thought about what I would do if Jalen Jordan somehow managed to break into my house in an attempt to kidnap Sean. I'd fantasized about surprising him and shooting him. I had a pistol near my bed at home, for the same reason I kept one at the office. If Jalen really came after Sean, I had no doubt I'd kill him.

"Really?" Richie said. "And how would you kill him? Gun? Knife? Run over him with a car?"

"I suppose I'd use a gun. Just shoot him in the head and be done with it."

"In front of witnesses? During the day or at night? Your place or his?"

"Don't make fun of me, Richie," I said as I realized that was exactly what he was doing. "This is serious. You didn't see the guy or talk to him. He threatened my son and I have every reason to believe he's capable of acting on the threat."

"I didn't mean to make light of the situation," Richie said. "My point is that I've never taken you for a killer. A bit intense and unpredictable at times, perhaps emotionally unstable occasionally, but I don't think you're the type of person who could simply walk up to another human being, put a gun to his head, and pull the trigger. Have you considered removing your son from harm's way until you can effect some type of resolution to this extremely unusual situation?"

I hated it when Richie went into his lawyer-speak mode. I much preferred plain, simple English.

"Effect some type of resolution?" I said. "What the hell does that even mean, Richie?"

"I might not have phrased that exactly the way I intended," he said. "What I meant was that perhaps the authorities will soon get a line on Mr. Jordan, especially now that you've gone to the patrol officer and expressed your concerns about the stop. I would expect the officer you spoke with to get a hold of the FBI agent immediately and tell him that there's a good possibility they might lose whatever evidence was in the van. I would expect the officer to tell the FBI agent they need to find a different way to get to Mr. Jordan, and they need to do it quickly. I would think they would set up surveillance on him and wait until he makes a mistake."

"They'll also start talking to his family and friends if he has any," I said, "and as soon as they do, Jordan will find out about it and Sean will be dead."

"And that's precisely why you move the boy out of harm's way."

"Where?" I said. "Where do I take him? Do I give up my practice and run away with Sean until Jalen Jordan is arrested for killing another child? And by the way, how do I live with the guilt of knowing I allowed a little boy to be killed without doing anything about it? Do I put my entire life on hold because this sicko threatened to hurt Sean? You know I'm not wired like that, Richie."

"Let me give it some more thought and call me this evening," he said. "In the meantime, don't kill anybody."

CHAPTER SIX

As I drove west along I-40 toward the Farragut exit, I wondered about something Richie Fels had said: *"I've never taken you for a killer. A bit intense and unpredictable at times, perhaps emotionally unstable occasionally, but I don't think you're the type of person who could simply walk up to another human being, put a gun to his head, and pull the trigger."*

What he'd said about me being intense and unpredictable at times, perhaps emotionally unstable, was true. He just didn't know *how* true, because he'd never seen me fight anywhere outside of a courtroom. Richie hadn't seen me on the football field, he hadn't seen me wrestle, and he hadn't seen me in a mixed martial arts competition.

He also didn't see what I did to my father.

It was nineteen years earlier—a cold, bleak night in November, the day before Thanksgiving. I was thirteen and going through the early stages of puberty. I'd put on some muscle weight, had grown a few inches, and my voice was changing. I'd also joined the wrestling team at school and had excelled at the sport.

I'd grown up fighting, mostly because of my size. I was smaller than a lot of guys, which meant they thought they could pick on me. They found out very quickly that I would fight back. My maternal grandfather, Delmar Royston, was a small, lithe man. He was a machinist during the week and an outdoorsman on the weekends until an aneurysm dropped him in his tracks when I was six years old. I remember him vividly, though, and I remember him telling me during a camping trip right before I started school, "Darren, buddy, it's just human nature that boys bigger than you are gonna try to dominate you. They're gonna try to make you do things they want you to do; they'll try to push you around. You can't let them, son. If you do, you'll spend your whole life mad at the world. First one that picks on you, punch him square in the nose. That'll discourage about ninety percent of the rest of them right there."

On that day before Thanksgiving, it was just me and my mom and my father. I was nervous. I was always nervous during the holidays, because I knew, just as my mother knew, what the holidays could bring. There would be angst, if not outright terror, along with drunkenness and, perhaps, violence.

My father, Billy Street, was a drunk. He started drinking Pabst Blue Ribbon at noon every day and he drank until he passed out sometime between nine o'clock and midnight. He'd been doing it for as long as I could remember. Billy tried to act like he owned a mechanic's business—he worked on cars in a run-down shop out back of our house—but all he really cared about was making enough money to drink. I remember one night when I was very young, maybe three or four, when my uncle Tommy walked into the house while my father was hitting my mother. Uncle Tommy beat him unconscious, and for several years, the violence stopped. The threats remained, but the violence stopped. Then Tommy went to prison, and it didn't take long for Billy to start up again.

Most nights, Billy would sit in the den in front of the television in an alcohol-induced haze and mumble to himself about whatever was troubling him at the moment. Some nights he would cry. But other nights, especially if he managed to get his hands on some liquor or some drugs, he became violent. He enjoyed removing his belt and lashing us with it. He struck me dozens of times with that belt—sometimes with the buckle—for offenses so miniscule that I rarely knew why I was being beaten. He beat my mother viciously. The beatings always came with threats of death should anyone dare to tell the police or anyone at school—or anyone at all, for that matter—and were always followed by remorseful wailing and pleas to God for forgiveness. It was a sickening way to live. I remember asking my mother repeatedly why she allowed him to get away with the things he did. Her answer was always some variant of "He doesn't mean it, Darren," or "It's really my fault, honey," followed by a vague reference to Jesus and how divine it is to forgive.

On that cold evening in November, my mother had closed her salon early to make a run to the grocery store so everything would be perfect for Billy on Thanksgiving. I'd spent a couple of hours with two of my friends that afternoon, but I'd asked them for a ride home early so I'd be around for the evening meal. I knew we would be the only people at our house over the holiday weekend. Billy had long ago worn out his welcome with the few remaining family members, and none of them would dare set foot in our house because they knew he would be deep in the bottle. Thanksgiving meant a Wild Turkey weekend for Billy, and he'd started taking shots of Wild Turkey chased by his beer as soon as the sun had gone down around five o'clock that Wednesday afternoon. By seven o'clock, when the three of us sat down for supper, he was spoiling for a fight, and so was I. I'd noticed the telltale signs over the past week—the escalation in the insults directed toward both my mother and me, the constant threats of violence, the suggestions that the world would be a better place if both of us were dead—and I'd readied myself mentally for the inevitable as best I could. My father wasn't a big man, nor was he especially strong. He'd spent fifteen years poisoning himself with alcohol, and at that moment, he was full-on drunk. I didn't know whether I could take him in a physical confrontation, but I was determined to try if I had to.

"What's this shit?" he slurred at my mother as she bowed her head and thanked the Lord for her family and the meal.

I stiffened when he said it. The tone in his voice was familiar; it told me something bad was about to happen. The muscles in my thighs began to twitch.

"What's what?" my mother said. A fake smile crossed her face, and I could see fear in her eyes.

"This shit right here," Billy said, pointing to his plate.

"You know what it is," Mom said, trying to maintain the smile.

"Don't get smart with me, bitch," Billy said. "I asked you a question!"

"It's spaghetti," Mom said. "We have spaghetti the night before Thanksgiving every year because that's what you always want. The sauce is your mother's recipe. You love it."

"Bullshit," Billy said. "I ain't no fuckin' guinea."

"I don't think anyone here is suggesting you're Italian, Billy," Mom said. "It's just that for as long as I can remember, you've always wanted—"

My fists clenched as I watched Billy pick up a fistful of spaghetti from his plate and throw it into my mother's face.

"Tryin' a feed me wop food day before a holy day," Billy said. "Fuck's the matter with you, anyway?"

"I'm sorry," Mom said as she reached for a paper towel and began wiping spaghetti sauce from her cheek. "I thought you'd—"

"Thought wrong, didn't ya, bitch? Matter of fact, you ain't ever thought right in your whole life. Trappin' me into this marriage the way you did. Havin' this damn kid."

I saw his hand reach below the table and knew he was undoing his belt buckle. He was drunk, so it took him a few seconds, long enough for me to get up from the table, grab the metal baseball bat I'd stashed behind the refrigerator a couple of days earlier, and stand between him and Mom.

"No," I said. "You're not going to hit her. You're never going to hit her—or me—again."

He stood shakily and freed the belt from the loops around his waist. "Well, lookie here," he mumbled. "Got us a hero in the house."

He raised the belt above his head, but before he could swing it, I hit him in the ribcage with the bat as hard as I could. I heard a bone break, heard the breath rush out of his body, and the next thing I knew he was on the floor by the table. He sat upright for a couple of seconds until I kicked him square in the chin and sent him straight over onto his back. His head thumped against the floor and he was still. I jerked the belt out of his right hand, tossed the bat aside, and for the next minute or two, I beat him with the belt while my mother watched me in silence from across the room. I beat his head and face with the strap for a good while, and then I took the strap in my hand and beat his torso and arms and legs with the buckle. After he finally managed to roll into a ball to try to protect himself, I straddled him and pounded him in the head with my fists. Years of anger, hatred, frustration, and vengeance came pouring out of me. When I finally stood up, breathing heavily, I looked over at my mother. She was standing against the refrigerator door with her arms folded and a look of resignation on her face.

"Just get him out of here, Darren," she said.

I dragged him by the ankles through the house, out the front door, and down the porch steps into the yard. It was cold and dark, the only light coming from the front porch. He was lying on his back, looking up at me through swollen eyes as puffs of mist rose from his bloody lips.

"You don't live here anymore," I said as I knelt beside him. "Do you hear me? Do you understand me, Billy? You don't live here anymore. Go to your druggie girlfriend's house. Go to your sister's. Go to hell for all I care. But if you come back here, I'm going to kill you. I mean it. You set foot on this property again, and I'll kill you."

* * *

My cell phone rang and jolted me back to the present. I looked at the screen, saw it was my mother, and answered it.

"This man who threatened Sean—what was he driving?" she said.

"I don't know. He was driving a van a couple of days ago, but the police impounded it. Why?"

"I think somebody might be watching us."

"Watching? What do you mean? Is somebody parked close?"

"I've had this feeling ever since I picked Sean up," she said. "I don't know how to describe it, just eerie, you know? Like someone was following me. I kept looking in the rearview and didn't notice anybody, but there's so much traffic coming out this way I probably wouldn't be able to pick anybody out even if they were following me. But I've been sitting in the living room looking out the window at the road and this car keeps going by. It just went past again."

"Are you sure? What kind of car?"

"I don't know, Darren. I don't know cars, and maybe I'm wrong, but I'm scared. Are you close?"

"Yeah. Just two or three minutes."

"Hurry."

"Which way was the car going?"

"Toward the interstate."

"Then it's coming toward me. Can you tell me anything about it?"

"A small car. Light blue, I think."

"Is that it?"

"I don't know cars, Darren!"

There was still plenty of light left, so I started watching the cars in the oncoming lane. About a minute after Mom and I talked, I saw a light-blue coupe coming toward me. It passed quickly but I got a clear look at the driver, a male with dark, long hair and wearing glasses.

It was Jalen Jordan.

CHAPTER SEVEN

My mother's first name was Shirley. She'd changed her last name back to Royston when she divorced Billy Street. She lived in a neat, fastidiously clean white house that sat on seven acres about five miles from Farragut High School in Knoxville. I was going so fast when I pulled into her driveway that I dug up some of her immaculately manicured lawn and slid off into the yard. I parked outside the garage and dialed my paralegal's cell number.

"Rachel," I said, "did Jalen Jordan list a cell number and an address on the intake form?" Every potential client who came into the office filled out an intake form that listed basic contact information.

"Just a sec," Rachel said. She came back on the line shortly thereafter and said, "He did."

"Give them to me."

As soon as I had Jordan's cell number, I dialed it. To my surprise, a male voice answered.

"Is this Jalen Jordan?" I said.

"You sound like Darren Street," he said.

"What the hell do you think you're doing?"

"Whatever do you mean, Counselor?"

"I just passed you on the road," I said. "You followed my mom and now you're driving back and forth, just like you did the other night."

"So your mom lives in that white house? I thought so."

"Stay away from my family."

"I haven't bothered anyone in your family. I just wanted to show you I was serious about what I said this afternoon, and I think I'm doing a pretty good job of it so far. I figured you'd call your wife and have her get Sean out of school, but I guess she was busy or you couldn't get a hold of her. Am I right? I was at the school before your mom was. I watched her lead little Sean out the front door, and then I followed her out here."

"I'm not going to represent you. Just leave us alone."

"Yes, you are. And like I said at your office, you need to do right by me."

"I'm not going to help you kill children."

"I don't know where you got the idea that I want you to help me kill anyone. I'm not asking you to help me do anything. All I'm asking is that you do what lawyers get paid to do. I want my constitutional rights upheld. Those police officers violated my rights, and your job is to hold them accountable for it."

"You're delusional," I said. "The underwear the cops found in the van is going to be tested, and when the tests come back and show that the underwear belonged to the two boys who were murdered, you're going to be arrested and held without bail. And under those circumstances, there isn't a judge on the planet who will rule that your van was illegally stopped and searched and suppress whatever evidence they found in it, including the underwear. The cops will come into court and lie, and the judge will accept everything they say as gospel. You can't win this. You're going to prison for the rest of your life, if they don't give you the death penalty."

"You spoke to the police officers, didn't you?"

"I talked to one of them."

"The man or the woman?"

"The woman."

"What did you tell her?"

"I didn't tell her anything. I just asked her about the stop."

"And did she tell you the truth? Did she tell you they violated my rights?"

"It doesn't matter!" I yelled. "Are you listening to me? It doesn't matter! They'll perjure themselves if it means bringing a child killer to justice. You're going to prison!"

"That's bad news for your little boy," he said.

"You sick son of a bitch. I'll cut your head off if you come anywhere near Sean."

"You're right about my mother being a bitch," Jordan said in that smug accent. "I really can't stand her. And did you see that hair? She looks like she's wearing a dead fox on her head. Now . . . as far as your family . . . I really won't get any pleasure out of killing your wife or your mother, so I'll probably leave them alone. But the boy is another matter. I'll get to him eventually. I'm sure I'll have to get out of here for a little while, but I'll cruise back through some day in the not-too-distant future and find a way to snatch little Sean up. He and I will get to know each other on an intimate basis, and then I'll strangle him and throw him into a river like a piece of garbage."

My heart was beating hard against my chest and my vision had tunneled. I started to yell another threat into the phone, but it had gone silent.

Jalen Jordan was gone.

CHAPTER EIGHT

I climbed out of the car and walked quickly around the house and in through the back door. Mom was waiting for me in the kitchen. Sean, who had his mother's sandy-brown hair and robin-egg-blue eyes, was standing right beside her.

"Hey, big guy," I said as I walked across the kitchen and picked him up.

I was probably overly involved in Sean's life, but I was unapologetic about it. After what I'd been through with my father, I suppose it was natural. I spent as much time with him as possible. I took him camping three or four times a year during the summer and fall. I took him to soccer or to basketball or to T-ball practices and games. I took him to movies and we went fishing and I played video games with him. I enjoyed cooking for him and sharing meals with him. I spent far more time with him than I did with my wife, and I enjoyed every second of it.

"What are we doing here, Dad?" Sean said. "Grandma says everything is okay but she never picks me up from school and Mom isn't here and I was wondering why we came here in the middle of the day because we don't ever come here except on Saturday or Sunday and today is Tuesday so I was wondering."

Sean was a smart little guy, and he was a talker. He'd always been a talker. I'd take him to movies, and he'd ask questions and make commentary from preview to closing credits. He was so distracting in the car that I had removed the middle bench seat from our minivan so Sean would have to talk from the back. It hadn't stopped him, though. It hadn't even slowed him. He just talked louder.

"I thought we might take a trip to Pigeon Forge for a couple of days," I said. "Stay in one of those chalets in the mountains. We'll go to the aquarium and find some other fun stuff to do. How's that sound to you?"

"What about school? You know they don't like for us kids to miss school because they say we get behind and then we might not be able to catch up and—"

"It's okay, Sean. I'll talk to them. Don't worry about it. A couple of days off from school never hurt anybody."

"Is Grandma going to go with us?"

"Sure, why not?"

"What about Mom?"

"She's working right now, but I told her to meet us tonight. Listen, why don't you go in the den and play some Mario? Your grandma and I need to talk."

"It was him," I said as soon as Sean got settled on the couch and was lost in the video game. "I saw him. The same guy that was at the office. He followed you here."

"I knew it," Mom said. She was sturdy and still pretty at fifty-six. Her chestnut hair was long, thick, and starting to go gray, her green eyes filled with worry. "Is he insane?"

"I don't think so, which makes him even more dangerous. We need to get out of here, find a good place to hide, and let me figure out what to do. Can your girls handle the shop for a couple of days?"

"Don't worry about the shop. What about Katie?"

"I don't think she'll even bother to come," I said. "I haven't said much about it, but things aren't all that great between us right now."

"Things have never been great between you. I'm not blind or deaf."

I shrugged my shoulders.

"We'll talk about Katie later," I said. "For now, pack enough for a couple of days. You drive your car, and I'll drive the van. You lead the way. Sean can ride with me since I have more experience dealing with all the questions that are going to come. Let's drive down to Maryville and then back to Pigeon Forge. Make a lot of turns, pull into gas stations, double-back a lot. I'll tell Sean we're playing a game."

"He'll know you're lying."

"I know."

"Why don't you call the police?" Mom said.

"And tell them what? That Jordan threatened my son? There's no real crime there, Mom. They can't do anything about it. Besides, the boys who were killed are being handled by the FBI. It's their case."

"You could ask them to keep an eye on him."

"You know as well as I do they're not going to keep an eye on somebody just because some lawyer asks them to. They'd laugh me out of the place."

"Tell them he's the man who killed those boys."

"I could lose my law license if I do that."

"That's crazy, Darren. That's absolutely crazy. What do you plan to do when we get to Pigeon Forge?"

"Let's do what I told Sean. Let's check into a chalet. There's a guy that lives in the mountains close to Gatlinburg I want to go see."

"Who is he?"

"Former client. He might be just what the doctor ordered."

CHAPTER NINE

James Tipton lived in a rundown trailer on the side of a mountain about six miles from the Ripley's Believe It or Not museum in Gatlinburg. I'd been to his place once before, back when he insisted that I come out and share a victory drink of his personal stash of homemade moonshine after I'd gotten him acquitted in a jury trial for slicing a man so badly that two hundred stitches had been required to close the knife wounds. The man had repeatedly run his truck into the back of James's car while James was driving down the road with the man's girlfriend in the passenger seat. James claimed he didn't know the woman had a live-in boyfriend, and she was such a miserable witness that the jury believed James and bought my argument of self-defense. Not that they shouldn't have bought it. It *was* self-defense. The guy bashed James's car four or five times, and then, when James pulled over and got out, the guy tried to fight him. The prosecution thought the knife wounds were excessive for a case of self-defense, and maybe they were, but was it James's fault that he was an excellent knife fighter and just happened to have a knife in the car with him? The jury was basically faced with making a choice between two pretty unsavory people, James and the victim. They chose James.

One of the things I was able to tell the jury about James was that he'd never been convicted of anything. As a matter of fact, he'd never even been arrested. But I'd heard from several people—cops, other lawyers, and clients—that James was a genuine bad ass. He came from a long line of criminals that began with moonshiners and bootleggers and had graduated to running drugs. James had apparently become territorial about it. A Sevier County detective told me that they suspected James of committing two murders—a couple of brothers who had gotten into the oxycodone trade and reportedly crossed James—but they hadn't been able to put together a solid case. The men were found in a barn on their parents' property. They'd both been skinned after their throats were cut.

It was just after dark by the time I got Sean and Mom settled into a chalet and drove to James's place. His trailer was brown and seemed to list to the right where the slope dropped off sharply and steeply. There was a black pit bull chained to a metal spike just to the left of the front stoop and the driveway had been "paved" with flattened beer cans, a little trick I'd seen a couple of times before and had always referred to as redneck asphalt. There were also hundreds of skulls around the place—cattle and deer skulls mostly with a few bear and cat skulls mixed in—along with dozens of sets of antlers. It gave the place a sort of gothic, medieval "venture forth at your own peril" vibe.

There was a dualie pickup in the driveway along with an old Dodge Charger, and I could see a Harley-Davidson motorcycle underneath a crumbling outbuilding. The dog went nuts when I pulled up, and within seconds, I saw James's slim frame appear on the stoop. It was just before dark, but I noticed the outline of a large pistol in his right hand. I got out of the car and said, "James! It's me, Darren Street."

He stuck the hand cannon into the waist of the blue jeans he was wearing and hurried down the stoop. I could see him grinning widely as he approached my car. James was a few years older than me—midthirties—a few inches taller than me at six feet, and had short black hair that was receding just a little. He wore a pencil-thin mustache that must have required a great deal of attention. He also had beautiful teeth, something that seemed out of place in his surroundings. He was shirtless, well muscled, and covered in tattoos.

"Well, I'll be damned," he said as he approached and stuck out his hand. "How the hell are ya, Counselor?"

I took the offered hand and smiled back at him.

"I'm good, James. You?"

"Shut up, Zeus!" he yelled at the dog. "I can't complain," he said as he turned back to me. "Come on in the house and take a load off."

"Is anybody here besides you?"

"Granny's inside," he said, "but she was about to leave."

Luanne "Granny" Tipton was probably in her early seventies. She had attended every meeting James and I had before his trial, and she had been in the courtroom during the trial and when the verdict was read. She was also at the after-party, drinking moonshine and dancing to bluegrass music right along with the rest of the Tipton clan. The Tiptons were a rough bunch, and I learned quickly that Granny was their undisputed matriarch. There were three boys: Ronnie, Eugene, and James, all of whom she claimed as her grandchildren, although I found out later that James really wasn't a biological grandchild. Granny, Ronnie, and Eugene lived about a half mile farther up the mountain. Granny lived in a nice home and the boys lived in beautiful cabins on either side of her. James was a self-described black sheep, and the trailer and his skulls seemed to confirm the image.

"It'll be nice to see her again," I said. "How's it been going?"

"Had me a live-in woman for a couple of weeks," James said, "but I kept going out to the bars and bringing other women home with me. She had some problems putting up with it."

"Imagine that," I said.

"Hell, Counselor, it wasn't like I was ignoring her. I always offered to let her join the party. She just wasn't into threesomes."

James was probably a sociopath, but he was a likeable sociopath. He had a loud, infectious laugh, and it rose over the barking of the dog and bounced off the surrounding slopes. We walked up the three stairs onto the stoop and stepped into the trailer, which was just as I'd remembered it—remarkably clean and well kept. He led me to the small kitchen where I sat down at a Formica-topped table. Granny walked in from the other end of the trailer.

"Well, as I live and breathe," she said as I stood to hug her. "Darren Street, in the flesh. What brings you up this way?"

"Hi, Granny," I said. Back when I was representing James, she insisted that I call her Granny. "I had a little break at the office so I thought I'd bring my boy to Gatlinburg for a day or two. Just thought I'd drop in and say hello."

"Well, it's good to see you," she said, "but I have to get going. It's bingo night at the Moose Lodge and my friends will be expecting me."

I said good-bye and James and I stood on the front porch as she walked out, climbed into the dualie pickup, and fired it up.

"Feisty as ever," James said as she drove out of the driveway. "I'll have to take you back up to her place one of these days, get you some of that ham and bacon she cures. She really likes you."

"The feeling is mutual."

"Let's go on back inside," James said. He stood over me after I sat down at the table and I noticed beads of sweat on his forehead. He was scratching his arms, too.

"Are you all right?" I said. "You sick?"

"What? Me? I'm fine, Counselor. Good as gold. Right as rain. What can I get you? I got beer, tequila, vodka, or I got some of that homemade corn whiskey that you liked in the freezer. Got some killer weed, too, if you're interested, probably some other stuff if you want."

"No drugs," I said, "but a shot of that moonshine and a beer chaser would be great."

"Coming right up," he said, and in less than a minute, the whiskey was warming my esophagus and stomach. I took a long pull off the beer and took another drink out of the Mason jar James had set in front of me. I drained what was left of the beer and asked for another. I hit the whiskey one more time, chased it.

"Rough day?" James asked.

"You wouldn't believe," I said. I took another swallow of the beer, waited for about a minute, and looked across the table at him. "Do you remember what you said to me when we were standing in the courthouse parking lot after the jury acquitted you of cutting that guy up?"

"I probably said a lot of things," he said, "mostly thank you, thank you, and thank you."

"You said if I ever needed anything, anything at all, that I should come to you."

James turned up the beer he was drinking, drained it, and slapped it down on the table.

"And by Gawd here you are," he said, wiping his mouth with the back of his arm.

"Here I am."

"What do you need?" he said. "What can ol' James Tipton, Junior, do for Darren Street, attorney-at-law?"

I wrapped both hands around the beer in front of me and leaned forward on my elbows. My eyes locked onto his and I said, "I need a man killed, I need it done immediately, and I'm willing to pay you fifty thousand dollars in cash."

CHAPTER TEN

When I got back to the chalet after leaving James Tipton's, I was half-drunk and so confused and exhausted that I felt as though I was living in a thick fog. Everything seemed to be happening in slow motion; I didn't seem to be able to comprehend anything fully. I'd driven aimlessly through the mountains around Gatlinburg and Pigeon Forge for more than an hour, ignoring the ringing of my cell phone, and when I finally pulled into the driveway at the chalet darkness had fallen. I walked in and smelled food cooking, but I couldn't identify what kind of food. My mother spoke to me from the kitchen, but she sounded like she was under water. Finally, she walked up to me and took my face in her hands.

"Darren," she said. "Darren! Are you drunk?"

"Maybe," I said. "A little."

"Damn it, Darren. What were you thinking? Where have you been?"

My mother's faith in God had waned over the years and her language had turned a bit toward the salty side. She turned away from me and crossed the kitchen, returning with a steaming cup of coffee she'd poured from a pot on the counter.

"Sit," she said, pointing to a stool at a breakfast bar adjacent to the kitchen. I took the coffee and started sipping as she moved back toward the stove. We sat in silence for five minutes while I got the coffee down.

"You cooked?" I finally said.

"Sean and I went to the store. It was something to do. Are you going to answer my question?"

"What question?"

"Where have you been? Did you find the old client you were talking about?"

She loaded a plate with baked chicken and mixed vegetables and sat it in front of me, but the thought of eating was repulsive. I pushed it away.

"I did."

"Did you find him in a bar?"

"No," I said. "At his house. He was home."

"So you went over there and drank with him?"

"Lighten up," I said. "I just needed to calm my nerves a little. He had some moonshine and maybe I drank a little too much. That stuff's like liquid heroin. Sneaks up on you. Where's Sean?"

"Fast asleep."

"Did he say anything about . . . about what's going on?"

"He just wanted to know why Katie isn't here. Have you talked to her?"

I took my phone out of my pocket and looked at it. I'd received more than a dozen calls—from clients, other lawyers, and from my secretary—but Katie wasn't among them.

"No. I tried her twice, but she didn't answer and she hasn't called."

I folded my arms on the counter and laid my head down as a mild wave of nausea passed over me. Mom came around the counter and started rubbing my neck.

"It's going to be all right, Darren," she said. "We'll figure it out."

"I think I might have done something really stupid," I said, my head still down. I'd been regretting what I'd done at James's house since the moment I pulled out of his driveway.

"What do you mean?" Mom said. "While you were gone?"

"Yeah. Hang on. I think I'm gonna . . ."

I got up off the stool; hurried over to the sink; and coffee, alcohol, and bile spewed from my mouth. I retched for five minutes before it finally passed. About halfway into it, I felt a cool washcloth being pressed against the back of my neck. When I was finished and had wiped my face and rinsed my mouth, I leaned back against the kitchen counter.

"What did you do?" Mom asked.

"I can't tell you," I said. "It could cause problems for you."

"You're not making any sense at all, Darren. You leave here and tell me you're going to find an old client who might be able to help. You come back drunk and acting like you don't have a damned bit of sense. Then you toss your cookies in the kitchen sink, and now you won't tell me what's going on? I'm your mother. Spit it out."

"Did I tell you Jalen Jordan paid me fifty thousand dollars?"

"You mentioned it."

"Did I tell you it was in the van? Under my seat?"

"I don't think you mentioned that. So?"

"It isn't there anymore," I said. "It's gone."

"Where did it go?"

"I gave it to the client I went to see. I gave it to James Tipton."

"Why would you give him fifty thousand dollars, Darren?"

I looked at her and saw the realization cross her face.

"You didn't," she said.

I nodded. "I know. It was stupid."

"Did you hire him, Darren?" Her voice took on a tone I rarely heard. It was a tone of incredulity. It meant the emotional dam was about to burst.

"I didn't know what else to do, Mom. I'm terrified for Sean."

"So you went out and hired this . . . this . . . *who is this guy?*"

"Tipton. His name is James Tipton."

"You said he's a client. Is he a thug? A criminal? Did you give him fifty thousand dollars to commit murder? Has my son involved himself in a conspiracy to commit murder?"

I dropped my eyes, no longer able to look at her. Hearing those words, hearing the fact that I'd committed a felony for which I could find myself imprisoned for the rest of my life made me ashamed of myself. I wasn't a killer or a vigilante. I was a lawyer, for God's sake. I was supposed to follow rules, not break them or make them up as I went along. What could I possibly have been thinking? My stomach began to knot again.

"Shit, Mom," I said. "Now what?"

"Now what? I'll tell you what! You're going back out to your van and you're going to drive back to this James what's-his-name's house and you're going to tell him you were temporarily overcome by insanity and you're going to get your money back and call this whole thing off!"

"But what if he—"

"Get!" she yelled, pulling me toward the door by the elbow. "Right now! Get back over there and call it off! And I don't care what you think about the police and I damned sure don't care about your law license. As soon as we get back tomorrow, you're going straight to the FBI."

CHAPTER ELEVEN

Silverware clinked against ceramic plates, customers talked quietly, and waitresses barked orders to line cooks at the Waffle House on Papermill Drive in Knoxville. Assistant US Attorney Ben Clancy sat in a corner booth and watched Special Agent Gary DuBose walk through the door and approach. Clancy smiled. He hadn't seen DuBose in a while, but the kid bore a strong resemblance to his old man, the late Knox County sheriff Joe DuBose.

"Good to see you, General Clancy," DuBose said, using the title conferred on district attorneys general by law enforcement officers. "I appreciate you meeting me this early."

"It's good to see you, too, Gary," Clancy said. "You're the spitting image of your daddy when he was a young man."

"Thank you, sir."

"I miss him," Clancy said. "He was a fine, fine man. The best sheriff this county has ever seen."

"I miss him, too. It's still hard to believe he's gone."

"He was always proud of you, I can tell you that," Clancy said. "And look at you. A DEA agent. How long have you been with them now?"

"Just over two years."

"Time certainly does slip away."

At thirty years old, DuBose looked like he'd been carved from a block of granite. Despite the morning chill, he wore only a tight black T-shirt, black utility pants, and black boots. His face was long and angled, his hair cropped close, his eyes forest green.

"I apologize for last night," Clancy said after they'd received coffee and ordered breakfast. "The phone woke me up. I'm one of those early to bed, early to rise people."

"It could have waited," DuBose said. "I just thought you'd be excited to maybe get a crack at Darren Street."

"Go over it for me," Clancy said. "And talk slowly. I'm getting old."

"About ten months ago," DuBose said, "I was assigned to the task force that's investigating the distribution of oxycodone in Knox and Sevier counties. One of the names that kept coming up was James Tipton, Junior. Actually, his entire family's name kept coming up. Everybody kept saying his grandmother is some sort of kingpin. The word is that they've been moving a lot of oxy up here from Florida and selling it wholesale to local distributors. None of them have ever been arrested, but James is a suspect in a couple of unsolved murders over in Sevier County. And two years ago, he was charged with aggravated assault for cutting a guy up with a knife, but a jury acquitted him at trial last year. Darren Street was his lawyer, and they apparently hit it off pretty well.

"We haven't been able to get squat on the family, but James apparently branched out on his own into Kentucky a while back. One of his sellers got popped up there, rolled on a distributor, and the guy put us onto James. We were fairly early into it. I had what I thought was some pretty solid intelligence but no wires or anything. What we were really interested in were the suppliers in Florida, so my boss suggested I go see him and rattle his chain, see if anything happened. We'd heard he was using his own product, and you never know, right? So me and a couple of my guys paid him a surprise visit at his little trailer up in the mountains one night. I told him it was just a matter of time before we had enough to indict him and that once we did, he was going away for at least thirty years and we would wind up arresting his whole family. I told him that if he would be willing to work for us and give us his suppliers, we'd figure out a way to keep his jail sentence to a minimum and maybe back off his family if they quit moving drugs. He's looking at a lot of time, though, General, and I know how you feel about making deals with those kind of people. I hope I didn't cross any lines, but I told him in exchange for a sentence reduction, he would have to give up his suppliers, work for us, and forfeit the money and property he's accumulated as a result of dealing drugs. He basically told me to go screw myself, but I could tell I scared him. So I left him my cell number and told him to call me if he changed his mind, otherwise I'd see him when we eventually got enough evidence together to indict him.

"Last night around nine I get a call from him and he wants to meet; he says it's urgent. So I drive to Strawberry Plains and meet him in this little bar and he tells me that the lawyer who represented him on the aggravated assault just tried to hire him to kill somebody, and he wants to know if I'd be interested in cutting a deal in exchange for information on the lawyer. I tell him I might, so he goes into this bizarre story of how Darren Street came to his house and offered him fifty thousand dollars to kill a man named Jalen Jordan because Jordan had supposedly threatened to kill Street's kid. He said Street already paid him the money."

Clancy dipped a piece of toast in an egg yolk, took a bite, and chased it with a cup of coffee.

"Interesting," he said. "It'd be nice if we had something besides the word of a suspected drug dealer and murderer to back it up."

"I asked him if he had a recording of any kind and he said he didn't. But I couldn't wait to call you, General Clancy. My dad would have given his right arm for a shot at Darren Street."

Clancy nodded. "I know. Street was extremely disrespectful to him." He motioned to the waitress for more coffee.

"This could be huge," DuBose said. "We catch Street in a murder conspiracy and jam up a drug dealer. Plus, from what Tipton told me, this Jalen Jordan might very well have killed those two little boys. Should we set up a meet with the FBI and put them on him?"

"We're already on him," Clancy said as DuBose's chin fell.

"So you knew about all this?"

"No, no," Clancy said. "You did the right thing by calling me immediately, Gary. Exactly the right thing. We knew about Jordan from an entirely independent source. We're all over him. But this with Darren Street is all new. I'll have to give some thought as to how we should deal with it. Do you know how Tipton left things with Street?"

"He said he agreed to do it and that Street gave him the money. They're supposed to meet again late this morning, and Street is supposed to bring some more information about Jordan. Pictures, address, descriptions of vehicles, that kind of thing. So what do you want me to do? Do we wire Tipton ourselves and sting Street?"

"You guys have what, four safe houses in and around the city?" Clancy said. "I'd like to talk to Tipton alone."

"Right," DuBose said. "We have four. Which one do you want to use?"

"The big one on Creekside Avenue."

"Not a problem."

"Go outside and call Tipton," Clancy said. "I have things I have to take care of at the office this morning, but set something up as soon as possible after noon. Just me, you, and Tipton. That's it. Don't say a word to anyone else. I'll get the check."

"Got it, General," DuBose said, and he slid out of the booth and headed for the door.

CHAPTER TWELVE

When I went back to Tipton's trailer after the tongue lashing my mother gave me, he wasn't home. I waited for an hour with that crazy dog barking and all of those skulls staring at me, but I eventually lost my nerve and decided to come back early the next morning. I went back to the chalet, set the alarm on my phone for 5:00 a.m., and arrived at Tipton's around 5:45. It was still dark and still frightening, but I was relieved to see Tipton's car in the driveway. I pulled up close to the front porch and got out. The dog was terrifying; he had the heavy chain stretched out tight, and I kept glancing over there. If he broke the chain or the pole or his collar, he would be on me in about three seconds and I was sure I'd be dead less than a minute later. I pounded on the door several times and yelled James's name. Finally, the porch light came on and James opened the door. He was wearing only a pair of boxer shorts, smelled strongly of beer and tobacco, and looked like death warmed over.

"I'm sorry to show up so early like this," I said over the ferocious barking of the dog, "but I've changed my mind. I don't want you to do it."

The look on his face was one of confusion mixed with pain. Judging by the way he looked, I could only imagine how badly his head was pounding.

"I'm gonna shoot that fuckin' dog," he muttered, and he turned away from the door as though he might really be going to get a gun.

"James! Wait! Don't shoot the dog, please. Just listen to me, okay? I changed my mind. I don't want you to do what I asked you to do last night. I don't want you to hurt anyone. Do you understand me?"

He started rubbing his face with both hands, but soon stopped and nodded his head.

"You understand?" I said. "You're not going to go back inside and forget I was here?"

"Nah, I gotcha, Counselor. Don't kill the fuckwad child rapist. You gonna do it yourself?"

"I'll probably just hide until the police catch up to him. They'll be onto him soon."

"What about your boy? Is he gonna be okay?"

"I won't let anything happen to Sean. I'll keep him hidden."

"And the money?" He pointed over his shoulder with his thumb. "You want me to get the money?"

"Keep it," I said. "For your trouble."

James nodded again. "You want to come in and have a cup of coffee?"

"Thanks, but I'm going to head on back to Knoxville. I have some things I need to do. Go back to bed, James. I'm really sorry I bothered you with all of this."

I drove back to the chalet, and Mom and I drank coffee while we waited for Sean to get out of bed. Once he was up, we packed up our vehicles, drove into Gatlinburg, and had breakfast. After that, we took Sean to the Ripley's Aquarium. We'd been to the aquarium a couple of times before. I usually loved it as much as Sean did, but I had a hard time concentrating on anything other than what I was going to do about Jalen Jordan. I knew he was out there somewhere. Was he waiting for me to make a mistake? To relax? Would he really kill my kid?

After we'd gone through the aquarium, I gave Mom my credit card and told her to take Sean and check into the Hilton Hotel in Knoxville.

"Entertain him for the rest of the day," I said. "I'll catch up with you later."

"What are you going to do?"

"I'm going to do what you told me to do. I'm going to talk to the FBI."

I drove from Gatlinburg to the FBI office in Knoxville. On the way, I called and asked to speak to Special Agent Freeman, the agent Officer Denton told me she'd spoken to. Freeman was gruff, but he agreed to meet with me. I walked into his office around eleven thirty.

"What can I do for you?" Freeman said in a businesslike tone. He had a smug half smile on his face, the kind of "my shit don't stink" look FBI agents are famous for.

"Have you ever heard of a man named Jalen Jordan?" I said.

"Not sure. Should I have heard of him?"

"He came to see me Tuesday afternoon and asked me to represent him in an assault case that was filed by the Knoxville police. I talked to him for a little while and decided I didn't like him. When I told him I didn't want to represent him, he threatened my son."

Freeman's expression didn't change a bit. He just sat there looking at me.

"And?" Freeman said.

"He said he'd hate to see somebody throw my son off a cliff out by The Sinks like those other two boys that have been killed."

"So?"

"I was hoping you might do something about it."

"Like what?"

"I don't know, whatever you can do. Put a tail on him. Keep a close eye on my son."

"Can't do it," Freeman said. "Don't have the manpower to baby-sit." He was acting so disinterested that I wanted to slap him to get his attention.

"Listen," I said, "I know you guys have the bag that was found in Jordan's glove compartment. It contained two pairs of boys' underwear. That underwear most likely belonged to the two boys who were murdered."

"And how would you know that?" Freeman said.

"I can't say."

"Attorney-client privilege, huh?"

"Exactly."

"So you wouldn't be willing to offer any testimony that Jalen Jordan confessed to you that he committed these two murders, am I right?" It was getting to the point where I wanted to do more than slap him—I wanted to jerk him up and punch him in the mouth.

"It was a privileged conversation," I said. "I couldn't testify if I wanted to. Any judge would toss it in a heartbeat."

"So again, why are you here?"

"I'm trying to get some help for my son," I said loudly. "Are you too thick to understand that?"

"And I just told you we aren't in the babysitting business. So the guy threatened your son. That isn't exactly a federal crime, is it? And you just told me anything Jordan might have said to you is privileged. So I don't see much point in continuing this conversation."

"Have you gone through the van yet?" I said. "Have you sent the underwear off to the lab? Can you tell me how long it's going to be before you arrest him?"

"I'm not in the habit of discussing ongoing investigations with defense attorneys," Freeman said, "and neither is any other FBI agent in his right mind. Listen, Counselor, you apparently caught a bad break when Jordan walked through your door. But there isn't anything I, or anyone else in law enforcement to my knowledge, can do to help you right now. My best advice would be for you to take your son on a little vacation until it's safe for him to return."

"A vacation?" I said. "Could you give me any idea as to how long this vacation would need to be?"

"Best guess? About two months. The lab is slow. And if you tell anyone I said that, I'll deny it."

"Two months?" I said. "I've practically told you that Jalen Jordan is your murderer and you're telling me it's going to take you two months to get him off the street? What if he kills another kid in the meantime? Somebody besides my kid?"

"Not gonna happen," Freeman said.

"How can you know that?"

"Because I know. You'll just have to take my word for it."

"But it's still going to be two months before he's arrested?"

"Give or take a week," Freeman said. "Listen, I've already told you more than I should, and I have a lot of work to do, so if you don't mind?"

I walked out of Freeman's office muttering and shaking my head. Two months? Freeman seemed to be sure of himself when he said Jordan wouldn't harm another child, which I took to mean they already had him under tight surveillance. But could I trust my son's life to them? Not a chance. Two months wasn't an eternity, but it was a hell of a long time to shut down a law practice. Still, if it meant Sean would be safe, I'd figure out a way. I'd take him somewhere until Jalen Jordan was arrested and then return. It would mean uprooting him from school, from his life, but it was better than the alternative.

I was certain my mother would do anything she could to help, but my wife was a different story. I reluctantly punched her number into my cell phone.

"Where were you last night?" she said as soon as she picked up.

"If you'd bothered to answer my call or if you'd bothered to try to call me, you would have known," I said.

"You're such a game player, Darren."

"I know. Game playing is my life. Listen, Katie, we really need to talk. Can you meet me somewhere?"

"I'm busy right now."

"Are you working?"

"I'm getting a pedicure."

"Can we just meet at home? It's important. Sean could be in real danger."

"Good lord, Darren, are you still on that? This isn't a movie, you know. You're not an actor. You're just a guy who hustles a living defending criminals. Nobody wants to hurt Sean."

"Maybe so, but I'm going to take him out of town for a couple of months. You can come if you want, or you can stay here. But Sean and I are leaving for a while."

"You're not taking my son anywhere," she said.

"I'm going to the house to get some of his things," I said. "If you want to talk about it face-to-face in a rational manner, show up there in an hour."

CHAPTER THIRTEEN

Ben Clancy loathed men like James Tipton. He believed them to be inferior physically—made up of defective genetic material—as well as mentally and spiritually. A man like James Tipton had no chance of spending eternity in God's kingdom. He was incapable of any sort of meaningful self-examination, which meant he could never truly repent, which meant he could never be forgiven. Clancy might be willing to minimize, or even ignore, some of Tipton's earthly transgressions in order to get a long-awaited and well-deserved shot at Darren Street, but Tipton, in the long run, was doomed to hellfire and torment.

When Clancy sent such men—and women—to rot in the federal penitentiaries scattered around the United States, he felt not a breath of guilt or remorse. In fact, Clancy walked away from every conviction, whether it be by guilty plea or a jury's guilty verdict, with a sense of satisfaction and an unshakable belief that justice had been served, because Ben Clancy regarded himself as an instrument of God, a David in a world haunted by Philistines. He spoke fondly and often of being a dispenser of God's justice during the Sunday school lessons he taught at Calvary Baptist Church in downtown Knoxville and tried to instill a sense of the avenging angel into the Boy Scout troops he counseled each year at camps in and around the city.

Clancy watched warily from a block away as Special Agent Gary DuBose and James Tipton walked into the safe house on Creekside Avenue in Knoxville. He'd arrived early and parked his car four blocks away, then walked around the outside of the safe house and checked out the neighborhood.

DuBose and Tipton were standing just inside the front door as Clancy approached.

"I'd like to speak to Mr. Tipton alone," Clancy said. He avoided Tipton; he had no desire to shake his greasy hand. Tipton was wearing jeans, running shoes, and a tan, Western-cut shirt. Clancy thought he looked like a pimp. "We'll talk in the backyard. Did you check him for recording devices?"

"I did," DuBose said. "He's clean."

The safe house was in an upscale residential neighborhood. The homes sat on large lots, and the lot of this particular house was surrounded by a ten-foot-high hemlock hedge. Clancy led Tipton to a spot near the hedge about a hundred feet from the house.

"I understand you're looking to make a deal," Clancy said.

Tipton seemed nervous. He was shifting his weight from one foot to another, and his eyes darted around the backyard.

"I lost my leverage a little while ago," Tipton said.

"What do you mean?"

"The lawyer, Darren Street, he came back by my place this morning. He said he'd changed his mind. Didn't want me to kill anybody. He said he'd figure out another way to handle it."

"My understanding is that Mr. Street asked you to kill a man named Jalen Jordan and paid you fifty thousand dollars. Is that correct?"

"That's right, but now he says he doesn't want me to do it."

"Did you give him the money back?"

"He told me to keep it. Said he didn't want anything to do with Jordan's money."

"So you still have it? Where is it?"

"Hidden out at my place," Tipton said.

"What did Street say he was going to do, exactly?"

"He said he was going to hide with his kid until he could get something figured out."

"Hide? Any idea where?"

"No."

"I've seen Agent DuBose's file on you," Clancy lied. "He's built a strong case against you for trafficking in oxycodone. You're looking at thirty years—minimum—in a maximum-security federal penitentiary. Since there isn't any parole, you'll serve a minimum of eighty-five percent of the sentence."

Tipton looked at the ground and dug at the grass with the toe of his shoe.

"But I think we could still make a deal," Clancy said.

"Is that right?" Tipton said. "What kind of deal?"

"You get what you want, which is to stay out of prison and we leave your family alone. I get what I want, which is a dead child killer and Darren Street's skin nailed to the side of a barn."

"That whole red bandana thing must have got pretty deep under your skin," Tipton said.

"Mention red bandana again and you and Darren Street will be sharing a cell," Clancy snapped.

Tipton held up his hands. "Take it easy," he said. "What do you have in mind?"

An idea had formed in Clancy's mind as soon as he heard that Darren Street had left Jalen Jordan's cash with Tipton. Some things would have to fall into place, but the idea had promise.

"Are you a hunter, Mr. Tipton?" Clancy said.

"Beg your pardon?"

"A hunter! Do you hunt and kill wild game?"

"I do."

"What do you hunt?"

"Deer, mostly. Bear every couple of years."

"I take a buck every year myself," Clancy said. "I assume you have a rifle?"

"I do."

"Scope?"

"Yes, sir."

"Is it accurate? Can you shoot?"

Tipton nodded. "I can take the head off a squirrel at a hundred yards."

"I've never let a drug dealer facing the kind of time you're facing walk away before," Clancy said, "but in your case I'm going to make an exception. You can keep your property and you can keep the money Darren Street gave you, but we're not going to give you another dime. We'll stay away from your family. And in exchange, you're going to do exactly—and I mean *exactly*—what I tell you to do."

Clancy reached into his inside jacket pocket and extracted an envelope, which he handed to Tipton.

"You'll find a prepaid cell phone in there and some photographs of the same man Darren Street wanted you to kill. I don't know yet how it's going to happen, but you will be ready at a moment's notice, day or night. I will call you on that phone and give you instructions. You will follow them to the letter. You want to make a deal with me? Fine. I'll deal. But this will be a high-stakes game, Mr. Tipton. Do I make myself clear?"

Tipton nodded again.

"Say it," Clancy said. "Say, 'This is a high-stakes game.'"

"This is a high-stakes game."

"You will deal only with me. You will not talk to anyone else. Say it."

"I will deal only with you. I won't talk to anyone else."

"If you make the slightest mistake," Clancy said as he pointed his finger at Tipton's nose, "if you suddenly grow a conscience, if you hesitate in the least, prison will be the least of your worries."

CHAPTER FOURTEEN

I was surprised when I heard the garage door opening. Katie had actually showed up. I went downstairs and walked into the kitchen just as she was walking in from the garage. The sight of her always made me hesitate for just a moment. She was an absolute knockout, completely out of my league. She was two inches taller than me and looked, for all the world, like a fashion runway model. Her hair was thick, sandy blonde, and wavy, and it cascaded down her shoulders to the middle of her back like a waterfall. Her face was structured perfectly: full, sensual lips, high, strong cheekbones, a petite nose, subtle chin and forehead. And her body . . . my God . . . it was a bottomless pool of pleasure. She was soft and firm, smooth and warm, athletic and voluptuous. She was wearing beige designer shoes, black designer shorts, a designer blouse that matched the shoes and shorts perfectly, designer jewelry that perfectly accented her designer outfit, and designer make-up that was meticulously applied and made her even more beautiful than she was naturally.

"I appreciate you coming," I said in the friendliest tone I could muster.

"I live here," she said. "Where's Sean?"

"He's with Mom. We're going to stay at a hotel downtown until I can figure out what to do."

"Don't you think you're letting this get completely out of hand, Darren?"

"Sit down, please," I said, gesturing toward the kitchen table. "Let me fill you in on what's happened."

She went to the refrigerator, retrieved a bottle of mineral water, and walked to the kitchen table.

"So fill me in," she said, and I started talking.

* * *

Katie and I met at a party at the University of Tennessee early in our senior year and very quickly wound up in the sack, half-drunk. The sex was incredible and became addictive. Thinking back on it, I suppose it was nothing more, or nothing less, than that elusive phenomenon people call chemistry. I couldn't get enough of the way she looked, the way she felt, the way she smelled. Wherever I was, whatever I was doing, everything stopped when Katie arrived. It was as though the universe revolved around her; she became the center of everything.

I'm not sure why she was so attracted to me. I like to think it was because I was smart and sexy and handsome, but ultimately, I think it was something neither of us really understood. I realized early on that there were things about her I didn't like—things I actually loathed—but inertia seemed to set in. The old "object at rest tends to stay at rest" thing. It was easier to stay with her than to break things off.

Before we knew it, we'd graduated. I went on to law school, and she barely made it into the master's program for exercise science. She didn't really want to keep going to school, but her father was willing to pay and it allowed her plenty of time to work out, which is what she loved more than anything. We moved into an apartment together, but the relationship steadily deteriorated. I was gone a lot, and when we were together, we argued constantly. We were about to call it quits a couple of months before I graduated from law school, but then she started having symptoms, took a pregnancy test, and *voila!*

Sean.

Katie's parents thought so much of me that they immediately offered to pay for an abortion. It was her body and her life, but I told her I didn't want her to abort the child. We'd find ways to bridge the gaps, to put aside our differences, I said. I told her I would do my absolute best to be a good father and husband. She was leaning toward the abortion for a while because the thought of having a huge belly was repulsive to her, but I eventually wore her down and we got married. It was a simple ceremony performed by a General Session Court judge at the courthouse in downtown Knoxville because her father—an extremely wealthy, notorious slum lord—told me he would burn every dollar he had before he would spend a dime marrying his daughter to a piece of gutter trash like me.

* * *

"And now you're going to shut down your office, take Sean out of school, and go where?" Katie said after I'd told her everything that had happened.

"I'm not going to shut down the office. I'll just have to reschedule everything, delay things for a while. I'll keep Rachel on and keep the doors open. It'll be similar to having some type of surgery or something. I'll go to the judges and explain what's going on and they'll move the cases back for me. And I was thinking I might call Peter Camp. I'm sure he'd let us stay with him and Jenny until they arrest this guy. He's in Nashville, so it isn't too far, and they have plenty of room."

"But you said the FBI agent told you he was sure no more children would be killed. Isn't that what you said?"

"I'm not willing to bet Sean's life on what an FBI agent said."

"And what about me?" Katie said. "My choice is to either give up my entire life until this imaginary crisis has passed or stay here while you and Sean go to Nashville. And if you do that, I wind up looking like a terrible mother, a terrible wife, and a terrible person."

"It isn't an imaginary crisis," I said, resisting the urge to tell her she was already a terrible mother, wife, and person. "This is as real as it gets."

"I think we should depend on the FBI," she said. "They're like gods or something."

"Are you serious? You're willing to bet Sean's life on what an FBI agent said because leaving until we're sure Sean will be okay would be an inconvenience to you?"

"Don't call me selfish," she said. "I hate it when you call me selfish."

"I didn't call you selfish," I said, "although calling you selfish is like calling a dog's ass ugly."

"That's it," Katie said as she pushed herself away from the table and stood. "I'm done. And I'm not agreeing to you taking my son anywhere. Bring him back here today or I'll call the police and have you arrested."

"For what? Trying to protect him?"

"For kidnapping," she said, and she turned and stormed out of the room.

CHAPTER FIFTEEN

Ben Clancy looked down at his ringing cell phone. The ID told him Special Agent Paul Freeman was calling; it was just before noon.

"Jalen Jordan is going into the mountains," Freeman said. "He and his mother are going to the bank to get him some money and he's going to try to lose us long enough to get to one of the trail heads in the national park. Then he's going to hike the Appalachian Trail north into New York or Maine."

The black bag teams Clancy had requested had placed listening devices all over Jalen Jordan's apartment, his mother's house, and in his mother's car. A GPS tracking device had been planted in Jalen's mother's car as well. Their phones were being monitored and records of their phone conversations, e-mails, and texts were being studied. The FBI and the US Attorney's Office knew what both Jalen and his mother were doing every second of the day and night. FBI agents had also been tailing Jordan and his mother, and they'd been doing so openly. They were pressuring Jordan, trying to force him into a mistake.

Clancy sat up straight when he heard the news that Jordan was going into the mountains. The world had suddenly become brighter.

God was smiling on him, offering him a beautiful opportunity. He forced the smile off his face.

"It might be perfect," Clancy said flatly.

"Perfect? How could it possibly be perfect?" Freeman said.

"It gets Jordan out of populated areas away from children, so we don't have to worry about him killing another child. If he goes to the Appalachian Trail, then he either goes north or he goes south. You say he's going north. Fine. We get eyes on him from the air and we put four or five agents on the trail close to him. Not too close, but close enough to make sure he doesn't get off the trail without us knowing it. Quantico has agreed to prioritize the DNA tests. It shouldn't be more than a week. Once we have the results, we take him down out in the wilderness and bring him back to civilization. Nobody will be in harm's way when the arrest happens. The more I think about it, the better I like it."

"So you're suggesting we gather some folks, gear up, and go camping?"

"Like I said, it's perfect," Clancy said. "Let him think he's gotten away, and when the time is right, we'll take him down."

* * *

James Tipton looked down at his cell phone and groaned. Clancy. Fucking Clancy again. It seemed like he'd been calling every ten minutes.

"Hello?"

"Do you have everything together?"

"Yes."

"It's time to go. Right now. Listen to me very carefully. Take your weapon, your binoculars, and a tree stand and drive to Gatlinburg. Turn left at traffic light number eight onto Historic Nature Trail Drive. Turn into the Rainbow Falls Parking area. Park and get onto the trail. Walk at least a half mile. Avoid contact with anyone and conceal yourself. Get into position in the stand and wait for Jordan."

"Are you kidding? Already?"

"Did I stutter? Right now, damn it!"

Tipton had made a deal with a representative of the government of the United States, but to him it seemed more like a deal with the devil. As he jogged from the parking lot on Circle Head Road toward the Bullhead Trail, carrying his deer rifle in his right hand and with a tree stand strapped to his back, he wondered whether he would be able to identify the guy, whether he could make the shot, and ultimately, what would happen later.

He cursed himself and the decisions he'd made. The drugs. The damned drugs. All Tipton had really given a shit about over the past two years was getting high. He looked forward each and every day to crushing the oxycodone pills, mixing them with water, and injecting them into his veins. The high was so raw, so euphoric, that it was almost indescribable. Everything around him seemed to intensify when he was high, and for the past couple of years, he'd been high almost all the time.

But now he was starting to pay the price. He'd managed to alienate most of his family, and they'd been nothing but good to him. He'd been high when he cut up and nearly killed a man a couple of years earlier. Darren Street had gotten him out of that one. He'd been high when he made the decision to branch out on his own, which had eventually led to a visit from the DEA agent named Gary DuBose. And now, here he was, running up a trail in the woods, about to kill a man he didn't know. Clancy had told Tipton the same thing Darren Street had told him—the man he was going to kill was the same man who had raped and murdered two young boys in the area over the past year. Tipton had no way of knowing whether that was true.

What he did know was that if he backed out, if he failed to deliver, then Ben Clancy and the DEA would send him off to federal prison for as long as they possibly could. Clancy might even kill him, or have him killed. The man was a zealot. Tipton had dealt with hard men in the past, men who were capable of cruel, even psychotic, acts. They had a certain air about them, almost a scent of danger. Clancy was a lawman, but Tipton believed without reservation that he was as merciless as any assassin.

It was now one thirty in the afternoon. The sun was high behind light, scattered clouds. A gentle breeze was blowing through the tiny leaves that had recently blossomed. Tipton was fifty yards off the trail, about thirty feet off the ground in his tree stand, just beneath the thin canopy of a blooming sugar maple. He had a clear view of the trail beneath him as it gradually descended to the point where he had stepped off into the woods. He hadn't seen a person, an animal, nothing. The lot where he'd parked his car was empty. Aside from the fluttering breeze, it was silent.

And then he saw a man walking up the trail toward him.

Tipton lifted the high-powered binoculars that were dangling from his neck and, using the focus wheel and the diopter, brought the image into focus. Clancy had provided Tipton with a dozen photos of Jordan taken from different angles in different light and Tipton had studied them carefully. It was him. He was wearing a long-sleeved, blue pullover shirt and was carrying a large backpack. There was a walking stick or thin pole in his right hand. Tipton watched him for a full minute as he came closer, then lowered the binoculars and reached for his rifle. He'd positioned his stand so he could rest the rifle against the trunk of the tree while he was taking aim. Tipton placed the crosshairs on Jordan's chest and took a deep breath. He let the breath out slowly and gently squeezed the trigger.

The rifle shot cracked, echoing off the surrounding mountains. Tipton watched through the scope as the bullet tore through Jordan's chest, lifting him slightly off his feet and knocking him straight over onto his backpack.

Tipton lowered the rifle to the ground using a piece of rope and quickly skittered down the trunk of the tree to the ground. He'd made the kill—he was certain Jordan couldn't have survived—but he still had to ditch the rifle and get out of there without being seen. A rifle shot in the mountains wasn't all that unusual, but you never knew when someone might be curious.

Tipton reached the ground and began to move in a half-circular path toward his car. Along the way, he found a spot to dump the rifle, just as Clancy had instructed. It was in a creek bed about a hundred yards from the body, a place that would certainly be searched by the FBI when they came. Tipton made it to his truck without seeing a soul, tossed the rest of the gear in the back, and was on his way less than twenty minutes after he'd fired the shot.

This part of the job was finished, but as he reached into his glove compartment and retrieved a flask of bourbon to calm his nerves, Tipton knew there would be much, much more to come. Tonight, he had to break in to Darren Street's garage and plant another piece of evidence. He pulled his truck onto the road and headed for his home on the mountain. There, in the medicine cabinet, he would find his oxycodone, and in the drug, he would at least find some temporary relief.

CHAPTER SIXTEEN

Ben Clancy was pacing along the wall at the back of the room. He could feel sweat running down his back, and he believed the performance he was delivering to be as good as any he'd ever delivered in front of a jury.

The office belonged to United States Attorney Stephen Blackburn, the man in charge of representing the federal government in forty-one Tennessee counties. It was just down the hall from Clancy's own office, but it was larger and more luxurious, almost regal. An American flag and a Tennessee flag flanked the desk and the seal of the Department of Justice, United States Attorney, hung on the wall. A Latin phrase on the seal, "*Qui Pro Domina Justitia Sequitur*," assured all who knew the translation that Blackburn was a man "who prosecutes on behalf of Lady Justice."

In the office along with Clancy were Blackburn, and FBI agents Daniel Reid and Paul Freeman. Six hours had passed since Jalen Jordan's body had been discovered by a hiker around three o'clock, and dozens of FBI agents had been scouring the mountainside ever since.

"How did this happen?" Clancy yelled. "How? We had him. We were all over him. We let him get out of our sight for an hour and he gets popped by . . . by who? A deer hunter who was poaching and mistook him for a deer? Another serial killer who just happened to show up and whack the serial killer we were tracking? An enemy of his who somehow found out he was going into the woods and also happens to be good with a sniper rifle? How is any of this possible?"

The agents simply looked away. They apparently had no answers. Clancy stopped pacing and glared at them.

"It had to be one of you or someone in your agency," he said. "We've got a vigilante in our midst."

Dan Reid, the special agent in charge of the Knoxville FBI office, sprang to his feet.

"Now you wait just a damned minute!" Reid yelled. "I'm not going to sit here and listen to you accuse me or any of my people of murder. I don't give a damn *who* you are. You want to make those kinds of accusations? Let's just talk about you, then. *You're* the one who made the decision to let Jordan go into the woods. You. You knew every move he was making because you wanted to be in the loop. Maybe you had something to do with this death."

Stephen Blackburn, gray-haired and in his midfifties, had been appointed to his office for a second four-year term by the president of the United States. Blackburn had originally gained his own lofty position because of his father's vast wealth and the political connections both he and his father had nurtured throughout their lives, but he was, nonetheless, a capable attorney and a shrewd assessor of problems. He was also a decent mediator.

"Hang on," Blackburn said, raising his hands. "Take it easy. Let's all just take a deep breath and calm down for a minute. Ben, I know you're upset, but Dan's right. It's way over the line to accuse him or anyone in his office of having anything to do with this. Same with you, Dan. And I can tell just from the looks on everyone's faces that we're all terribly upset about this. But let's take a minute and think it through. Go back to the beginning. How did we get onto Jalen Jordan in the first place?

Who, outside of the people in this room and the FBI, knew about what we were doing? Who knew about what was inside the van? Who knew we were having the boys' underwear tested? Who could have possibly had a reason to kill him and could have known where he was? Did anyone talk to the parents of the boys who were murdered?"

"I did," Freeman said. "I told them about the underwear. I showed them photos."

"Did you mention anything about a suspect?" Blackburn said.

"I told them we may have a suspect, but I didn't mention any names."

"Who else?"

"The Knoxville PD officers who arrested him—Olivia Denton and Terrance Casey," Reid said. "They know about it. So would their superiors and anyone they might have told between then and now. They arrested him more than a week ago. It could have spread through the entire department by now. Some of our forensics people know. So do some administrative people and, of course, the folks at the lab, plus anyone those people may have told. It becomes a matter of exponential progression. Dozens of people, maybe a hundred, could know by now."

Reid turned back to Clancy. "You said you were going to talk to politicians if they wouldn't give us a priority bump at the lab. Did you do that?"

"He came to me," Blackburn said. "I took care of it myself."

"If a good deal of the Knoxville PD knows, then it's just a matter of time before there's a leak and the media gets wind of it," Clancy said. "Once they find out we suspected Jordan of killing the two boys that were found at The Sinks, they'll start baying like hounds. The conspiracy theories will fly, there'll be accusations of vigilantism. And what if they find out we were on Jordan twenty-four-seven and let him walk away into the woods?"

"Like I said, that was your call," Reid said. He'd sat back down, but his face was still pink.

Clancy pointed a pudgy finger at Reid.

"Do you think you're going to use that against me somehow? Take me down with it? I've been in politics at some level or another my entire adult life. There's nothing I can't handle."

"Except maybe a red bandana," Reid said.

The air seemed to go out of the room for a full thirty seconds. Nobody said a word.

"I'd advise you to tread lightly," Clancy said.

"If I may," Paul Freeman said "I think I have something to add. Something that might be productive."

"By all means," Blackburn said

"Speaking of red bandanas, and I don't say this to upset you, Ben, Darren Street showed up at our office yesterday afternoon, and looking back on it now, it seems more than a little strange."

"What did he want?" Clancy said.

"Basically, he wanted protection for his son. He told me Jordan had come to see him on Tuesday and wound up threatening his boy. He's bound by the attorney-client privilege, so he can't repeat what Jordan said to him, but in a roundabout way, he pretty much told me Jordan confessed to killing the two boys and then threatened his son. I told him we couldn't help him."

"So you're saying Darren Street is a suspect?" Clancy said.

"I'm just saying the timing is odd. I don't see how he could have known Jordan would be on the trail, though."

"Maybe he bugged Jordan's place," Clancy said. "We did."

"That's pretty far-fetched."

"It might be, but right now, it seems like a good place to start," Clancy said. "I say we turn our attention toward Darren Street, look as far up his skirt as possible, and see what we find. And while we're at it, let's talk to the Knoxville police, starting with the two officers who arrested Jordan."

Clancy looked around the room. Everyone was silent. He looked at his boss.

"Steve?" he said. "What do you think?"

"Sounds like a plan," Blackburn said. "Let's get to it."

CHAPTER SEVENTEEN

On Friday, I walked into the chambers of the Honorable Zachary P. Holloway. I had six cases pending on Holloway's docket and needed to move them back until after Jalen Jordan was arrested. Holloway was a large, light-skinned black man with a pleasant disposition outside of the courtroom. Inside, he acted very much like an irritable grizzly bear.

He was sitting behind his mammoth desk, munching on a salad that was in a Styrofoam container. His black robe was hanging on a coat rack in the corner. A television on a stand behind me was broadcasting the noon news.

"Forgive me for not standing and shaking your hand," the judge said as I walked in. "I've had a bit of a cold and don't want to pass it on to you."

"I appreciate that," I said.

"Have a seat, Mr. Street. What can I do for you?"

"Well, Your Honor, I have an unusual request. I really hate to impose, but I have to ask you . . ."

Something a newscaster was saying caught my attention and I turned and looked at the television.

"Ask me what?" the judge said.

"I'm sorry, just a second."

"The victim has been identified as twenty-four-year-old Jalen Jordan of Knoxville," the newsman on the television said.

I stood and said, "I'll be damned."

"What? What are you talking about, Mr. Street?" the judge said.

My attention had shifted completely to the TV. "The body was found by a hiker near the Appalachian trail yesterday afternoon," the newsman said as Jordan's slimy face flashed across the screen. "Our sources indicate he was shot with a high-powered rifle from some distance away. Stay tuned for updates as more information is made available."

I felt a smile cross my face. I couldn't help it. I heard myself say, "Ding dong, the bastard's dead."

"I beg your pardon?" Judge Holloway said.

"Did you hear the same thing I just heard?" I said. "Did you just hear that a twenty-four-year-old man was found dead near the Appalachian Trail and his name was Jalen Jordan?"

"I'm not sure. I wasn't listening that closely. But why would the death of anyone bring a smile to your face? And did you just say, 'Ding dong, the bastard's dead'?"

"I'm sorry, judge," I said. "He threatened to kill my . . . ah, never mind. You don't want to hear it, but believe me, I have a reason to smile. Now, if you'll excuse me, I have to make some phone calls."

Judge Holloway was staring at me, open-mouthed with a fork full of salad in his right hand, when I turned and walked out the door. I practically floated out of the courthouse and dialed my mom's number as soon as I was on the sidewalk outside. She'd been staying with us at the hotel and had been willing to do whatever it took to ensure Sean was safe.

"Have you heard?" I said when she picked up the phone.

"Heard what?"

"Jordan's dead; somebody shot him."

There was a brief silence. "Are you sure, Darren?"

"I just saw his face on the news. He's dead, Mom. The dirty, rotten, filthy son of a bitch is dead, and I couldn't be happier. I feel like I could fly."

"So what do we do now?"

"We go back to our lives. But first we celebrate. Check out of the hotel and meet me at Calhoun's. Lunch and alcohol is on me."

CHAPTER EIGHTEEN

A week later, life was seemingly back to normal. It was also rather unpleasant, because Katie was continuing to act like Katie.

I watched my wife get out of the luxury sports car I was paying for and walk quickly into a small restaurant called Baldacci's about fifty miles north of Knoxville off I-75. It was dark, around eight thirty. Katie was wearing a sexy little black dress and a pair of fuck-me pumps, neither of which I'd ever seen before, and carrying a clutch purse covered in rhinestones. The private investigator I'd hired two months earlier had told me Katie was having an affair with a man named Leonard Bright, who was fifteen years her senior. He owned, among other things, the Mercedes-Benz dealership in Lexington, Kentucky, which was a two-and-a-half-hour drive to the north. He also lived in Lexington and was a lifelong bachelor. The investigator didn't know how they'd met. I figured they'd met at the gym where Katie worked out and did her personal training, but I didn't really care.

Katie thought I'd gone to Nashville to a continuing legal education seminar because I'd lied to her two weeks earlier in order to give her this opportunity. I wasn't sure at the time whether she'd go to Lexington or whether he'd come to Knoxville, but now I realized they were splitting the difference. I borrowed a car from the lawyer who would soon be handling my divorce and followed Katie from our neighborhood. She dropped Sean off at her parents' multi-million-dollar mansion on the Tennessee River and drove straight to the restaurant. I wasn't certain she was meeting the guy from Kentucky, but from the way she was dressed, I doubted she was meeting a girlfriend. I'd never heard of Baldacci's, but I assumed it was an Italian place, and if Katie was eating there, it was undoubtedly expensive. There were only about a dozen cars in the parking lot, and after Katie walked into the restaurant, I did a quick recon. There was a Mercedes-Benz with a dealer tag from Kentucky.

I parked near the Benz and got out of my minivan. I was wearing clothing appropriate for a nice restaurant: a navy-blue suit, a white button-down shirt, and shiny black shoes. I walked in the front door, quickly scanned the place, spotted Katie, stepped straight to the maître d', and said, "I'm meeting my wife and a friend. She's right over there." I walked to the table, less than thirty feet away, and was on them before they realized what was happening. I pulled a chair back and slid into it.

"Hi, sweetie," I said to Katie as soon as I sat down at the table. "Sorry I'm late. Introduce me to your friend."

She looked like she'd been caught in the path of an oncoming train in the middle of a trestle. Her mouth formed a perfect circle. Her expression made me think of a frightened blowfish. I turned to her dinner partner.

"I'm Darren," I said. "My wife seems to be temporarily unable to communicate. I understand your name is Leonard Bright. Should I call you Leonard? Len? Lenny Baby? Or maybe I should just call you the dickhead geezer who thinks he can roll into town and bang my wife anytime he wants to."

Leonard was smiling, which I found infuriating. I was within a millisecond of punching him in the mouth when I suddenly felt the presence of large men standing behind me, one at each shoulder. I looked around and recognized one of them, but I couldn't immediately identify him.

"Darren Street," he said.

"Yeah. What do you want?"

"Stand up and place your hands behind your back. You're under arrest."

"Arrest? I didn't touch him. Didn't threaten him."

Then I figured out who the guy was. Freeman. The FBI agent.

"Stand up," Agent Freeman said. "I'm not going to tell you again."

"What the hell are you arresting me for?" I asked as I stood.

"The murder of Jalen Jordan," Freeman said, and he slapped the cuffs on me and led me out of the restaurant.

PART II

CHAPTER NINETEEN

They led me out the door and put me in the back of a silver Ford Crown Victoria. Neither Katie nor her boyfriend had gotten a chance to say a single word. Two agents I didn't know climbed into the front. Agent Freeman got into the backseat beside me. We pulled out of the restaurant and pulled onto the interstate, headed back south toward Knoxville.

"Tell me this is some kind of joke," I said as the car gathered speed. I had never been arrested, never been cuffed, never been in a police vehicle. My mind was racing, but I was so confused and so scared I couldn't concentrate on any single thing. I couldn't believe I was being arrested. And for Jalen Jordan's murder? How in the hell could this happen?

"No joke," Freeman said. "We're booking you for first-degree murder. The judge won't be back in court until Monday morning so we can't arraign you until then. I thought we'd take you down to Maryville, let you spend the weekend in scenic Blount County."

"That jail is a shithole," I said.

Freeman chuckled. "Yeah, it is. By the way, we're executing search warrants at your home and your office simultaneous to this arrest."

"In other words, your goons are tearing my house and office apart."

"I prefer colleagues to goons, but yeah, they're tearing the places apart."

"They won't find anything."

"Are you sure?"

"There's nothing to find. I didn't kill anybody."

Freeman turned his head and looked at me.

"You need to rethink that," he said, "and I'm going to be a nice guy and tell you why. You practically announced to an officer of the Knoxville Police Department that you were going to kill Jalen Jordan. You threatened to strangle your wife. You've been highly agitated."

"You talked to my wife?"

"She doesn't like you much, Darren. You should probably start thinking about divorce. No, wait, you're going to be in prison for the next fifty years, so I suppose *she's* thinking about divorce. Where were you last Thursday afternoon?"

"Let's see," I said. "I'm handcuffed and riding in the backseat of a car with three FBI agents. At least I'm assuming those two guys in the front are FBI agents. I'm not free to go, am I?"

Freeman smiled sarcastically and shook his head.

"Then this is a custodial interrogation and Miranda applies. You haven't Mirandized me, Agent Freeman."

"Would you like to be Mirandized?"

"I'll leave it to your discretion."

"You have the right to remain silent," Freeman said. "That means you can sit over there and not say another word and there won't be a thing I, or anybody else, can do about it. If you choose to keep talking, you need to understand that anything you say can and will be used against you in a court of law. You understand that, right? You're charged with murder, and if you say something in this vehicle that will help us convict you of that murder, all of us will show up at your trial and repeat what you said in front of the jury so they can use it as evidence in their deliberations. And finally, you have the right to be represented by an asshole like yourself. And by asshole I mean an attorney. If you can't afford an asshole, the judge will pick an asshole for you and the taxpayers of the Unites States will foot the bill for the toilet paper. Do you understand the rights I've just explained to you?"

"That may have been the most clearly elucidated explanation of the Miranda warnings I've ever heard," I said. "Especially the asshole–toilet paper part. I really enjoyed that."

As the seconds passed, the realization that I was in the custody of the federal government began to set in. And they weren't charging me with littering in a national park; they were charging me with murder. The state had put my uncle away for twenty years for a crime he didn't commit. This was the feds. They were the baddest of the bad, the guys who could reach out to other countries and grab up drug dealers and terrorists, try them quickly, and put them so far underground they were never heard from again.

"Good," Freeman said. "So where were you last Thursday between, say, noon and three o'clock?"

I thought about it. Thursday was the day after Mom and I had come back from the chalet. I'd spent the afternoon fishing with Sean because Mom had needed to go to her beauty salon and catch up. It wasn't much of an alibi.

"I think I'll keep that to myself," I said to Freeman. "But I will say this again. I didn't kill anybody."

"Our hastily convened grand jury begs to differ," Freeman said. "And I suppose you know who presented the case to them."

My fingers began to tremble slightly. I hadn't thought about it, but now that he mentioned it . . .

"That's right," Freeman said. "I can see your face getting darker. Your old buddy Ben Clancy. He can't wait to get you in front of a jury. He told me he's thinking about wrapping a red bandana around his head and wearing it to court every day."

CHAPTER TWENTY

The Blount County Jail, like most county jails across the country, was, indeed, a shithole. Six hundred inmates were usually housed there from what I'd read in a newspaper account of a lawsuit that had been filed against the county. It was designed for 250.

Agent Freeman walked me from the sally port through two thick, steel doors into a booking area that looked, believe it or not, similar to a circulation desk at a public library or the nurse's counter inside an emergency room. Four thickly muscled deputies stood ready to process the next number, and since it was Friday evening, business appeared to be steadily picking up. Around the central desk, recessed in the concrete block walls, were eight holding cells, each with large, Plexiglas windows in the doors so the guards could see what the inmates were doing. I stood with Agent Freeman and his two pals next to a wooden bench against the wall until we were waved up by a deputy. He asked for my full name, date of birth, and Social Security number and then asked Agent Freeman about my charge.

"He's charged with first-degree murder," Freeman said entirely too loudly as he handed the deputy some paperwork.

I cringed and felt my shoulders involuntarily slump. I looked down at the floor. The deputy pushed a button on his headset and said something quietly. The next thing I knew, I was flanked by two deputies who were even bigger than the ones behind the desk. They had to be juicers—steroid users. I'd seen plenty of them at the gyms where I'd worked out over the years. They quickly ran a chain around my waist and shackled my legs in irons, then attached a chain to my handcuffs, ran it through a D-ring on my waist chain, and then did the same thing with the leg irons. I was now pretty much trussed except I was still upright. Had they laid me on my back and gutted me, they could have stuffed me with some cornbread, put me in an oversize oven, roasted me for a few hours, and served me to the inmates as a late night supper. Next came the mug shot and the fingerprinting, both of which were pretty much painless. Despite the fact that I was terrified of what might happen to me and utterly dumbfounded by how I could possibly have wound up being charged with Jalen Jordan's murder, I was doing my best to maintain, however miniscule, some sense of humor.

That changed when they strip-searched me.

I was taken into a shower room with the three large deputies and Freeman in tow. I didn't know where the other two FBI agents went and didn't care. Once we got in there, they uncuffed and unshackled me and told me to strip. They took each piece of clothing as I handed it to them, catalogued it, and put it in a box. They took my watch, my wallet, and my wedding ring. Once I was completely naked, the largest guard told me to open my mouth. He looked inside my mouth with a flashlight and then told me to run my hands through my hair. I suppose he expected drugs to come falling out. Next I had to turn my head both ways so he could look in and behind my ears, and then, the denouement:

"Squat and cough," the deputy said.

I did it.

"Turn and face the shower. Bend over. Spread your butt cheeks."

A feeling of humiliation like nothing I'd ever experienced washed over me like a tidal wave as I bent over and reached back.

"Turn on the water, take a shower, and make it fast."

When I was finished, the guard handed me a towel. I dried off in front of them, and he handed me a striped jumpsuit and a pair of slippers. I put them on, and as soon as the jumpsuit was buttoned they replaced all of my restraints. Then he put a band on my wrist that identified me as a federal inmate, handed me a rolled up, thin foam pad along with a rolled up sheet and blanket, and said, "Let's go. You get one call."

They guided me toward a bank of four phones on a wall. One of them removed the chain from my handcuffs so I could reach the phone. I dialed my mother's cell. I let out a deep breath when she answered after the second ring.

"Mom, it's Darren," I said.

"The caller ID says Blount County Jail," she said.

"That's where I am. I've been arrested."

"Arrested? For what?"

"It doesn't matter right now. Listen, Mom, I don't think I have much time on the phone. I need you to get ahold of Richie Fels immediately and tell him where I am. Tell him to come running."

"Is it serious, Darren? Are you in a lot of trouble?"

"It's bad. Call Richie." I made her write down Richie's cell number and read it back to me. "Keep calling until you get him, okay?"

"I will. What about Katie and Sean?"

"Katie already knows. Sean is with Katie's parents."

I felt a finger poke me between my shoulder blades.

"Enough," a voice said. "Hang up."

"I have to go, Mom. Call Richie. I love you."

"I love you, too."

A guard took my arm and we started walking. At this point, apparently, Agent Freeman disappeared. I didn't even notice he was no longer with us until several minutes later when I looked over my shoulder and only the three Blount County guys were with me. We walked down a long corridor, turned left, and walked down another long corridor until it ended. The sounds of the guards' boots echoed off the walls and ceiling. The guy who had looked in my mouth and ears pushed a button, and a couple of seconds later the lock buzzed and the steel door retracted into the wall. We walked into a large room that reminded me somewhat of the small basketball gyms where I'd played in church leagues when I was a teenager. A guard was sitting at a metal desk just to our right when we walked in.

"Two-zero-seven," the guard said.

There was a row of gray metal cell doors in the wall across the room. Each door had a twelve-inch square window about five feet off the ground, and a face was peering out from the other side of nearly every window. There was a set of steel stairs to the far right that led to a narrow balcony and another row of metal cell doors directly above the doors at ground level. There was a lot of shouting going on. Men were calling to each other; others were yelling at the guards; still others were simply yelling. I did my best to block it all out.

"Up the stairs," one of the guards behind me said.

I climbed the stairs and walked about thirty feet down the balcony.

"Stop. Turn to the right."

I did what the man said. One of the guards stepped to the window and peered inside.

"Step back, Hillbilly," he barked.

The cell door buzzed. A guard beside me said, "You're gonna love Hillbilly." Suddenly, my shackles were off and I was inside the cell.

"Turn around and face the door."

I turned. There was a sliding sound, metal against metal, and a slit, about two feet long and about five inches high—something I would later learn was called a "pie hole"—appeared in the door.

"Put your hands through."

I offered my hands and a second later was free of the cuffs. I pulled my hands back inside the cell and the slit slammed shut. I turned around. The cell was maybe seven feet wide and nine feet long. To my right was a stainless steel toilet and sink. To my left were two steel bed frames, bunk bed style. Sitting on the bottom bunk in a pair of boxer shorts was a lean, long-haired, bearded man who looked to be around forty-five. His upper body was covered in tattoos, and he smelled like piss and sweat.

He looked at me like he wanted to slit my throat. The guy reminded me of Charles Manson. Then, without saying a word, he folded his fingers behind his head and lay back on the bunk.

CHAPTER TWENTY-ONE

Richie Fels, appearing exhausted and smelling of bourbon, showed up around ten thirty that Friday night. Three guards escorted me from the cell to a small interview room that contained a table and four plastic chairs. The shackles, waist chain, and handcuffs had all been put back in place and I remember thinking for the hundredth time that evening just how surreal things had become as I listened to the clangs and rattles while I shuffled down the hallway.

"Are you sober enough to do this?" I said as I sat down across from Richie. He was still wearing his work clothes, *sans* the tie. His button-down shirt was white and the sleeves were rolled up just beneath his elbow. Navy-blue suspenders secured what I assumed were pants of the same color. A white T-shirt was visible beneath the unbuttoned collar and a white tuft of hair sprouted from beneath the shirt. I knew exactly where he'd been. He'd been drinking at a restaurant downtown called Lola's. I'd spent many Friday evenings eating and drinking with Richie and his pals at Lola's. I felt the flimsy, plastic chair I was sitting in shift beneath me and wondered how Richie's was supporting his three-hundred-pound frame.

"I can leave right now if you'd like," Richie said. "Actually, nothing would please me more. You've killed my buzz."

"Sorry," I said. "I'm sure you'll catch another after you leave."

"Do you have a copy of the arrest warrant?" Richie said.

"They didn't give me anything, but they said they were searching my house and office, too."

"I guess you'll get everything soon enough. Your mother said you weren't specific about the charge. What is it?"

"First degree," I said.

Richie's eyes widened. "Murder? First-degree murder?"

"Yeah. Can you believe it? And it's the feds."

Richie took his wire-framed glasses off and rubbed his nose for a few seconds. He replaced the glasses and said: "Who'd you kill? Allegedly?"

"Jalen Jordan. And for the record, I didn't do it."

"Is that the man you were telling me about a week or so ago?"

"Been more than a week, but yeah that's the guy. The one who came into my office and tried to hire me and when I refused, he threatened Sean."

"Didn't he get shot in the national forest over by Gatlinburg?"

"That's what they say."

"Ambushed? From some distance away?"

"Those are the reports I've heard."

"We'll have to talk about your experience as a sniper at some point. Right now, as much as I hate to, we need to talk about money. I can't represent you on a first-degree murder case for free, Darren. I just can't do it."

"I wouldn't expect you to. Wouldn't want you to. How much are you thinking?"

"I don't know what kind of case they have," Richie said, "but since you're sitting here, they must have something at least moderately strong. We're looking at a thorough, expensive investigation, and we're definitely looking at a trial. Since it's the feds, you realize who will be prosecuting the case, don't you?"

"Yeah. It'll be Clancy. I thought about that earlier."

"He'll be extrazealous about this one. He'll want to hang you from the highest tree he can find."

"But you won't let him do that, will you?"

"I'll certainly try not to, but back to the fee, I'm thinking you're looking at a minimum of two hundred thousand, and that will be if I do it for half my normal hourly rate."

I nearly fell out of my chair. Richie? Asking me for $200,000? Our relationship apparently wasn't quite as strong as I'd believed it to be.

"I don't have that kind of money, Richie."

"What kind of money do you have?"

"We just bought a house, so almost all of my cash went to the down payment, but even if I sold it—which Katie would never agree to—there wouldn't be much equity. I've got maybe fifty thousand stashed in an investment account, another thirty in an IRA, but Katie is having an affair and I'm about to go through a divorce. Everything will probably be locked up for a while, and when the divorce is over, by the time the lawyers get paid, there won't be much left."

"So you can't pay a retainer? Nothing on the front end?"

"I'm sure my mom would help me out, but she doesn't have a lot and I hate to ask her. I'll pay you in installments for the rest of my life if I have to, Richie."

"If you don't wind up getting a life sentence."

"I'm innocent. I didn't kill anybody."

"Even if you don't get convicted, you're going to be sitting in here for a year before they try you."

"You don't think I'll make bond?" I knew the answer to the question before I asked it, but I was desperate, hoping against hope that Richie would offer some encouragement, some reason to be optimistic.

"It's a first-degree murder case, Darren. Think about it. You're going to walk into the arraignment Monday morning and Clancy is going to tell the judge you're a danger to the community. The judge will look at you and say, 'You're charged with first-degree murder. He's right.' You might as well accept the fact that everything has changed. You're not getting out of here for a long time. If they convict you, you're going into the federal penitentiary system and you might never get out. Even if they don't, you're going to be suspended by the Board of Professional Responsibility and your reputation is going to be ruined. You can hope for the best, but you better start planning for the worst."

I sat there for a moment, stunned by the sudden realization that what he was saying was true. Prior to that day, I'd always taken my clients' situations for granted. If they were in jail, they were in jail. No big deal to me. I was always able to walk out the door. But no more. I realized that I was in a fight for my life. If I went down on this charge, I would rot in prison. I thought about Sean and tears filled my eyes. I couldn't speak for a couple of minutes.

"Help me, Richie," I finally said. "Please? Help me."

"I'm sorry," he said, and I could see he was beginning the lawyer's process of emotionally shutting down. There would be no more empathy from Richie Fels. I felt myself beginning to grow angry. I thought Richie was my friend. We'd chased windmills together, ate and drank together, swapped war stories. We were supposed to be colleagues, but he had obviously changed. Maybe it was the years of alcohol abuse. Maybe the stress of practicing criminal defense for decades was taking a toll on him. He'd become impressed, almost enamored, with himself and his press clippings. Friendship apparently meant nothing to him because now, when I needed him more than I ever needed a friend, he was going to abandon me because I couldn't come up with an astronomical fee.

"No, you're not," I said. "You're not sorry."

"I just can't do it if you can't pay, Darren," he said. "It'll take so much time, it just wouldn't be fair to the other people in my firm and to my other clients. Besides, you practically made me a witness when you came into the office last week. You told me you were thinking about killing the guy."

"I didn't mean it," I said, horrified that he would say something like that out loud in a jail interview room. I'd always conducted my interviews in jails under the assumption that the rooms were wired. "And I didn't kill him."

"The federal defenders are good lawyers," he said. "You'll get a good defense."

"They work for the government. The United States of America signs their checks. I don't care what you say, it's an inherent conflict of interest."

"Maybe you can get one of the other lawyers in town to take it," Richie said. "I'm sure it'll be a highly publicized case. Somebody will want the recognition."

"I need a lawyer, not a glory hound."

"Yes, well . . ." Richie laid his hands flat on the table in front of him and pushed himself up. "This is getting more awkward by the moment. I feel badly, Darren. I really do, but I just can't make such a huge commitment without adequate compensation."

"Money talks," I said. "Right?"

He nodded. "Right."

"And bullshit walks. So take your bullshit and walk. Get the fuck out of my sight."

CHAPTER TWENTY-TWO

Back in the cell, I lay on the upper bunk in the semidarkness. I could hear the constant shouting from the cellblock, and the smell of the man lying in the bunk beneath me was almost overwhelming. The guard had called him "Hillbilly," and I could hear him breathing steadily. He hadn't moved when I climbed into the bunk.

Earlier, I spread the foam roll, wrapped the sheet around it, and covered it with the blanket. It offered little comfort; I could feel the cold steel of the bed frame coming through the foam. When I laid my head back on the pillow, it was the thickness of a towel.

There was a dull ache in my stomach, and I realized I hadn't eaten since noon, which was roughly eleven hours earlier. Had I been at home, I would have simply wandered into the kitchen, opened a cupboard or the refrigerator, and picked out something to eat. But there was no kitchen here, no refrigerators. There was only a stainless steel toilet and a sink. I had no desire to use the bathroom, but the thought of the sink made me thirsty. I sat up for a few seconds, then climbed over the side of the bunk to the floor. I bent over the sink and let the tepid water pour into my mouth. I swallowed a bit, realized it tasted metallic, and spit the rest out. I turned back to the bed and noticed that Hillbilly was standing next to the bunk. He was staring at me silently, like a predator in the night. I stared back at him, unsure of what I should do.

"You don't drink unless I say you can drink," he growled in a thick, southern drawl. "You don't shit, you don't piss, you don't eat, you don't do a damned thing unless I say it's okay."

I tried to maintain my stare and an air of toughness while I sized him up. He was an inch, maybe two, taller than me, but I probably outweighed him by five or ten pounds. I looked at his hands and didn't see a weapon. I'd always heard that prisoners challenge each other on a regular basis in order to establish a hierarchy, something very similar to wild dogs in a pack, but this was a surprise. I'd been in the cell for only a couple of hours. Hillbilly and I hadn't said a word to each other.

"And what if I tell you to go straight to hell?" I said in a voice that wasn't nearly as confident as I'd hoped it would be.

He turned sideways slightly, a fighter's angle.

"I'm gonna give you one chance to get on your knees and ask for my forgiveness," Hillbilly said.

"I'm not hitting my knees for anybody."

He was on me in a split second. He apparently favored boxing, because he stayed on his feet and caught me with a left hook that landed close to my chin and nearly knocked me out. I stumbled back against the door and pulled my arms in for cover while he punched me in the face and the ribs. I felt my lower lip split against my teeth and one of the blows to my ribs sent such a sharp pain through me that I believed for a second I'd been stabbed.

As I stood there with my back against the cell door, the thought of this animal beating me unconscious—and the fear of what he might do after I was unconscious—sent a surge of adrenaline rushing through me. My head cleared and I managed to get my forehead into his chest and bull rushed him back across the cell. He groaned as his lower back smashed into the steel sink and I took the opportunity to bash him in the face with my right elbow. His left hand came up and grabbed my cheek, and I could feel his thumb trying to gouge my left eye. I started trying to knee him in the groin, but the angle wasn't right. By that time he'd slid off the sink and we were in the far corner of the cell away from the door. I managed to slip behind him and get my arms around his waist. I lifted his feet off the floor and took him down between the bed and the sink. He didn't seem to have much experience with grappling, so I was able to control his legs and upper body while I wormed my way toward getting him into a choke hold. I got my right forearm beneath his chin, wrapped my legs around his waist, grabbed my right wrist with my left hand, and clamped down on him like a boa constrictor. Within ten seconds, he was out. I rolled off him and stood. I noticed movement and looked at the door. Two guards were standing outside the cell. They'd apparently been watching the fight.

"Good God awmighty, boy," one of them said. "You done whipped Hillbilly."

"That's a first," his buddy said. "Hillbilly's been whippin' people on this block for years."

"Let me out of here," I yelled as I beat my fist against the Plexiglas window. "Open the door. I need medical attention."

"You look all right to me," one of them said.

Just then, I felt a hand touch my shoulder and spin me around. I saw a bright flash, and everything went dark.

CHAPTER TWENTY-THREE

The guards left us in the cell together. I don't know how long I was unconscious, but I awakened with my head in the corner of the cell and my body twisted at an odd angle. Hillbilly was sitting on his bunk staring at me. I pushed myself up into the corner, slowly stood, and waited for him to come, but he didn't move.

"Show's over," he yelled at the guards, and they finally moved away from the cell door and went back down the stairs.

"You ain't bad," Hillbilly said after they were gone. He was rubbing his chin where I'd cracked him with my elbow.

My jaw felt like it was locked tight, I could feel both of my eyes swelling, and my rib hurt like hell.

"I'm not asking you for permission for anything," I said. "You're not going to bully me."

He chuckled, and I could tell it hurt. He was as sore as I.

"What?" I said. "What's funny?"

"You talk like a city boy. You educated?"

"I went to college."

"They teach you how to survive in jail?"

"Nah, that particular subject wasn't in the curriculum."

"You did okay on your first test."

"Yeah?"

"Rule Number One is don't be anybody's bitch. You let them, people in here will eat you alive. They'll take your money, your commissary, your cigarettes, your stamps, anything they can get from you. You have to stand up for yourself. If you have to fight, you fight. If you don't, you're gonna get robbed every time you turn around."

"What else?" I said. Richie had been right earlier. I was stuck for at least six months, maybe a year before I even went to trial. I had no control. I knew my trial date would depend on the judge's calendar, the US attorney's schedule and my lawyer's schedule. Even if I asserted my rights under the Sixth Amendment and demanded a speedy trial, courts had held that sixteen months was a reasonable delay on a murder case. I needed to learn as much as I could about how to deal with my present situation.

"Don't show weakness. Don't *ever* show weakness. Don't trust anybody. That means other inmates, your cellmate, and especially the guards. Don't ask dudes why they're in prison unless you get to know them real good. Don't show emotion. Don't ever stare at anybody. Don't talk bad about another inmate because it's going to get back to him. You can be friendly with other races, but not too friendly. Be loyal to your own race. Don't join a gang. Stay away from drugs and booze. Don't call anybody punk or bitch unless you're ready to fight to the death. And if you're in a shower with a bunch of dudes, wear boxers."

I felt like I should be taking notes.

"You gay?" he said.

"No."

"That's good. If you're lying, keep it that way. That shit you hear about people being raped in prison all the time ain't true. Inmates will stab you, but they won't rape you. The gays get segregated in most places, but you need to stay away from them. They ain't nothing but drama queens, big trouble. Did you bring money for a commissary account?"

"They picked me up at a restaurant in Knoxville. It was a surprise, out of the blue. I have maybe thirty bucks in my wallet and a credit card."

"You're gonna need basic things like soap and a toothbrush and underwear and socks. You have to buy all that from the commissary, and believe me, it ain't cheap. The food in this place is shit, so if you want anything extra to eat, you have to buy snacks from the commissary. You can put up to five hundred dollars in your account, but don't ever tell anybody how much you have."

"How often do we get out of this cell?" I asked.

"The block is maximum security, which means you must have done something pretty damned bad to get yourself put in here. We get out of the cell once a day for one hour. That's the only time you can use the phone. The only way to call out is collect, and it's expensive. Nobody can call in, and they won't bring you a message. The guards are punks. Most of them are cruel; they love to pound on dudes. Don't ask them for anything and don't trust them."

I shook my head and let out a deep sigh. Twenty-three hours a day locked up in this cage with Hillbilly? My legs suddenly felt weak.

"I'm going to get back on the bunk now," I said. "Am I going to have to fight you again?"

"I don't reckon."

I walked over, climbed stiffly onto the steel platform, and rolled onto my back.

"They charged me with first-degree murder," I said after a few minutes. "But I didn't do it."

There was no answer. After a couple more minutes, I said, "Why are you in here?"

"You don't know me that good," Hillbilly said. "Now shut up and let me go to sleep."

CHAPTER TWENTY-FOUR

I'd been inside the United States District Courthouse in downtown Knoxville plenty of times, but I'd always walked freely through the front door. On this day, I was cuffed and shackled as I was hustled through a sally port and down a hallway to a holding cell.

I'd never cared much for representing criminal defendants in federal court. The judges were all bluebloods who had far too much regard for their own intellects, and their holier-than-thou attitudes seemed to permeate the atmosphere and infect the other people who worked in the building. The United States attorney, the assistant US attorneys, the agents of the FBI and DEA, the US Marshals, even the judges' clerks seemed to think they were a cut above everyone who didn't spend their days serving Uncle Sam.

When I walked through the door into the courtroom, I almost gasped. The place was packed. I'd been isolated all weekend, and other than a couple of wiseass comments from a guard on our block about me being "some hotshot lawyer," I hadn't given much thought to the journalistic possibilities of my situation. But as I looked around, it began to dawn on me. I was a young, white criminal defense lawyer, a local boy with a clean record, a family man. I was accused of first-degree murder. The reporters reminded me of jackals scrounging for carrion.

The worst of it, though, was my mother. She was wearing a navy-blue business suit, her head held high, standing right behind the defense table. I mouthed, "I love you," to her as I walked across the courtroom.

I hadn't heard a word from Katie, which didn't really surprise me. The only way for me to contact her was by phone during my one hour out of the cell each day, which was usually closer to thirty minutes. I would have to call collect, and she would have to accept the charges. I was sure she wouldn't, so I didn't even try. To her way of thinking, what had happened to me would be nothing but an advantage for her since she knew I'd discovered her affair. She wouldn't give a damn about what Sean thought or heard or saw on television; as a matter of fact, I felt fairly certain she had probably gleefully informed him that I'd killed someone and would most likely never return.

But the thing that was weighing on my mind most heavily was who would wind up representing me. I'd thought about different lawyers in town, but nobody really stood out besides Richie, and he was obviously no longer an option. I couldn't afford a heavy hitter from Nashville or Memphis, and paying a low fee and hiring a bad lawyer was probably worse than having no lawyer at all. Mom didn't have the money to hire an expensive lawyer, and even if she did, I wouldn't have wanted her to spend it on me. I'd pretty much decided at that point that I could handle the case myself as long as they appointed me a decent mouthpiece. And Richie had been right about one thing. The federal defenders were generally excellent lawyers. The positions were highly competitive because they paid far better than state public defenders. Most of the federal defenders I'd known had been law geeks, the type who edited their law review in law school and who graduated at the top of the class and went on to clerk for federal judges.

A marshal led me to the defense table. I looked at Ben Clancy, pink-cheeked and puffy, who was sitting at the prosecution table like a toad on a rock, acting as though he wasn't aware I was in the room. He was wearing a shiny gray suit with a red kerchief. The kerchief had the same paisley design as the red bandana I'd used to help defeat him. The judge was already sitting on the bench. I looked up at him and felt an even deeper wave of anxiety pass over me. His name was Donnie Geer, a tall, lean, sixty-year-old egomaniac who wore wire-framed glasses and still dyed his hair red. I'd done battle with Geer several times, and in his courtroom, I'd always lost. One does not beat a federal judge on his own turf. I'd managed to get him reversed twice in the Sixth Circuit Court of Appeals, however, both times on Fourth Amendment issues. He should have respected me, but instead, he loathed me.

Geer looked down at me from his perch on high and said, "Mr. Street, it genuinely disturbs me to see you standing there."

"I'm not real happy about it, either, Judge," I said.

"You're charged with first-degree murder," he said.

"Yes, sir. I understand."

"What have you done about retaining counsel?"

"I spoke to an attorney, but I'm embarrassed to say I'm not going to be able to afford anyone. It's a first-degree murder case, I'm not guilty, and we're going to end up going to trial. The attorney I spoke to asked for a figure I couldn't begin to pay, and given the circumstances, that price seems to be the bottom line for a competent criminal defense lawyer."

"Are you asking the court to appoint a lawyer to represent you free of charge?"

"I don't think I have a choice."

"Forgive me, Your Honor, but that seems hard to believe," Ben Clancy said from my right. "Mr. Street has been practicing law for several years now, and from everything I've heard, he seems to be quite busy, quite successful. As a matter of fact, if I'm not totally misinformed, he recently moved into a half-million-dollar home. And surely he has financial accounts, investments, things of that nature. The federal defender program is designed to help indigent defendants, people who have no means to hire a lawyer. I don't believe for a second that Mr. Street is indigent."

"I might be able to work out some kind of financing arrangement with an attorney if I was going to be able to continue to work," I said to the judge. "But I don't see that happening. Does Your Honor intend to set me a reasonable bail?"

"He's charged with first-degree murder," Clancy said. "We have a strong case against him. He's a danger to the community."

"I've lived here my entire life," I said. "My family is here. I've never been charged with any kind of crime until this. I'm not a flight risk, judge. I plan to prove myself innocent and go back to practicing law."

"You're representing yourself right now," Judge Geer said. "That's never a good idea. And the answer to your question is no. I'm not going to set you a bail. Mr. Clancy is right. The indictment charges you with a premeditated murder by ambush. I'm going to ask you to fill out an application for an appointed lawyer. If you meet the criteria, I'll approve the application. If not, I'll expect you to hire a lawyer and have him here the next time you appear in court, which will be a week from today. We'll do a formal arraignment then."

I cringed at the thought of waiting a week to find out who my lawyer was going to be, but there wasn't a damned thing I could do about it. The marshal took me by the arm and led me toward the inmate exit. I looked back over my shoulder at my mom, who was standing there with tears running down her cheeks. Just as we cleared the door, another marshal appeared. He was carrying a sheaf of papers, which he handed to me with a smile.

"Looks like your wife isn't impressed," he said.

I looked down at the papers. Katie had either been preparing or she had flashed some money at a divorce lawyer over the weekend, probably money given to her by her parents or her geriatric boyfriend. I read through the papers quickly: a petition for divorce that asked for all of our assets plus full custody of Sean; a temporary injunction barring me from going anywhere near my home, my wife, or my child; and a petition to terminate my parental rights.

It was Monday at ten in the morning. It looked like I was in for a hell of a week.

CHAPTER TWENTY-FIVE

Grace Alexander, at thirty years old, was the youngest federal defender in the Knoxville office. She scanned through the e-mails on her phone, looked up at the clock on her office wall, and drew in a deep breath. She let it out slowly, then started tapping a pen on the top of her desk.

Twenty-four hours earlier, Grace had been assigned to represent Darren Street. It was a huge case as far as publicity, and that was exciting, but it was also a first-degree murder, and the stakes were high for her client. She hadn't yet met Street, but she was about to meet his mother. The woman had been calling for days, asking whether the judge had appointed a lawyer for her son. Yesterday, she'd been told yes, and she had asked immediately to speak with Grace.

Grace had dealt with mothers of clients in the past. For the most part, she'd found them to be unrealistic excuse makers, blind to the things their offspring had done, and unwilling to accept that their babies were headed to prison. But this one had seemed reasonable on the phone, so Grace reluctantly agreed when she asked if she could come to Grace's office and talk.

Grace stood as the woman walked in. She was attractive, around fifty, with brown hair and green eyes.

"Miss Alexander?" the woman said.

Grace could tell immediately that she was expecting someone older. She looked dismayed.

"Yes."

"I'm Shirley Royston, Darren's mother."

"It's nice to meet you."

Grace motioned to a chair, and Ms. Royston sat down.

"How can I help you, Ms. Royston?" Grace said.

"I just wanted to come here and look you in the eye and tell you my son is innocent," Ms. Royston said.

It was all Grace could do to keep from rolling her eyes.

"Yes, ma'am," she said.

"I was with him all during that week because his wife was too self-absorbed to give a damn about her own child. He didn't kill anyone, Miss Alexander. The problem we're going to have, I believe, is that we don't have . . . oh, what's the word I'm looking for? When you can prove you were somewhere else when something happened?"

"An alibi?"

"Exactly. We don't have an alibi "

Of course you don't, Grace wanted to say. *Nobody ever has an alibi when they're guilty.*

Instead, she said, "Why not?"

"From what I understand," Ms. Royston said, "Mr. Jordan was shot and killed on Thursday afternoon that week, sometime in the early afternoon. Darren was fishing with his son, Sean, during that time, but I doubt that there's a videotape of it."

"Maybe he stopped and bought gas or something," Grace said. "I'll ask him when I go talk to him tomorrow."

"So you haven't talked to him yet?"

"No, ma'am. They just told me about the case assignment yesterday afternoon, right before you called. I'm planning to meet with several people today and find out what I can, and then I'll go to Maryville and talk with him tomorrow."

"Would you like for me to fill you in on what happened leading up to the shooting?"

"By all means."

Grace listened as Shirley Royston recounted the unbelievable tale of what had happened to her son that week. She took detailed notes, nodded a lot, and asked a great deal of questions. When Ms. Royston was finished, Grace said, "Wow, that's quite a story."

"You don't believe me?"

"I didn't say that," Grace lied. "I just said it's quite a story. So while all of this was going on, someone else apparently shot Jalen Jordan on a trail in Gatlinburg."

"That's right, and we don't have any idea who it was or why he or she did it. We were just relieved to know that Sean was safe."

"And this was after Darren had talked to the FBI?"

"The day after, I believe. Are you going to be able to get Darren out of this?"

"I have no idea, Ms. Royston. It's too early to make any kind of prediction. I have no idea what kind of proof they have, but my experience with the federal government has been that if they indict and arrest someone, they have a pretty strong case, or at least they think they do."

"How well do you know Ben Clancy?"

"Fairly well on a professional level. Not at all personally."

"Do you like him?"

"I don't really like to talk about people, Ms. Royston."

"So you don't like him. Please do me a favor and look up the history between Mr. Clancy and my son. There's a case—*State of Tennessee versus Tommy Royston*—that should tell you everything you need to know. Tommy was my brother, Darren's uncle. Ben Clancy convicted him of murdering his wife when he knew all along my brother didn't do it. Darren hates him."

"Does Darren hate a lot of people?"

"No. Darren is a good person, Miss Alexander. An extremely good person who has worked hard to get to where he is. No one has given him a thing. His father was awful. He used to beat him terribly. He beat both of us terribly, and I think Darren developed some issues because of that. Darren was the one who finally stood up to his father. He was only thirteen, but one night when Billy—that was Darren's father's name—started in on me, Darren beat him up with a baseball bat and dragged him out of the house. He told him he had to leave, that he was never going to hurt either of us again, and he meant it. I think Darren would have killed him if it had come down to it, but Billy was a drunk and a coward and he just left and never came back. Darren probably suffers from post-traumatic stress disorder, and he has a bit of a hero complex. I think that's why he got into criminal defense law, that and what happened to my brother."

Beautiful, Grace thought. *My new client beat his father with a base-ball bat and has some issues.*

"I appreciate you helping me understand, Ms. Royston," Grace said, "but it would probably be best if you didn't say anything about Darren's mental or emotional issues to anyone else."

"What? Oh, right, of course. I don't want you to get the wrong impression. I just told you that because . . . oh, well, I don't know why I told you other than I want you to understand why Darren might have overreacted at first to his son being threatened. But he didn't kill anyone. I've never known him to own a rifle and I don't think he's ever been hunting. And besides, how could Darren have known where Jalen Jordan would be that Thursday? He wasn't spying on him. We were hiding from him."

Grace nodded and looked at the clock on the wall. She had another meeting in ten minutes.

"Ms. Royston," she said, "I really appreciate you coming in to talk with me, but I have another—"

"Wait, please. Would you mind telling me just a little bit about yourself? The rest of my son's life is apparently going to be at stake. I'd like to know something about the person who is going to be representing him."

"Of course," Grace said, not really wanting to tell the woman anything. "What would you like to know?"

"I'm not sure. How old are you, for starters?"

"I'm thirty."

"And how long have you been out of law school? Five years or so?"

"Right. Five years. I graduated from the law school at Vanderbilt University, and then I clerked for Judge Donald Kincaid in Memphis for two years. I applied for the federal defender program and was lucky enough to get a job in Knoxville. I've been here for three years."

Grace saw Ms. Royston's eyes pass over her left hand, which did not display any rings.

"Do your parents live here?"

Grace smiled and shook her head.

"No, ma'am. My parents are in San Diego. My father is a colonel in the Marine Corps, a career officer. My mother teaches journalism at San Diego State University."

"So you've traveled a lot."

"We actually spent a lot of time in San Diego because that's where my dad's unit is headquartered. He was gone a lot, but it wasn't all that bad."

"Are you close to your parents?"

Grace thought about her answer for a second, and then said, "Why is that important, Ms. Royston?"

"I'm sorry, I shouldn't pry. It's just that Darren and I are very close. We always have been, mostly because of what we went through with his father, I'm sure. And the thought of him sitting in a jail or a prison . . . the thought of him being convicted of a murder . . ."

Ms. Royston's voice trailed off and tears began to stream down her face.

"Please, Miss Alexander," she said, "please don't let Ben Clancy destroy my son. I'm terrified for Darren because I know what Clancy is capable of."

"I'll do what I can, Ms. Royston," Grace said, growing more uncomfortable by the second as this stranger wept in front of her. She reached into a desk drawer, brought out a box of tissues, and offered it to her client's mother. "But I have to warn you, it isn't easy to win against the United States government in federal court."

Ms. Royston stood, wiping her eyes with tissue.

"I'll go now," she said. "I'm sure you're very busy. Just please, please remember that Darren is innocent. He's worth fighting for."

Grace watched her turn and walk out the door. When it closed, she said under her breath, "Right. Your son is innocent, and I'm the Easter Bunny."

CHAPTER TWENTY-SIX

On Thursday, the guards showed up at my cell, slapped the cuffs and shackles on me, and led me to the attorney's room. Sitting at the table was a young, pretty-in-a-prudish-kind-of-way, green-eyed blonde wearing a pink blouse and designer glasses that were perched on a perfect nose. I sat down across from her and didn't say a word.

"Are you trying to intimidate me?" she said after a minute or so.

"Who are you?" I said.

"I'm your lawyer."

"No, you're not. You're a kid."

"I'm also your lawyer. My name is Grace Alexander. I'm with the Federal Defender's Office and I've been assigned to your case."

"How old are you?"

She looked at me like she might spit in my eye. "I'm old enough to have graduated from high school, college, and law school. I'm old enough to have passed the bar and gotten a job in the Federal Defender's Office. I'm old enough to have tried fifteen trials to a jury, two of which I managed to win. I'm old enough—"

"Excuse me," I said. "Did you just say you're two and thirteen as a trial lawyer? Two wins, thirteen losses?"

"Most of them were drug cases where the government was offering thirty years. My clients felt like they might as well go to trial and take a shot with a jury. They were really no worse off having gone to trial and lost, and it gave me some valuable experience."

"Wow, good for you," I said. "Tried any murders?"

"Two."

"Lose both of them?"

"Sure did."

"Why?"

"Because my clients were guilty."

She was young, but she was poised, and I'd known criminal defense lawyers who absolutely never tried a case to a jury. They were terrified of juries and resolved every case by plea agreement. This young lady had tried fifteen cases, and even though I was giving her a hard time, I was impressed.

"I can't tell you how comforted I am that you've been assigned to my case."

"Yes, well, perhaps you should have saved some money so you could hire a real lawyer."

"If I'd known I was going to get charged with first-degree murder, I would have saved every dime I ever earned. Even that probably wouldn't have been enough."

"Probably not," she said.

"I'm not guilty, you know."

"Good for you. It always makes me feel better about representing someone when they come right out and tell me that, even if they aren't telling the truth, and my experience has been that about ninety-nine percent of them aren't telling the truth."

"I'm telling the truth. I didn't kill anyone."

She folded her hands on top of the table and held my gaze. Her eyes were flecked with black, extremely pretty.

"Judge Geer is going to arraign you formally Monday morning at nine," she said. "You can forget bail. I already talked to him and it isn't going to happen. I spoke to both him and Mr. Clancy, and it looks like the soonest we can get the trial done will be six months from now, probably late September."

"What do you think of Clancy?" I said.

"I think he's a snake in the grass. He'd do anything to win a case, and he feels a special sort of loathing for you."

"So you know what we're up against."

"I know exactly what we're up against. Eight of my fifteen trials have been against Ben Clancy."

"Have you beaten him?"

"Not yet, but back to what I was saying. The judge has agreed to have you transferred to Knoxville so it will be easier for me to talk to you, but the Knox County sheriff says since you're charged with first-degree murder, you have to stay on a max block. That means the same drill as here—twenty-three hours locked down in the cell. I also met with your mother yesterday, so I know basically what happened, although I'm going to need to hear it from you several times."

"Why several times?" I said.

"Because it's such a wild story that if you're lying, you won't be able to keep everything straight."

"Fair enough."

"I don't want to get into it here today because I don't really trust this place, but if you can figure out a way to get a cell to yourself when they move you downtown it would help a great deal as far as you and I being able to speak openly. I've never known of the Knox County sheriff to put listening devices in the attorney's room, but from what your mother told me about you and Clancy, we should probably be extra careful."

"Fine," I said. "Extra careful."

"I'll see you soon," she said. She stood, closed her briefcase, and within a minute, the only thing left was the scent of her perfume.

"I didn't kill anybody," I said to the walls. "I need you to know that, and I need you to believe it. I didn't kill Jalen Jordan."

The guards came in and led me back to the cell. As soon as they'd unlocked the handcuffs and closed the pie hole, I turned around and looked at Hillbilly.

"Let me ask you a question," I said. "If you wanted to get a cell to yourself, how would you go about it?"

CHAPTER TWENTY-SEVEN

They moved me about twelve hours later. I was asleep in the cell at four in the morning when the guards came. They hustled me through the building, back through booking and the sally port, and chained me to a cold, steel ring inside a white van. We arrived at the Knox County Jail in downtown Knoxville in less than forty-five minutes, where I had to go through the entire booking procedure again. The sadistic bastards even strip-searched me again, made me squat and cough, spread my butt cheeks, and shower in front of them. There was absolutely no reason for them to do it—I'd been removed from a cell and had been supervised every step of the way—but they did it anyway. They gave me a fresh gray-and-white-striped jumpsuit, flip-flops, and the same thin bedding and led me to another maximum security cellblock. I was as humiliated as I'd been the first time they made me squat and cough, but this time there was another emotion pushing its way to the front: anger. I was already tired of being herded and humiliated and treated like an animal, and I was only a few days into it. Just as we were walking up to the cell door, one of the guards, who looked like all the rest of the guards—a white, muscle-bound skinhead—said, "Joe DuBose hired me, dickhead. I can't wait for you to give me an excuse to bust your skull open."

I turned and looked at him, thinking I should probably keep my mouth shut. But the anger was sizzling, Hillbilly's advice was echoing, and I couldn't restrain myself.

"DuBose hired you?" I said. "What were your qualifications? Inbred ingrate? Is your mother your cousin? Do you read above a first-grade level? Doesn't everybody start in the jail and then move out to patrol? Joe's been dead two years and you're still here. You must be a real mover and shaker."

He grabbed a handful of my hair, slammed my forehead into the metal cell door, and punched me in the kidney. The blow to my head and the punch took me to one knee, but I managed to get back to my feet.

"I'm going to beat this charge," I said through clenched teeth, "and then I'm going to come back here and stomp your ass. I'm sure you'll still be around."

He spun me around, pushed me flat against the cell door, and stuck the index finger of his right hand into my forehead just above my nose. The other guard who had walked with us had stepped to the side a few steps. I glanced at him but couldn't read anything on his face.

"You ain't gonna stomp nobody," the DuBose hire hissed, "and you need to remember something. I fucking *own* you when you're on this block." The volume of his voice was building slowly. His face was turning pink; the veins in his neck and forehead were bulging. He was putting on a show for all of the inmates on the cellblock who were watching and listening. "This is MY block!" he yelled. "MY FUCKING BLOCK! You disrespect me on MY FUCKING BLOCK and I'm going to FUCK YOU UP! I'm going to put you in the FUCKING hospital. You got that, you pansy-ass, criminal-loving faggot?"

I thought "criminal-loving" must be a reference to my career as a defense attorney, and in that moment, it actually amused me. I suppose it was the completely overwhelming nature of everything that had happened over the past few days—the feelings of total helplessness and humiliation, the fear, the confusion, the anger—coupled with his ugly, spitting, yelling, redneck presence in my personal space that caused me to suddenly react without giving any thought to the consequences.

I truly didn't care what happened when I head-butted him. I moved my head quickly to the side, which caused his finger to slip off my forehead and caused him to move a bit closer to me, and I slammed my skull into the bridge of his nose as hard as I could. I felt the cartilage in his nose give, saw the shower of blood, and within seconds, the two of them were on me, quickly followed by two more. They beat me savagely. Luckily, I was either knocked out or I passed out from the pain in less than two minutes.

* * *

A week later, after the arraignment, Grace Alexander showed up unexpectedly in the afternoon. I was in an "admin"—an isolation cell—chained to two thick, steel rings sticking up out of a concrete floor, when she arrived. I was sitting on the floor, but there was a concrete bench that served as a bed that ran along one wall and she sat down on it next to me.

"No wonder I had such a hard time getting in here to see you," she said. "I had to practically get a court order. What happened?"

I lifted my head slowly. It hurt to breathe, let alone speak, but I managed to say, "You told me to get a cell to myself."

"What? What are you talking about? Who did this?"

"A guard did it," I said. "A couple of guards, maybe three or four. I'm not really sure. But I started it. It was the only way to guarantee a cell to myself. I had to fight the guards."

"Fight the guards?" she said. "You mean physically fight them? You're supposed to be a lawyer. Lawyers fight with principles and words."

"This isn't court," I said, "and I'm an inmate, a prisoner. I'm not a lawyer in here. After you left last week when I was still at Blount County, I went back to my cell and asked my cellmate how I could get a cell to myself. He told me that if I start messing with the guards they'll put me in a cell by myself so there won't be any witnesses when they come beat the hell out of me. He said I have to fight them and fight hard, but if I chill out after a while, they'll eventually quit beating me. They'll also leave me in a cell by myself. It's a respect thing. I don't really understand it yet, but I'm working on it."

"You should be in a hospital," she said. "I'm going straight to the sheriff."

"No, don't do that. You'll ruin what little I've managed to accomplish so far. These guards won't respect me if you go crying to the sheriff. And I don't need to be in a hospital. They know what they're doing. I'm bruised all over, but there isn't anything life-threatening. None of them want to get caught up in a killing."

"So this is how you . . . how you—"

I managed to crack a smile.

"I did it all for you, my dear. Just so we could be alone."

I started to chuckle but my ribs were bruised so badly I couldn't. I must have cringed because her eyebrows curled into a look of sympathy.

"I heard what happened after court your first day," she said. "Serving you with divorce papers when you walked out of the courtroom. That was really low, even for Clancy. They couldn't have done it without his prior knowledge and approval."

"He's capable of much worse."

"I wasn't all that familiar with the situation between you and him," she said, "so I did some research yesterday. I'm not sure I could have done what you did. It took a lot of courage."

It was almost intoxicating, having her in the cell close to me. She was wearing clothes that were less formal than what she'd been wearing when I met her in Blount County and when she came to court— tight, faded jeans tucked into midcalf leather boots, a purple blouse, a white scarf tied loosely around her neck. Her hair was down, falling loosely in waves to her shoulders. The glasses still gave her a librarian, prudish kind of look, but she was a pretty prude. Her skin was smooth and unblemished, her fingers long and slim. And she smelled so good, so fresh, like a flower, lilac maybe. The combination of the look and the smell represented to me the freedom I'd taken for granted such a short time earlier. Grace Alexander became, in that brief encounter that day, a symbol of hope, and I think I began to love her for it.

"Courage?" I said as I pulled myself back to the moment. "I'm not sure courage is the right word. I was angry more than anything because of what he'd done to my uncle. I was reckless sometimes. It seems to be part of my nature."

"You ousted him from the DA's office. The red bandana campaign was a stroke of genius."

"He beat himself," I said. "He didn't take his opponent Morris seriously because he'd become so arrogant. He certainly didn't take me seriously. He regarded me as an insect, something to squash. He still does. Do you know he used to keep a miniature replica of an electric chair on his desk?"

Grace shook her head.

"Can you imagine? That's the way he thinks of himself, though. Judge, jury, and executioner. I assume you've been in his new office?"

Grace nodded. "Sure. Plenty of times."

"No electric chair?"

"I haven't seen it."

"Then Blackburn must have told him to tone it down. He hasn't changed at all, though. I could see it in his eyes in court. He's going to do anything he can to convict me and send me to prison for the rest of my life."

"Speaking of, I got a partial witness list from him this morning."

"Yeah? Who's on it?"

"Your wife, for starters. Your secretary, the victim's mother, a Knoxville cop named Olivia Denton, another cop named Bob Ridge, an FBI agent named Paul Freeman, a man named James Tipton, Junior, a man named Hobart Godsey, plus the medical examiner and any other experts they might call."

"I wonder how they got to James Tipton," I said.

Tipton being on their list wasn't good. I'd thought he would be a witness for me, that he would come in and tell the jury that I'd tried to hire him but then I'd called it off.

"He's the former client, right? The one you went to see?"

"Right. There's no way he would come to them voluntarily. I was going to ask you to interview him and consider calling him as a witness. I wonder what in the hell he's going to say."

"I'll put an investigator on it and find out," she said.

"And who is Hobart Godsey?"

"I don't know," she said. "I just got these names. I was hoping you could help me out."

"No idea," I said.

"There's something else I've found that bothers me," she said.

"What's that?"

"You've told me you don't hunt. You don't own a rifle, have fired one only a few times, and you don't ever hunt."

"Right, so?"

"The FBI found a tree stand in your garage when they searched your house. It's on Clancy's discovery list. He's going to introduce it at trial."

"What? A tree stand? In my garage? Where in my garage?"

"Doesn't say exactly. Why would you have a tree stand in your garage?"

"I don't. I mean I didn't. There was no tree stand in my garage."

"You haven't been in the house all that long, right? Any chance it was left by the former owners?"

"It was new. We bought it new. I'm telling you, there was no tree stand in my garage. They must have planted it."

"Who? The FBI? We're not really going to go down that road, are we?"

"Whoever is trying to frame me for this murder must have planted it," I said.

"Fine, think about it some more and we'll talk about it again soon. In the meantime, I know a lot of lawyers don't like to do this, but I'd like to hear the truth from you, Darren. Tell me everything. Exactly the way you remember it."

I leaned back against the concrete, took as deep a breath as I could without cringing, and started talking. I told her the whole story, from the meeting with Jordan to being arrested at the restaurant. When I was finished, she put her hands on her knees, dropped her chin, and started staring at her boots.

"As I see it, then," she said, "our defense will be—and this is the macro version—that Jalen Jordan threatened to kill your son during a conversation you and he had at your office. He then went to your son's school and waited until your mother picked your son up, and then he followed them to your mother's house. You were already alarmed, but when you found out he had followed your mother and Sean to your mother's home you became even more terrified. In a moment of desperation, you went to James Tipton's house—a former client whom you knew to have violent tendencies—and you gave him fifty thousand dollars to kill Jordan. The next morning, however, you went back and called the whole thing off because, as I understand it, your mother told you to and you came to your senses. After that, you hid out for a couple of days and by complete coincidence, somebody else killed Jordan. Is that right?"

"That's pretty much it," I said quietly.

"And you also let Tipton keep the fifty thousand dollars."

"I did."

I shook my head and took a slow, deep breath. For the millionth time, I asked myself, *What were you thinking? How could you possibly have wrapped yourself up in this?* The facts were an absolute nightmare for any lawyer, any defendant. If I'd been representing someone who told me a similar story, I'd have started talking to him or her about making the best deal possible and entering a plea.

"Do you realize how difficult this is going to be, Darren?"

"I know it looks bad, but I'm innocent. I didn't do it. That's a fact . . . the most important fact."

"Do you have any idea who killed Jalen Jordan?"

I shook my head. "I don't. I really don't."

"Then we're in for a war," she said, "and to be honest, if I was betting, my money would be on Ben Clancy. But I took it upon myself to put a bug in the ear of a friend of mine at the *Knoxville News Sentinel*."

She reached into her briefcase, pulled out a section of the newspaper, and held it up for me to see. A banner headline on the front page said "Did Accused Lawyer Shoot Serial Child Killer?"

"They're going absolutely crazy over this," Grace said as I skimmed through the story. It speculated that Jalen Jordan was the only suspect in the murders of the two boys and that the FBI had evidence in its possession that was taken from Jalen's van and matched the boys' DNA. "Every paper, every television station, the Internet, it's going viral."

"That's nice," I said, "but the accused lawyer didn't shoot *anybody*."

She folded up the paper, looking slightly offended, put it back in her briefcase, and stood to leave.

"It's a start toward jury nullification," she said. "A damned good start. And you're welcome."

CHAPTER TWENTY-EIGHT

I'd been in jail for exactly two weeks before my mother was able to get in to see me. She came into the visiting room at the Knoxville jail with the skin on her face looking a bit loose and shadowy circles beneath her eyes. She was on the other side of a piece of Plexiglas and we had to speak through old, hand-held phone receivers that crackled and cut out completely on occasion. As soon as she saw me, tears fell from both of her eyes.

"Don't cry," I said. "This is hard enough."

"You look terrible, Darren. What are they doing to you in here?"

"Nothing I haven't deserved. And you don't look so good yourself."

"What are they doing? Are they beating you?"

"Not so much now," I said. "The news coverage about Jalen Jordan has eased things up a lot."

"Why haven't you called me?"

"Because I only get out of the cell for about a half an hour a day, and every time I get out they tell me the phones aren't working. Besides, it's ridiculously expensive and we both need to accept that I'm in here for a long time. We need to deal with it. Calling you would only make me miss being free even more than I already do."

"Please call me once in a while," she said. "I want to hear your voice."

I nodded and asked the question that had been tormenting me. "How's Sean?"

She looked down and folded her hands together.

"I don't know," she said. "Katie won't let me see him."

"Miserable bitch," I said. "Small-minded, cheating, geezer-screwing bitch. I can't say it surprises me, though. Do you plan to do anything about it?"

"Of course I'm going to do something about it. Sean needs me now more than ever. Can you imagine what Katie is saying about you? She'll have him thinking you're Hitler reincarnated before it's over."

"He doesn't know who Hitler is, Mom."

"Well, Godzilla reincarnated then. Or some kind of evil dragon."

"Do you know the process? You have to file a petition in juvenile court and ask the judge to order Katie to let you see him. You'll have to hire a lawyer."

"I've talked to more lawyers in the past week than I care to remember. They're really sleazy, Darren. Are you like that?"

"I don't know. I hope not. I try not to be sleazy, but sometimes it just sort of comes with the territory."

"I've spoken to a couple of lawyers besides the people I talked to about being able to see Sean. I think I can hire somebody for you."

"Don't even tell me their names," I said. "I have a perfectly good lawyer, and she's free. You've met her, right? You've talked to her a couple of times."

"I have . . . I've met her and she seems very bright and very capable. But she's so young."

"I was young when I got Uncle Tommy out of prison."

"You had help, though. You had Richie."

"She has help, too, Mom. First of all, she has me. I'm not exactly in my right mind these days, and I realize that, but I still have a lot of experience as a lawyer and I can help her out if she needs it. There are also older lawyers in her office. I know a couple of them and they're very good. If she needs help with something, I'm sure all she has to do is ask. And they have their own investigators. I think she'll do a good job. She's already tried fifteen cases and she's been on the job only three years. Most lawyers don't try fifteen cases in their entire careers. And the last thing I want you doing is spending your life's savings on lawyers. Do you know how many miserable scumbags have come into my office over the past seven years depending on their mommies to pay their way out of trouble? I'm not going to be one of those guys."

We sat there looking at each other for a few minutes, mother and son, barely able to comprehend the situation that faced us. Thinking about what Katie had done made me want to scream, to jump up and start destroying everything around me, but I knew it would result only in my being thrown into the admin cell for a couple of days. And at some level, I'd known Katie would do what she'd done as soon as they led me out of the restaurant in handcuffs. She had seized the high ground now and was lobbing artillery shells on me. She'd blow me to bits if she could. Had the situation been reversed, I like to think I would have put Sean's needs first and I would have made sure he had contact with his mother. But the situation wasn't reversed. It was what it was and I had to accept it. Besides, when I thought about it, I realized that I didn't want Sean seeing me confined by the concrete and the steel and the bars and the windows. I didn't want to talk to him through an ancient phone. He wouldn't have understood why I couldn't lift him in my arms and kiss him on the cheek and hug him like I always had. He wouldn't understand why his dad couldn't leave and come home with him. As I thought about him, tears began to well in my eyes and I swallowed hard. Don't show weakness. Don't ever show weakness.

"You've lost weight," Mom finally said. "Are you eating?"

"A little more now than I was," I said. "We get one hot meal every three days and that's either hot dogs and tater tots or fish sticks and tater tots. The rest of the time it's cold bologna sandwiches. The place is so overcrowded they don't have room in the budget for decent food."

"Can I do anything to help?"

"You can put some money in my commissary account. I need underwear and socks and stamps and pencils and paper, and I can buy a snack every now and then if I want."

"Will they let you have a television?"

"No."

"Books?"

"If you send them to me."

"How long can you keep your office open without taking new cases?" Mom said.

"A few months. I hate to close the doors, but the lawyer police will probably force me to shut it down pretty soon."

"Lawyer police?"

"The Board of Professional Responsibility."

"What do they have to do with this?"

"Since a federal judge has declared me a danger to the community, I guarantee you they'll do the same thing. They'll shut my practice down, and Rachel will be on the street."

"Darren," Mom said, almost in a whisper. "The FBI has come by to talk to me a couple of times. They're coming to my shop in the middle of the day. They're scaring my help and my customers."

I shook my head. "I'm sorry, Mom."

"They're threatening me, Darren. They're threatening to arrest me as a coconspirator or as an accessory. They're saying they'll subpoena me to a grand jury if I don't talk to them."

"They probably will," I said, "but they've already indicted me. Dragging you in front of a grand jury won't do them much good."

"What do you want me to do if I get a subpoena?"

"Tell them the truth, Mom. Just tell them the truth."

I knew the sheriff's department listened in and occasionally recorded conversations in the visiting booths, and I figured I was probably a top priority candidate.

"So you want me to tell them about—"

I held up my hand.

"The truth," I said. "I'm going to have to tell the jury what happened when we go to trial. You do the same thing. Okay?"

She nodded and put her hand on the glass. I covered it with my own.

"Okay," she said. "Then you believe the truth will set you free?"

"It has to, Mom. I don't think I can deal with the alternative."

"I love you, Darren. Stay strong."

"I love you, too."

CHAPTER TWENTY-NINE

As the days and nights dragged endlessly by, I found myself becoming more and more feral. I was locked up in my sixty-three-square-foot concrete box twenty-three hours a day, sometimes twenty-four. When they let me out for "recreation," I was simply moved to a ten-foot by ten-foot, steel-mesh cage just outside the cellblock that had a phone on the wall. There was another cage next to it, and every once in a while they'd bring another inmate in, but I ignored them. To me, they were enemies, placed in the cage by Clancy or the sheriff for the sole purpose of engaging me in conversation so they could later appear in court and testify that I had confessed.

All of the simple pleasures of life that I'd taken for granted—going to work, sleeping in a comfortable bed, taking long, hot showers, eating decent food, feeling the sun on my face, marveling at the beauty of the moon, having a beer with colleagues playing with Sean, *talking*—were gone. I was living an existence so different from what I'd known—so utterly deprived of normal stimulation—I sometimes feared for my sanity. At first I tried to console myself with the thought that I'd be out soon, but thinking about being out made being in even worse, so

I stopped. I thought about Sean often, but that, too, was painful, and before too long, I found it difficult to remember what he looked like.

The guards left me pretty much alone after those first few weeks, especially after the story about Jalen Jordan being a child killer broke. I had a cell to myself, so I stopped calling them names and challenging them every two or three days. The only exception was the Joe DuBose hire that I'd head-butted my first day on the block. His name was Belcher—it was stitched into his black uniform right above the pocket on the left side of his chest—and he seemed to derive a great deal of pleasure from calling me faggot: "Rec time, faggot." "Here's your supper, faggot." "Why don't you ever say anything anymore, faggot?" "Please, faggot, give me a reason to come in there and whip your ass." I ignored the taunts, which I suspect made him hate me even more, but given the circumstances, there really wasn't much more he could do to me.

After about a month in isolation, I quit shaving. I hadn't had a haircut in a while and saw no reason to make arrangements. (There was a civilian barber who would come to the block and cut hair every two weeks.) I became used to the rats and the roaches—I even spoke to them on occasion—and I became used to the mold on the walls and the foultasting water. I became used to feeling unclean, to taking only one shower a week, and to eating food barely fit for human consumption. I became used to the extreme changes in temperature inside the cellblock. I became used to the constant din of men in close confinement who are scared and uncertain and who express their fear either by yelling or singing or moaning or fighting or simply by banging their fists against the metal in the cells. I took refuge occasionally in the books my mother sent me, but I found it difficult to concentrate. I became terrified of fire breaking out in the cellblock. I did push-ups and crunches and pull-ups. I shadow boxed for hours at a time. It wasn't conscious, but I seemed to be preparing myself for something both mentally and physically. War, perhaps?

I called my mother on Thursdays when they let me out of the cell if the phones were working, but as time went by, we had less and less to say to each other. Katie was fighting her hard over being able to see Sean. She'd spent thousands of dollars on a lawyer—supposedly a friend of mine—and still hadn't even been granted a court date. As for the divorce, I'd filed a handwritten answer to the petition for divorce and had managed to get a judge to agree to postpone the proceedings until after my trial. I knew if I was convicted, I'd probably never see Sean again.

Grace came to see me once a week and would give me updates on the case. It wasn't going well, she said. James Tipton had refused to talk to her investigator, and when the investigator pressed the issue, Tipton threatened to shoot him. We had no idea what his testimony would be, but we figured it had to be something about me trying to hire him to kill Jordan.

Grace's investigator had also found the witness named Hobart Godsey. As it turned out, his nickname was Hillbilly and he'd been in the cell with me at Blount County. Both Grace and I knew what that meant. Ben Clancy would call him at trial to say I admitted to shooting Jalen Jordan. Hillbilly, the hypocritical bastard, was going to be their jailhouse snitch.

Grace also told me that Clancy had expert witnesses lined up to testify. One was a ballistics expert who was going to testify that the bullet that killed Jalen Jordan came from a rifle that FBI agents found near the crime scene. The other was a fingerprint expert who apparently was going to testify that my fingerprints had been found on some money that had been turned over to the feds by James Tipton. I didn't understand why that mattered if they were trying to prove that I'd committed the murder, and Clancy wasn't telling Grace any more than he absolutely had to.

We went to court a couple of times for motions, and I sat there listening as the lawyers fought over the rules by which we would conduct the trial for my life. The most important motion was the one Ben Clancy filed asking the court to order that no mention would be made of the fact that the underwear found in Jalen Jordan's van had, indeed, contained DNA that matched the two murdered boys. Judge Geer granted the motion, and as much as I hated to admit it, he was probably right. Our defense wasn't that I killed Jalen Jordan because he was a killer of children and had threatened my child. Our defense was that I hadn't killed him at all. Still, allowing the jury to hear that Jalen was a budding serial killer of children would most likely have prejudiced the jury and may have caused them to let me go because they thought he needed killing, no matter who had done it.

The week before the trial started, Grace came to see me on a Wednesday. The clean, fresh smell of her was almost overwhelming. I smiled at her and tried not to stare. Sometimes when she came to the cell, I had to force myself not to look at her because I knew there was hunger in my eyes and I didn't want her to see it. She was leaning against the sink while I sat on the edge of the bed frame.

"I'm sending a barber in here on Friday," she said. "You need to go back to your lawyer look. Clean-shaven, short hair. I want you looking good in court. And I've arranged through the sheriff to let you shower on Monday morning. Use soap, Darren. Your mother is bringing clothes. They'll let you change in the holding cell before we start jury selection."

The words came at me in a frenzy. As I spent more and more time in isolation, I found it took a bit of time for my brain to be able to absorb and decipher spoken information.

"Are you all right?" Grace said.

"I'm fine. It just takes me a minute to get used to someone talking to me. I'll get the haircut. I'll shave. I'll use soap. I'll come in there looking like a million bucks."

She smiled, which was something I'd grown to love. A simple pleasure.

"Are you ready?" she said.

"Are you?"

She nodded. "I think so. I know so, actually. I'm as ready for this trial as I've ever been. I want to ask you about Sean one last time. He's your alibi, but I know how you feel about putting him on a witness stand. I just want to make sure."

We'd been through this before. I'd taken Sean fishing on the Tennessee River bank the Thursday Galen Jordan was killed. We'd been out there for about four hours, and I hadn't bought gas or been anyplace that would have captured my presence on tape. We'd checked into whether cell phone tower evidence would be gathered and introduced, but I hadn't made any calls and the towers could only put me within a twenty-mile radius. Jordan had been killed less than twenty miles from where I was fishing.

"I'm not putting him through that. He's six. Clancy will chew him up."

"I have to be honest, Darren. I'm concerned. I still don't know exactly how they're going to tie you to it other than some of the things you said. I don't know what James Tipton's testimony will be. He's refused to talk to my investigator. He actually threatened to shoot him the last time he went to Tipton's house. I think Tipton might come in there and lie."

"Why would he do that? Not only did I save his ass on the aggravated assault, I gave him fifty thousand dollars for nothing. He doesn't have a reason to lie about me."

"Don't forget who we're dealing with."

"You mean Clancy?"

"I've suspected him of coaching witnesses, of basically manufacturing testimony, in the past, but I haven't been able to prove anything. He's so good at it that I haven't even been able to accuse him of any misconduct. But considering how much he hates you, nothing he does will surprise me."

"He's going to railroad me into prison for the rest of my life, isn't he?" I said.

Pressure began to build in my chest, and I suddenly found it difficult to breathe. Grace noticed immediately and sat down beside me. She reached over and took my hand. Her touch was electric.

"Take it easy," she said. "Everything is going to be all right."

"No, it isn't," I said. "He's done this before. He's going to steamroll us."

"You have to believe in the process."

"Is that all you've got? Believe in the process? We're talking about the rest of my life, and my lawyer is feeding me platitudes."

"I know you're hurting, Darren," she said, "and I believe you when you say you didn't kill him. I really do. I don't know how Clancy is planning to prove you were on the trail that day or how you might have known Jalen Jordan was going to be there, but the fact remains that you certainly did some questionable things, and we're going to have trouble explaining why that tree stand was in your garage if you're going to testify that you know very little about hunting and shooting. Defending you is going to be quite a challenge."

"And now you're going to tell me that in spite of my stupidity, you're going to do the best you can, right?"

"That's right. I'll do my absolute best for you."

"And then you'll go home. No matter how it turns out for me, you'll get to go home."

"If it turns out badly, we'll keep fighting. I won't quit, Darren. I won't let them just throw you away forever."

I turned toward her. Her face was only inches away, her hand still clutching mine.

"I'm afraid, Grace," I said. "I hate to say that out loud. I hate to admit it to you, to myself, to anyone, but I'm really, really afraid."

Her face moved toward mine and I closed my eyes, feeling ashamed that I'd admitted to being afraid. A few seconds later, I felt the pressure on my hand release and she stood, walked to the door, and pressed the button so a guard would come and let her out of the cell.

"I know you're scared," she said. "So am I. But remember what I said. I won't desert you, Darren. No matter what happens next week, I won't ever quit."

The door clanked and opened, and suddenly, she was gone.

CHAPTER THIRTY

Grace's cell phone rang, and her eyes opened. She had drifted off to sleep on her bed, covered in notebooks and files and papers. Her laptop lay open next to her. She reached over and picked up the phone. The caller ID was blocked. It was 11:57 p.m. Darren's trial would begin in nine hours.

"Hello?"

"Your client is innocent," a male voice said. "There were fewer than half-a-dozen people who knew Jordan was heading for the trail that day, and your client wasn't one of them."

"Who is this?" Grace said.

"One of the people who knew."

The voice was gravelly, and the words were slightly slurred. This was someone who was probably drinking. Maybe a whacko, but maybe someone who was having an attack of conscience.

"Tell me who you are," Grace said.

"It doesn't matter who I am. I'm not going to come forward and risk my career for you or for your client. Listen to me. After Jalen Jordan was stopped by the Knoxville police, and after those two pairs of underwear were found in his van and turned over to us, we put a surveillance net around him so tight he couldn't have picked his nose without us knowing about it."

"So you knew he was going hiking?"

"He wasn't going hiking. He was running away. He was going to get onto the Appalachian Trail and head north into New York. He wanted to disappear."

"And you just let him go? Or did one of you shoot him?"

"Nobody on our side shot him. I don't care what you think or what you may have heard, the FBI doesn't murder people. Clancy was the one who made the decision to let him go. He made the call. It had to go up the chain a little ways, but a decision had to be made quickly and they let him make it. We were going to get some people on the trail close to Jordan and make sure he didn't get away and didn't hurt anyone, but we didn't even have a chance to do that, because between the time we knew he was going and he actually went out to the trail, somebody else was able to get out there, get into position, and pick him off. We're only talking about an hour and a half here, total. Somebody had to know exactly where he would be, and there's just no way your client could have been that person. If he'd been doing close surveillance on Jordan, we would have known about it because we were all over Jordan."

"So what's the bottom line?" Grace said. "Why are you calling me?"

"Bottom line? Clancy is your man. He's behind this. Figure out what he did, and your boy walks away."

"But I can't go off half-cocked and accuse an assistant United States attorney of being involved in a murder without some kind of solid proof. They'll take my license, maybe put *me* in jail."

"I know you can't. But I thought it might help if you at least knew your client didn't do it. Maybe Clancy will slip up, open a door for you."

"Clancy doesn't slip up."

"Then all I can tell you is that after your boy is sent away for life, keep digging. Eventually, maybe you'll find what you're looking for."

CHAPTER THIRTY-ONE

The *United States of America versus Darren Street* began the following Monday morning at precisely nine o'clock. By noon the next day, a jury had been picked. When we came back after the lunch break and Judge Geer asked Ben Clancy to make an opening statement, he said, "The United States waives its opening statement," which meant he intended to hide his strategy from us to the very end and let the case play out in front of the jury.

Grace stood, and for the next half hour, she began the process of trying to soften the blow of what I'd done. I'd hired a hit man and then reneged, she said. I'd paid him in Jalen Jordan's own money and left the money with him. Yes, I'd made some ill-advised threats, but I'd done so under great duress. The victim had threatened my son, and I had reason to believe he would follow through. But I was innocent of the charge. I did not shoot Jalen Jordan. I could not have known he was on the trail that day. I did not own a rifle nor had I fired one more than a few times during my entire life. I was innocent.

Innocent.

Innocent.

Ben Clancy began his parade of witnesses with the man who'd found Jalen Jordan's body. He described the body's position, and a couple of photos were introduced. Then came the uniforms, the first responders who described the scene in further detail. Next up was the first FBI agent on the scene. He identified Jalen Jordan. Then came the medical examiner, who told everyone what they already knew—the man was dead. He described in detail the massive damage inflicted by the Winchester .270 bullet that tore through Jalen Jordan's heart. Clancy was excellent, I had to admit it. He was thoroughly prepared and didn't let the trial drag. He got to the point quickly with each witness, elicited the testimony he wanted, and then shut his mouth and sat down.

Grace cross-examined the witnesses, but there really wasn't much to question. She was establishing a rapport with the jury, though, and I liked what I saw. She was attractive, confident, polite, and articulate. During her opening statement, she'd made it a point to walk over to me and to put her hand on my shoulder, thereby showing the jury she didn't think I was a killer, that she wasn't afraid of me. She repeatedly called me "Mr. Street" instead of "the defendant," an elementary trial tactic used by defense lawyers to humanize their clients, and I felt that overall, she'd done a good job of downplaying the evidence that had been introduced by the end of the first day. Clancy hadn't yet tied me to anything, and I walked out of court and went back to the jail feeling a tiny glimmer of hope.

To begin the day on Tuesday, Clancy called a crime scene expert, who reconstructed the killing for the jury. There was a great deal of scientific testimony about bullet velocities and trajectories and the use of a bullet trajectory laser. The expert testified that Jalen Jordan was shot by someone who was sitting in a tree stand (they found marks left by the stand in the bark of the tree trunk and introduced photos) approximately twenty-four feet off the ground at a distance of 103 yards away. Grace attempted to cross-examine him about the skills it would take to put a bullet in someone's heart from that distance, but the judge cut her off, ruling that the questions were outside the witness's field of expertise.

The crime scene expert was followed by an FBI agent who had found a rifle in a creek bed not far from the crime scene. The rifle was a Ruger .270 with a stainless steel barrel and a high-powered Leupold scope. I'd never seen it before. The FBI agent, whose name was Riley, said he had learned through his investigation that the gun was originally purchased from a gun dealer in Maryville by a man named Carl Jones ten years earlier.

"Did you speak with Mr. Jones?" Ben Clancy asked Riley.

"I did not. Mr. Jones died three years ago. I went to the address we had listed for him and spoke to his widow. She told me she sold the gun to a friend of her husband's named Bill Miller three months after her husband passed away."

Clancy handed the agent a piece of paper.

"Will you identify this document for the jury, please, Agent Riley?"

"It's a bill of sale for the rifle from Mrs. Jones to Bill Miller. It says she sold the rifle to him for three hundred dollars."

"And what did you do next?"

"I contacted Bill Miller."

"And what was the result of your contact with Mr. Miller?"

"Pretty much the same thing," the agent said. "Mr. Miller said he sold the gun to a friend and fellow hunter."

Clancy held up another document.

"And will you identify this document, please."

"It's another bill of sale, this one from William Miller to James Tipton, Junior. It says Mr. Miller sold the rifle to Mr. Tipton for two hundred dollars two years after he bought it from Mrs. Jones."

"And finally, Agent Riley, did you participate in a search of the defendant's home the night he was arrested?"

"I did."

Clancy held up a photograph and asked the bailiff to hand it to Riley.

"Would you identify this photo, Agent Riley?"

"Yes, this is a photo of the tree stand we found in the defendant's garage. It was located behind a sheet of plywood against the south wall."

"And does this photo depict the tree stand as you found it in the garage?"

"It does."

Clancy then turned and picked up a tree stand from beside his table.

"And is this the tree stand you found in the defendant's home, Agent Riley?"

The bailiff handed the stand to Riley.

"Yes. This appears to be it."

Clancy asked the judge to introduce both the photo and the tree stand into evidence, and the judge did so.

"Thank you, Agent Riley," Clancy said. "Please answer Miss Alexander's questions."

Grace leaned over and whispered in my ear, "Okay, for once and for all, do you swear to me you've never seen that rifle?"

"Never," I said.

She stood and moved to the lectern.

"Agent Riley, during your search of Mr. Street's home, did you find any documentation that Mr. Street had ever purchased a tree stand? No receipts, credit card statements, things of that nature?"

"No, we didn't."

"And I assume you looked thoroughly. That would have been a nice little piece of corroboration, wouldn't it?"

"I think it's a pretty solid piece of evidence on its own."

"Were my client's fingerprints on it?"

"No."

"DNA?"

"No."

"And do you have any way of proving that this particular tree stand is the same tree stand that was used during Jalen Jordan's murder?"

"The measurements match up generally with the marks on the tree, but we can't definitively say it was the same tree stand that the murderer used, no."

"Thank you. And in your search of Mr. Street's home and office, did you find any other single piece of evidence that would implicate him in this killing?"

"Nothing that I'm aware of."

"Now, moving to the rifle, were Mr. Street's fingerprints on it?"

"No."

"DNA?"

"No."

"And your investigation revealed that the rifle used to kill Mr. Jordan passed from a gun dealer to a man named Carl Jones, who subsequently died, correct?"

"That's right."

"And then Mrs. Jones's widow sold it to a man named Bill Miller, correct?"

"Correct."

"And then Mr. Miller sold it to a man named James Tipton?"

"Yes."

"And you have bills of sale proving this chain of ownership."

"We do."

"And the chain of ownership stops with Mr. Tipton, correct?"

"Not exactly."

The tone in his voice caused me to sit up immediately. I wanted to stop Grace, to get her attention, to tell her to be careful. Something was up. She was about to be snagged in a trap.

"I don't understand," Grace said. "Do you have further documentary proof that the rifle changed hands again?"

"We don't have documentary proof, but we have other proof."

Don't ask him anything else, I thought. *Stop right now and sit down.*

"Proof of what?"

"That the rifle changed hands again. James Tipton sold it to your client two days before Jalen Jordan was murdered."

There was a gasp in the courtroom, followed by an extended murmur. My head dropped involuntarily, and I felt as though I was deflating.

"I move to strike his answer," Grace said.

"On what grounds?" Judge Geer said.

"Since the agent obviously has no documentary proof, his answer must be grounded in hearsay. He's repeating what he heard from Mr. Tipton. It's inadmissible."

"She led him right to it," Clancy said from his table. "And besides, Mr. Tipton is on the witness list; he's going to testify that he sold the rifle to Mr. Street. We also have an expert who is going to tie Mr. Street to the money he paid for the rifle through fingerprint evidence."

So that was it. The big lie that would convict me. The essential piece of the puzzle that Clancy needed to put me on the convict train. They were saying I bought the murder weapon from James Tipton two days before Jalen was shot. I felt like I was going to vomit.

"I'm going to withhold ruling on your objection until I hear these other witnesses the government is planning to call," the judge said to Grace. "Technically, I suppose you're right about the statement being hearsay, but if they put on the evidence they say they're going to put on, I believe the issue is moot.

Grace nodded and looked back at the agent.

"I don't have anything further for this witness," she said.

That was how the second day ended. I walked out of court in a shock-induced daze. Up to that point, I hadn't really believed Clancy would be able to tie me directly to the murder. But he'd done it, and in spectacular fashion.

CHAPTER THIRTY-TWO

Grace came to my cell that night around eight. She looked as though her favorite pet had just been run over by a car.

"I'm sorry, Darren," she said as soon as she walked in. "I can't believe I made such a stupid mistake."

I knew what she was referring to. She'd asked the FBI agent, Agent Riley, a question when she didn't know the answer. It was a cardinal sin for a trial lawyer. You simply don't ask witnesses questions, especially on cross-examination, to which you don't know the answers.

"Doesn't matter," I said. "Clancy was right. They were going to get it in through Tipton eventually. All Riley did was speed up the process."

"And create an 'oh my God' moment in front of the jury. He might as well have hit me in the face with a shovel."

She was right about that. It had been one of those rare moments in a court proceeding where everyone in the room was figuratively knocked off their feet.

"I guess the circumstances could have been better," I said. "If we'd known it was coming we could have tried to lessen the blow a little, but we didn't have any way of knowing."

"We should have gotten to Tipton."

"You know how it is, Grace. Prosecution witnesses don't have to talk to defense lawyers in criminal cases."

"He's going to lie, isn't he?"

"Of course he's going to lie. I didn't buy that rifle from him and I've never seen that tree stand in my life. The question at this point is why is he lying? And the answer has to be that Clancy is coercing him somehow. He has something on James, something that must terrify him. He's one of those old school thugs, or at least he used to be. One of those guys who would rather cut off an arm than talk to the police. Have you checked him out thoroughly?"

Grace shrugged.

"As thoroughly as we can, I suppose," she said. "I've followed up on everything you've told me. My investigator has poked around some. Tipton's grandmother is apparently some kind of Ma Barker or something. The story is that she and her grandsons run an oxycodone smuggling operation from her farm in Sevier County. But we haven't been able to get anything out of the DEA about a drug investigation into Tipton or his family. I talked to Clancy right before I came here, and he swears there is no drug case pending against anyone in Tipton's family and that they haven't offered Tipton anything in return for his testimony. The only reason he got involved was because they traced the rifle back to him."

"I wonder if Tipton killed Jordan," I said, "and if he did, why?"

Grace shook her head and sat down next to me on the bunk.

"I don't even want to think about the answer to that question," she said, "because it's just so frightening. Is Ben Clancy capable of manipulating all of this? Could he possibly have set all of this in motion just to frame you for a murder?"

"You're damned right he's capable," I said. "I think he's a straight-up sociopath."

"Then may God help us," Grace said, "because the legal system isn't going to."

CHAPTER THIRTY-THREE

Clancy's first witness the next morning was a ballistics expert who testified that the bullet that killed Jalen Jordan was fired from the rifle that James Tipton had supposedly sold to me. The testimony was almost entirely well-established science. There was nothing Grace could do to refute it. After the ballistics expert was excused, Clancy began the process of methodically stepping on my throat.

My paralegal and secretary, Rachel, was trembling and nearly in tears when she described the encounter with Jalen Jordan in my office that day, how she brought me a fee contract and placed $50,000 in the office safe only to bring the money back to me later and see me tear the contract into pieces. She described me as "extremely upset" and admitted to Ben Clancy that I answered a question she asked me about Jalen Jordan with, "Before or after I kill him?" Grace objected on the grounds that the evidence was hearsay, but the judge allowed it as an "excited utterance," which is an exception to the rule against hearsay. Grace tried to cauterize the wound by having Rachel tell the jury what a wonderful guy I was, but it didn't seem to work well.

My old friend, Knoxville Police Captain Bob Ridge, reluctantly testified that I was "highly agitated" when I spoke with him on the phone and that I told him my son had been threatened by Jalen Jordan. Same objection. Same ruling. When Grace cross-examined him, Bob took the opportunity to tell the jury how highly he thought of me. It seemed to sit better with the jury than Rachel's remarks, and for a few moments, at least, I once again felt a tiny glimmer of hope.

Officer Olivia Denton testified that I called her and told her my son had been threatened by Jalen Jordan. She met with me, she said, and during the meeting I told her that I was going to have to "deal with him outside the system." Grace again objected on the grounds that the evidence was hearsay, but the judge again allowed it, calling it an "excited utterance" and a "statement against interest." A pattern was developing. Grace wasn't able to do anything else with Officer Denton because the judge had ruled before the trial that any mention of the underwear found in Jalen Jordan's van was inadmissible. When he made the ruling, I knew he was right, but at that moment, I wished we could turn the jury's attention to what a scumbag Jalen was. We desperately needed to stop the bleeding.

Next up was my beloved Katie, looking perfectly cosmopolitan in her designer duds.

"State your name, please," Clancy said.

"Kaitlyn Street. I go by Katie."

"And what is your relationship to the defendant, Mrs. Street?"

"I'm married to him for the time being, but I filed for divorce right after he was arrested. The court has delayed the divorce until this trial is over, but as soon as it's over, I'll be changing my name back to Kaitlyn Reece, which was my name before we were married."

"And you and Mr. Street have a child together, correct?"

"Yes. His name is Sean. He's six years old, almost seven."

"Mrs. Street, do you recall a day back in April when you received a telephone call from your husband regarding a threat that had been made against your son?"

"I'll never forget it," Katie said. "Darren threatened to strangle me with his bare hands."

"Objection," Grace said. "Hearsay."

"Sustained," the judge said.

"Is it fair to say that your husband was upset during that phone call?" Clancy said.

"I've never heard him more upset,' Katie said, "and believe me, I've heard him say some crazy things."

"What did your husband want when he called?"

"He wanted me to walk out of my job and go to Sean's school and pick him up. He said Sean had been threatened by some man who came to his office."

"Did you go immediately and pick up your son?"

"No, of course not. Darren has a tendency to overreact to things. He goes nuts sometimes, and he's overprotective of Sean. Darren's father was hard on him, so he's the opposite with Sean. He won't discipline him or anything."

"So after you told him you weren't going to pick up Sean that day, what happened?"

"You mean after he threatened to come to my work and strangle me with his bare hands?"

"Objection!" Grace said.

"Sustained. Disregard the answer." Judge Geer said to the jury.

"What happened after you hung up?"

"He disappeared for three days, that's what happened," Katie said. "He took Sean with him. This was on a Tuesday, and I didn't see either one of them again until Friday night."

"And Mr. Jordan was murdered that Thursday?"

"Yes, I think so."

"Where did your husband go?"

"I have no idea. I think maybe he was hiding."

"But he returned on Friday?"

"Yes."

"Thank you, Mrs. Street."

Grace approached the lectern. Before she got there, she said, "You're a liar, aren't you, Mrs. Street?"

"Objection!" Clancy said. "Argumentative."

"Let me rephrase," Grace said. "You're dishonest, aren't you?"

"Same objection."

"Okay, let's try this, and before Mr. Clancy starts objecting, let me just say that these questions go directly to Mrs. Street's credibility. You're an adulteress, aren't you, Mrs. Street? You were having an affair with a man named Leonard Bright for several months before your husband was arrested for this crime, were you not?"

"I don't see how that's any of your business," Katie said.

"Will the court instruct Mrs. Street to answer the question, please? Were you or were you not having an affair with a man named Leonard Bright for several months prior to your husband being arrested for this crime?"

"Answer the question, ma'am," Judge Geer said.

"Darren was insensitive," Katie said.

"Is that a yes?"

"He called me names."

"So you're an adulteress. You admit that. You were dishonest and were sneaking around with another man during your marriage."

"We're getting a divorce. I was the one who filed."

"Yes, and you had the divorce papers served on your husband right outside the courtroom following his initial appearance, isn't that right?"

"Mr. Clancy was the one who suggested that," she said.

I turned and looked at Clancy, who had suddenly become fascinated with his tie clasp.

"Can you tell the jury of one instance when your husband has been violent toward you or your son, or anyone else for that matter?"

"He told me he beat his father up and threw him out of the house when he was a teenager," Katie said.

"That was to protect his mother and himself from being beaten, wasn't it? You took an oath to tell the whole truth, Mrs. Street."

"I don't know if he or his mother were beaten. I wasn't there."

"Back in April, after your son was threatened, you say your husband disappeared and you didn't see him for three days, is that correct?"

"That's right."

"But it isn't true, is it? You saw him on Wednesday afternoon. He had taken Sean into hiding because he was concerned by the threat Jalen Jordan had made, and he came to your home to talk to you about it. And during that conversation, didn't you mention something about suing the FBI if your son was killed?"

I kept glancing at the jury and they were looking at Katie like she was a bug they wanted to squash. It was a small victory, but at least it was a victory, and Grace seemed to be genuinely relishing the opportunity.

"I don't have any idea what you're talking about," Katie said.

"Fine. Just so the jury understands, your husband called you, upset that someone had threatened your son, and asked you to pick your son up at school. You refused because you said the place where you work was having a sale and you didn't want to leave."

"He was overreacting."

"How could you possibly know that?"

"Because that's what he does, especially when Sean is involved."

"He loves his son very much, doesn't he?" Grace said.

"I don't know. I guess he does."

"And he was only trying to protect him, wasn't he?"

"I don't know."

"He's been a good husband, a good father, a good provider, hasn't he? He's spent a great deal of time with Sean?"

"I don't know what you want me to—"

"And yet you've filed a petition to terminate his parental rights, isn't that true?"

"He's a murderer," Katie said. "I don't want him anywhere near Sean."

"He isn't a murderer unless the jury finds him guilty," Grace said. "You, on the other hand, are already guilty of being one of the worst people I've ever had the displeasure of cross-examining. Nothing further."

CHAPTER THIRTY-FOUR

Katie was followed by Richie Fels, and it was all I could do to keep from leaping over the table and pummeling him right there in front of the judge and jury.

"Would you tell the jury about your encounter with Mr. Street on the day in question?" Ben Clancy said.

"He called my secretary and demanded to see me immediately," Fels said, "and then he came storming in like he owned the place. He walked into my office and dropped a hundred-dollar bill on my desk, apparently in hopes of buying my silence."

"Objection, speculation," Grace barked.

"Sustained."

"Before we go any further, Mr. Fels, I'd like to give the jury some sense of your background. You've been practicing criminal defense law exclusively for how many years?"

"Nearly thirty-eight," Richie said. "I've published several articles in various law journals and have also written a text book on ethical issues in criminal cases. I've tried hundreds of cases in my career, everything from first-degree murder to driving under the influence. I'm listed in several publications as one of the top-rated criminal defense lawyers in the country."

"And you've been friends with the defendant for quite some time, haven't you?"

"Yes. Darren came to me several years ago and asked me to help with an appellate case involving his uncle. I agreed, and we became friends. I've admired his work."

"And just in the interest of full disclosure, in that case you referred to a second ago that involved Mr. Street's uncle, I was the prosecutor. I was on the other side."

"Correct."

"And you won. You secured Mr. Street's uncle's release from prison."

"We did."

"So you don't exactly have an ax to grind with Mr. Street, do you?"

"No, I certainly don't. I'm here only because I believe it's the right thing to do."

"All right, then, will you please continue telling the jury about your encounter with Mr. Street on that Tuesday afternoon?"

"He came in and dropped a hundred dollars on my desk. It was obvious that he was quite distraught. He told me a breathless story about a man who came to his office seeking representation who wound up threatening his son. He believed the threat to be legitimate, and wanted advice on what he should do. I told him if he thought the threat was genuine, he should take his son somewhere out of harm's way until he could get the police involved or until the threat was contained in some other way."

"And how did he respond?"

"He said he was thinking of killing the man."

Grace sprang to her feet and objected, but just as he had throughout the trial, Judge Geer found an exception to the hearsay rule and allowed the statement to stand.

"Please continue," Clancy said.

"I again told him I thought he should simply move the boy, but he said, 'Richie, you know I'm not wired like that.'"

"Was there anything else?"

"Not really. He left shortly thereafter. The last thing I told him before he walked out the door was not to kill anyone, but then, just a couple of days later, I saw that this man had been shot, and I realized it was the same man Darren had been talking about. I made some calls to the Board of Professional Responsibility in Nashville and talked to the good folks there about my ethical responsibilities in this situation, and we agreed that it was my duty to come forward. So I called the FBI, and now here I am."

Grace moved to the lectern a couple of minutes later. I'd told her what an ass Richie had been, and I knew she wasn't pleased. She'd told me she was looking forward to going after him.

"There's a long history of deep animosity between Mr. Clancy and my client, isn't there?" she said.

"Objection," Clancy said. "I fail to see the relevance of my relationship with the defendant."

"He brought it up, judge. He opened the door when he asked about the appellate case."

"I'll allow it for a short time," the judge said. "Tight leash, Miss Alexander."

"The fact is that Mr. Street was infuriated by Mr. Clancy's conduct during Mr. Clancy's prosecution of Mr. Street's uncle, correct?"

"Darren was quite upset, yes."

"In fact, he was so upset that he dedicated himself to helping Mr. Clancy's opponent in the next election for district attorney general and Mr. Clancy lost by a narrow margin, isn't that right?"

"I suppose it is."

"So if there's anyone in this trial with an ax to grind, it's Mr. Clancy, correct?"

"That's enough, Miss Alexander," the judge said. "Move on."

"It's also correct that you have grossly exaggerated your testimony, isn't it? You've taken Mr. Street's comments to you entirely out of context."

"That isn't true," Richie said.

"You've already said Mr. Street was upset. He was upset because Jalen Jordan had threatened to kill his son and throw him off a cliff, isn't that right?"

"I believe he said something like that, yes."

"And this threat had been made within just a couple of hours of Mr. Street's visit to your office?"

"I believe so."

"And he came to you because he believed you to be his friend, correct? He trusted you?"

"I think he did."

"You were friends, weren't you?"

"Probably more colleagues than friends, but we knew each other."

"He told you he'd given some thought to killing Jalen Jordan, correct?"

"He did."

"But you didn't take him seriously, did you?"

"I was concerned."

"Really? Why didn't you call the police?"

"I . . . I don't know. I didn't really see it as my place to call the police."

"You didn't go to the FBI until after Mr. Street had been arrested, did you, Mr. Fels?"

"I believe it was a couple of days after they picked him up, right."

"And a couple of days after you spoke to Mr. Street at the jail. He wanted to hire you, didn't he? He wanted his old friend, a man he trusted, to represent him in this case?"

"His mother called me and asked me to come to the jail."

"And you told him you would need a minimum of two hundred thousand dollars to take the case, correct?"

"I don't remember the exact fee I quoted him."

"Why? Because you were drunk?"

"Objection!" Clancy said.

"Sustained."

"The truth is that you came to the jail and asked for an extremely high fee. Mr. Street thought you were his friend and would find a way to work something out, but you weren't willing to do that. So the two of you got into an argument and you left, correct?"

"It is true that I left. I certainly did."

"And after the argument, you suddenly had an attack of self-righteousness, called the FBI, and have now come into a federal courtroom and exaggerated, if not outright lied, because Mr. Street ruffled your feathers, isn't that right?"

"Objection!" Clancy shouted.

"That's enough, Miss Alexander," the judge said.

"Fine, I'm finished," Grace said. "You're some friend, Mr. Fels. And I want it on the record that I'm filing a disciplinary complaint against you for violating the attorney-client privilege and for committing perjury here today."

She turned away from the lectern and sat down next to me. I could feel the heat coming off her. We were probably losing the trial, but Grace was definitely finding her courage.

Fels was the last witness of the day, and by the time he was finished testifying, I could barely stand up to walk out of the courtroom. I looked for my mother, but she was being sequestered outside the courtroom because she was to be a witness—my only witness besides me. There was no one else in the courtroom who was on my side. Uncle Tommy was dead, and our small family had been fractured and separated by my father's alcoholism many years ago. My father, too, was dead, having run a car into the trunk of an oak tree two years after I kicked him out of our home. I hadn't spoken to him in the interim and didn't attend his funeral.

I'd never felt so alone.

CHAPTER THIRTY-FIVE

When they came for me the next morning, I felt like I was being led to the gallows. I knew James Tipton would be the first person on the stand, and I knew what he was going to say. I just didn't know why.

As soon as court was convened and everyone was settled, the clerk called Tipton's name. He walked in looking uneasy and out of place in a brown suit.

Clancy: "State your name for the jury, please."

Tipton: "James Tipton, Junior."

Clancy: "Mr. Tipton, are you familiar with the defendant, Darren Street?"

Tipton: "Yes, sir."

Clancy: "Tell the jury how you know him."

Tipton: "He was my lawyer when I was charged with aggravated assault a couple of years ago. We ended up taking it all the way to a trial and the jury found me not guilty last year. He and I became friends. He's even been up to my home a couple of times."

Clancy: "So how do you feel about Mr. Street now? Do you like him?"

Tipton: "I like him a lot. He's a good man and a good lawyer. I feel real sorry for him, though. I hate that he put himself in this spot."

Clancy: "I suppose it's probably difficult for you to testify here today then, is it not?"

Tipton: "Very difficult. Very hard."

Clancy: "Mr. Tipton, back on April sixteenth of this year, did you see the defendant?"

Tipton: "I did."

Clancy: "How did that come about?"

Tipton "He showed up at my house around seven-thirty, eight o'clock in the evening."

Clancy: "Were you expecting him?"

Tipton: "No. He showed up out of the blue. My dog started barking and I looked outside and saw a minivan, so I went out onto the porch and Darren hollered at me."

Clancy: "Tell the jury about the encounter you had with the defendant."

Grace stood up and objected that Tipton's testimony was unreliable and inadmissible hearsay. Clancy countered that the things Tipton was going to testify to were admissible because they were "statements against interest," another exception to the hearsay rule that allows witnesses to repeat statements they heard if the statements were supported by corroborating circumstances and would tend to expose the person who made them to criminal liability. The judge agreed with Clancy.

Clancy: "Go ahead, Mr. Tipton."

Tipton: "Well, like I said, he kind of showed up out of nowhere. He came in the house and we sat down at the kitchen table. He seemed a little upset, so I asked him if he'd like a beer or maybe a shot of moonshine and he said he would, so I got us both a beer and grabbed a jar of moonshine out of the freezer. He took a couple of long pulls of the moonshine and drained a beer real quick and asked me for another one. So I asked him if something was wrong, and he said this man had come to his office and tried to hire him. He said the man gave him fifty thousand dollars for what Darren thought was a pretty minor case at first. But he said he needed the money so he took it. Then he tells me that during the conversation, the man tells him that he's the guy that killed those two little boys they found out by The Sinks and just a few minutes later he threatened to kill Darren's son."

Clancy: "Stop right there, Mr. Tipton. I move to strike the last sentence and ask the Court to instruct the jury to disregard what the witness just said."

The Court: "I can't unring the bell, Mr. Clancy. He's your witness. You were supposed to instruct him."

Clancy: "I did, Your Honor. I went over this very thoroughly with him."

The Court: "Mr. Tipton, you will make no further reference to the boys who were found. They have nothing to do with this trial. If you mention them again, I'll jail you for contempt. Is that understood?"

Tipton: "Yes, sir."

The Court: "Continue, Mr. Clancy."

Clancy: "At some point in the conversation, did Mr. Street ask you for something?"

Tipton: "He did. He asked if I had a rifle I'd sell him."

Clancy: "And what did you say?"

Tipton: "I said, 'Darren, you're my friend. If you need a rifle, I'll sell you one, but don't tell me what you're going to do with it.'"

Clancy: "Did you eventually sell Mr. Street a rifle?"

Tipton: "I did."

Clancy: "And how did you happen to come by this rifle in the first place, Mr. Tipton?"

Tipton: "I bought it from a buddy of mine I used to hunt with by the name of Bill Miller."

Clancy: (Shows the witness the rifle previously entered into evidence.) "Is this the rifle you sold to Mr. Street?"

Tipton: "It appears to be."

Clancy: "How much did Mr. Street pay you for this rifle, Mr. Tipton?"

Tipton: "He paid me five thousand dollars in hundred-dollar bills."

Clancy: "Didn't you think that was a little expensive for a rifle?"

Tipton: "I did, and I told him as much, but he insisted. He said he'd gotten it from the man who came into his office and didn't want it."

Clancy: "What happened to that money, Mr. Tipton?"

Tipton: "I turned it over to you all when you came around accusing me of killing Jalen Jordan."

Clancy: (Showing the witness a stack of bills.) "Does this appear to be the money Mr. Street paid you?"

Tipton: "I can't say that's it for sure, but it looks like it."

Clancy: "So let's get this all straight for the jury, all right? You initially purchased the rifle from a friend of yours named Bill Miller. Mr. Street came to you in April. He was upset and told you this story, then he asked you if you would sell him a rifle. You agreed, and he paid you five thousand dollars. He left, and you didn't see the rifle again until a week later when you were picked up and questioned by FBI agents after Jalen Jordan was murdered. At that time, you admitted that you'd bought the rifle from Bill Miller, told the agents you'd sold it to Darren Street, and turned over the money he paid you for the rifle. Is that correct?"

Tipton: "That's about it, yes, sir."

Clancy: "Had you used the rifle recently, Mr. Tipton?"

Tipton: "Not since hunting season, back in December."

Clancy: "Do you know whether the scope was aligned properly? Was it zeroed-in, as they say?"

Tipton: "The scope was zeroed. I keep all my weapons in perfect shape."

Clancy: "Thank you, Mr. Tipton."

Grace didn't even pick up her notes. She went straight to the lectern and stared at Tipton for a long minute.

"You committed this murder, didn't you, Mr. Tipton?" she said.

James's shoulders dropped and he folded his hands in his lap. I didn't know what he'd expected when he walked into the courtroom, but Grace's posture and the tone of her voice very quickly told him it wasn't going to be pleasant.

"No, ma'am," James said.

"Mr. Street came to you and originally offered you fifty thousand dollars to kill Mr. Jordan, didn't he?"

"No."

"He gave you the money, too. He didn't give you five thousand, he gave you fifty thousand. Where is the other forty-five thousand dollars, Mr. Tipton?"

"I don't know what you're talking about."

"Mr. Street came to you originally because he knew you had violent tendencies. You've been known to cut people up with knives, haven't you?"

"I was acquitted of that charge."

"But you still cut a man so badly that almost three hundred stitches were required to close the knife wounds, isn't that right?"

"It was self-defense."

"How many other people have you cut up, Mr. Tipton?"

"I haven't been charged with anything else."

"How many others have you cut up? How many others, besides Jalen Jordan, have you killed?"

"None. I haven't killed or cut up anybody. And I didn't kill Jalen Jordan."

"Mr. Street knew you were capable of violence, he was frightened for his son, so he came to you and asked you to commit a killing. It was a mistake, and he realized that quickly and came back first thing the next morning, didn't he? He came back to your trailer and he told you he didn't want you to harm anyone. He told you to forget what he said the night before and he said you could keep the money he'd already given you."

"Today is the first time I've seen him since I sold him the rifle."

"Did you plant the tree stand in his garage?"

"Beg your pardon?"

"You heard me. Did you toss the rifle in a place where it would be easy for the FBI to find it and then plant the tree stand in Mr. Street's garage so the FBI would find it, too?"

"I don't know what you're talking about."

"You set him up. You're taking part in framing Mr. Street. Why are you doing this, Mr. Tipton?"

"I'm not."

"Do you sell drugs, Mr. Tipton?"

"No, ma'am."

"Does anyone in your family sell drugs?"

"No."

"Do you use drugs?"

"No."

It went on like that for another forty-five minutes. Grace hammered away and Tipton denied. She accused him of committing the murder. She accused him of killing two men in Sevier County. She accused him of being a drug dealer and a pimp and a burglar and now a lying snitch, but Tipton was like Teflon. Everything she said just sort of slid off him. He stayed calm and didn't allow himself to be baited. She asked him three times whether he'd been promised anything by the government in exchange for his testimony, and he said no. He was there, he said, only because he'd been accused early on. He was there only because he'd sold me a gun, which I'd apparently used to commit a murder and then had been stupid enough to hide poorly.

I knew he was lying and Grace knew he was lying and Clancy knew he was lying, but he was good enough at it that I didn't think there was anything the jury could really lock on to and say, "This guy isn't telling the truth." Clancy had coached him effectively and he'd coached him thoroughly.

In the end, Tipton walked out of the courtroom like an automaton, staring straight ahead. He hadn't looked at me a single time during his testimony, and I could only wonder what Clancy had done to coerce him into lying.

CHAPTER THIRTY-SIX

Once Tipton was finished, I checked out mentally for a little while. His testimony was almost completely false, but with the other witnesses Clancy had called and the way he had framed the narrative of the trial, I couldn't shake the feeling that I was doomed. It was as though the people around me were moving and speaking in a thick mist. I could hear them, but the things they said didn't completely register and I didn't fully comprehend what was going on. I was aware that Clancy called a fingerprint expert who testified that my fingerprints were on the money James Tipton had turned over to the FBI. He then called the property manager of the chalet Mom, Sean, and I stayed in and used credit card receipts to prove that I was near Tipton's home that night. His final witness was Hillbilly, who told the jury that I told him I'd murdered Jalen Jordan because he had threatened to harm my son. He said I told him I enjoyed seeing the bullet tear into Jalen's chest and that I would do the same thing again under the same circumstances. Again, Grace was a valiant warrior. She completely discredited Hillbilly as a jailhouse snitch, but things had gone so badly I almost felt sorry for her.

After Hillbilly was excused, Clancy stood up and said, "The United States rests, Your Honor."

My mom took the stand and told the truth, and sitting there listening to her after all that I'd heard over the previous three days, I knew the story Ben Clancy was putting forth was far more compelling than the one we were telling. When Grace finished with her direct examination of my mother, Clancy stood up and asked her three questions: "Do you love your son, Mrs. Royston?" "Would you do anything for him?" "Would you lie?"

Looking back on it, I was a terrible witness. Six months in what amounted to solitary confinement may have allowed Grace and me to talk privately, but it certainly hadn't sharpened my social skills. I was stiff and unsure of myself on the witness stand. I was embarrassed and humiliated that I was there in the first place. And the things I had to say were almost unbelievable, even to me. I blurted out the information that during my interview of Jalen Jordan, he had admitted to me that he had already killed two boys and that he was totally unreasonable—almost delusional—about what the outcome of his assault case would be. After being sternly chastised by the judge, I went on to explain that he had threatened Sean, that he knew personal information about him, and that, yes, I was highly upset. Did I say all of those things to Rachel and Katie and Olivia Denton and Bob Ridge and Richie Fels? Yes, unfortunately, but I didn't really intend to kill Jalen. I was terrified for my son. Jalen *followed my mother home*, for God's sake. Did I attempt to hire James Tipton? Yes. Did I give him $50,000? Yes. I gave him *fifty*, not five. He was lying about that, along with nearly everything else.

Because I called it off the next morning.

I swear I called it off the next morning.

I didn't kill him. I couldn't have killed him. I didn't own a rifle and had very, very limited experience with shooting. Yes, I had Jalen's address, but no, I didn't stalk him. There was simply no way I could have known he was going to be on the trail that day. No, I didn't own a tree stand. I'd never been deer hunting.

I didn't kill him.

Ben Clancy's cross-examination of me was surprisingly brief. He acted as though nothing I'd said held any importance at all, that I was simply another murderer lying through his teeth to save his own ass. He did stumble once, though, when he said, "Why would James Tipton come in here and lie to this jury?"

"Because you have something on him and you've threatened him," I said.

I saw just a hint of surprise on his face, and I knew I was right. Clancy had coerced James somehow. But he recovered quickly, wrapped up his cross-examination, and before I knew it, the trial was over. Clancy and Grace delivered their closing arguments, the judge instructed the jury, and three hours later the marshals came to the holding cell and took me back to the courtroom.

The jury had reached a verdict.

As I walked in from the holding area, I took a look around the courtroom. It was packed, not a single seat open, with people standing against the walls. Most of them, I knew, were reporters. I saw Richie Fels and Rachel, my secretary. My mother had managed to get a seat right behind me. There was no sign of James Tipton or Katie. Marion Jordan wasn't there, which surprised me a little, but there had been very little mention of the man I'd been accused of killing. Clancy hadn't introduced photos of him and nobody had taken the stand to tell the jury what a great guy he was. I started thinking at that moment that a better strategy for me from the beginning would have been to lie and say, "Yeah, I killed the son of a bitch. He deserved it." I would have had a better chance of walking out the door.

I walked over next to Grace and we stood while the jury, seven men and five women, filed in. The foreman was a man named Israel

Gillette, who was in his midfifties and worked as a mechanical engineer for Eastman Chemical Company in Kingsport.

"Mr. Street, will you and your counsel please rise?" Judge Geer said.

I stood, but it was difficult. My thighs were like jelly and my heart was beating so hard I could hear it. My hands were shaking so badly that I folded them in front of me, hoping no one would notice.

"Have you reached a verdict?" the judge said.

"We have," Gillette said.

"On the sole count of the indictment, murder in the first degree, how do you find?"

"We find the defendant, Darren Street, guilty."

My throat constricted, and I found it difficult to breathe. I fell back into the chair, slumped forward, and leaned on the table while the judge thanked the jury for their service and people whispered loudly behind me. I heard my mother sobbing.

A couple of minutes later, the judge asked me to stand again. Grace put her hands on my arm and helped me up. I looked toward the judge, but I couldn't really see him.

"Mr. Street, as I'm sure you're aware, the only sentences for first-degree murder in federal court are life and death. Mr. Clancy didn't file a death notice, and based on the evidence I heard, with the threat to your son, I can see why. But the jury has found you guilty of first-degree murder, and it is my duty to sentence you accordingly. Therefore, you are hereby sentenced to life in prison without the possibility of parole. The Bureau of Prisons will determine where you serve the sentence. Marshals, take him away."

"It isn't over, Darren," Grace said as the marshals flanked me and started guiding me out. I could barely manage to put one foot in front of another, but I also didn't want to break down completely in front of all of those people. For a couple of minutes, I withdrew so deeply into myself that I imagined I was an embryo, safe inside my mother's womb, but the embryonic sac was quickly pierced when we walked around a corner and Ben Clancy suddenly appeared.

"Do you remember what you said in front of the press that day they let your uncle out of jail?" he said. "I wasn't there, but I was told immediately. You said, 'Fuck Ben Clancy. He isn't going to be around much longer.' Well, fuck you, my friend. I'm still here, and you're going to a federal max for the rest of your meaningless life."

I stood there staring back at him. I would have spit in his face if I'd been able to muster the strength. He pushed a pudgy finger into my chest.

"And guess what?" he said. "I'm not finished with you yet."

CHAPTER THIRTY-SEVEN

Clancy was right. With the jury's finding, my life had become meaningless. I can't even begin to adequately describe the feelings of hollowness and despair I experienced during the few remaining weeks I was in the Knox County Jail. I fell into a deep depression, slept most of the time, and rarely ate. I didn't call my mother when they forced me to go to the rec cage, and the one time she tried to visit me I refused to go to the visiting room. I was simply too ashamed to face her.

Grace came to see me the day after the trial, but I could barely look at her and don't remember much of what she said. I didn't think she'd done a poor job of representing me at trial; as a matter of fact, I thought she was excellent. But I was in shock, literally, from the reality that now faced me. She told me I would be transferred eventually to the federal penitentiary in Atlanta, where I would be processed and then sent on to Oklahoma, where I would be processed further before being assigned to my final destination. The last thing she said to me was, "I'll handle the appeal. We'll keep working. We won't quit, I promise."

And as for Sean, that, too, was over. The only way I would ever see him again was if my mother somehow was able to obtain visitation rights and then bring him to whatever federal maximum security prison I was going to be shipped to. Clancy had been right about that, too. I knew the feds classified prisoners based on a point system, and I knew that a first-degree murder conviction would run my point total high enough to get me sent to maximum security prison. They wouldn't send me to Florence or Marion—the so-called "super max" prisons—but wherever they wound up sending me, it was going to be an ongoing nightmare.

And then early one morning, Belcher showed up outside my cell door and started banging.

"Get your ass up, faggot," he yelled through the door. "Time for you to stop breathing the air in my block and move on down the road."

He and another guard hooked me up and shackled me, and I shuffled along the hallways to a holding cell near booking and the sally port. A clock on the wall in booking said it was 4:00 a.m. Two federal marshals, wearing gray uniforms, black caps, and black combat boots, came into the cell about an hour later. They replaced my handcuffs and shackles and chained everything together. They attached a "black box" between my hands that covered the lock on the handcuffs. The box also forced my hands into an extremely uncomfortable position. They pulled the chains so they were extremely tight and then moved me to another holding area—they called them bullpens— where there were about twenty other inmates, similarly cuffed and shackled. During that short walk, I realized it wouldn't be long before my wrists and ankles would be raw and my hands and feet would be numb. I noticed that only a couple of inmates had black boxes on their cuffs, and I found out later that the boxes were used only on maximum-security guys.

About half an hour later, a group of six marshals came in. A county deputy unlocked the cell door. "Let's go," one of the marshals said, and I shuffled out to the sally port, bent slightly at the waist because the chain that connected my cuffs and shackles was so tight. Waiting in the sally port was a black-and-white unmarked bus. It looked like a generic

Greyhound. Standing outside the bus were four more marshals holding assault rifles. The windows were tinted so darkly I couldn't see inside.

There was a marshal standing near the door of the bus gazing down at a clipboard. As we approached, he looked up and said, "Which one of you is Darren Street?"

I was about six men back, about ten feet from the door. I didn't say a word.

"Did you hear me?" he yelled. "Which one of you worthless maggots is Darren Street?"

"I'm Street," I said, surprised my voice worked.

He walked straight to where I was standing. He was a big guy, maybe six feet four, and he towered over me. He leaned down and put his nose about an inch from mine.

"You ever heard of diesel therapy, boy?" he said.

"No." I tried to look through him, past him, anything but at him.

"You're about to get you a dose," he said. "A mighty big dose."

He backed away from me and said, "On the bus!" The line started moving slowly as the inmates in front of me shuffled to the door and awkwardly climbed on board.

"Back to front," I heard a voice say from midway down the aisle after I got on. "You, sit right there. You, right there."

The back of the bus was full of inmates, about 80 percent of them black. I followed the herd and plopped into a small metal seat next to an extremely overweight black guy with dreads that hung to his shoulders. He reminded me of Medusa. The rest of the inmates filed onto the bus and sat down. There were steel mesh dividers at both the front and the back of the bus. The marshals sat on the other side of the dividers, four of them facing us. Their seats looked much more comfortable than ours. Just before we pulled out of the sally port, the big marshal stood in the front and faced us.

"Anybody that gets up out of the seat is going to get hurt," he said. "There ain't no potty breaks on this bus. You can talk, but you best keep it down. Chow in four hours."

The bus pulled out, and a few minutes later we were on Interstate 40 headed west. We passed Interstate 75 about twenty minutes later. To get to Atlanta, we would have gone south on I-75. We were headed toward Nashville. My feet and hands were both tingling in less than an hour because the cuffs and shackles were so tight. I heard men talking in quiet tones around me. Most of them were speculating on where the bus was going and when it would stop next. Others were complaining about their hands and feet. After we'd passed through Nashville and were near Jackson, a marshal came down the aisle and started dropping white boxes in everyone's lap. I opened the box and looked inside. There was a bologna sandwich on white bread, a small orange, and a half pint of milk.

"You best be careful what you eat," the guy next to me said.

"Yeah? Why's that?" I said. It was the first time I had spoken to an inmate since I'd shared a cell with Hillbilly.

"I heard the man say diesel therapy. You gonna be on this bus eighteen, twenty hours a day for a while. What goes in gotta come out, right? You eat too much and you'll be sittin' in your own shit."

"Are you serious?" I said.

"I don't know what you did, but you must've pissed somebody off bad. I've known dudes they done it to. They gonna drag your ass all over the country, man. Where you supposed to be going?"

"Atlanta."

"You'll probably hit LA and Oklahoma and lord knows where else before you get to Atlanta. You better just hunker on down and get yourself ready mentally, because they tell me there ain't nothing quite like it. It's worse than the hole because you got the cuffs and the shackles on all day every day. You're gonna be in holding cells in different jails and prisons for a couple hours a night, then back on the bus for another eighteen or twenty. You ain't gonna see a hot meal or a shower or phone for weeks, maybe months. I heard of one dude they kept on the bus for more than a year, man. Damn near killed him."

I shook my head and locked at the floor, wondering what else Clancy could do to me. He'd taken my freedom, and now it appeared he wanted my soul.

CHAPTER THIRTY-EIGHT

Grace Alexander watched Steve Morris walk through the rows of long tables toward her. He was a stocky, powerful man of forty or so, medium height, dark-brown hair parted on the side and cut like a politician's. He was wearing a charcoal gray suit with a gray tie and a white shirt. Very professional looking. Businesslike. She'd never met him, although she'd seen him many times and had heard him speak through sound bites on television screens. She'd read his quotes in the newspaper, and she knew him to be, like nearly all prosecutors, politically conservative. He had been, back before he unseated Ben Clancy, an effective trial lawyer who handled complex medical malpractice cases. Grace wondered how much of a pay cut he'd taken when he was elected district attorney general of Knox County.

"Interesting place for a meeting," Morris said as he approached and offered his hand.

"It's a shame, really," Grace said. "There used to be people in libraries. This one is like a ghost town now."

The branch library was on the outskirts of Knoxville, a rarely used depository of printed information. Grace had called Steve Morris the day before and asked if they could meet. He'd agreed immediately.

"I'm sorry about Darren," Morris said as he sat down across from Grace. "I'm sure he understands why I couldn't reach out to him, but from everything I read and heard in the media and from people around the courthouse, you did an excellent job."

"I'm convinced he's not guilty," Grace said. "Clancy used perjured testimony to convict him. The entire thing was set up. I think Clancy may even have had something to do with the murder itself."

"Can you prove any of that?"

"Not yet. That's why I called you. Darren needs a friend. A real friend who has power and is willing to use it to help him."

"He was convicted by a jury, Miss Alexander, after a very public trial. That isn't something that's easily undone."

"I need to find out what Clancy had on his star witness, the man named James Tipton, Junior. Tipton lied through his teeth in court, but I couldn't expose it because I'm not sure why he did it. Our investigators are slammed, they have more work than time, and besides, they're not really that good. I can't go to the feds because asking the feds to investigate an assistant US attorney is like asking the army to investigate a general. If they find anything, they'll just cover it up and Darren will rot. But you have access to investigators, don't you? Do you have anyone you can trust who can look into this?"

Morris folded his arms across his chest and looked out the window to his right. He pondered the scenery for a minute or so and then looked back at Grace.

"I don't really see myself getting involved," Morris said.

"Why?" Grace said. She felt anger rising in her chest and told herself to remain calm. "Why don't you see yourself getting involved? I thought Darren was your friend. Didn't he help you beat Clancy? Wasn't he the difference in the election? Because from everything I've read, and I've read a lot, he was extremely influential. He practically put you in the district attorney's job."

"And I've thanked him for it a hundred times over. But Darren didn't help me get elected so he could take advantage of my power or influence or whatever I may have. He helped me because he thought I was the best man for the job."

"And he despised Ben Clancy."

"Yes, yes he did, and for good reason. But what you're asking me to do is extremely dangerous in a lot of ways. If you think about it, I could possibly wind up with a federal obstruction of justice charge if Clancy somehow got wind that I was second-guessing him and going behind his back talking to his witnesses."

"So don't let him find out. Be discreet. Use informants. Lie, cheat, misdirect. Do that law enforcement thing."

"I'm glad to hear you think so highly of what we do, Miss Alexander."

"I'm sorry," Grace said. "I'm getting upset. I need help. Darren needs help, and nobody is willing."

"It sounds to me like you've allowed your relationship with your client to cross over the line from professional to personal."

"My relationship with Darren is irrelevant here. An injustice has been done, and I believe a crime has been committed by a federal prosecutor. Maybe more than one crime. I'm simply looking for some help in holding him accountable."

Morris stood and gave Grace a patronizing smile.

"A federal grand jury heard the evidence against Darren and indicted him," Morris said. "A federal petit jury of twelve men and women heard the evidence in court, heard the arguments of counsel, applied the law to the facts, and found Darren guilty of first-degree murder. If you think the jury got it wrong, your remedy is to appeal to the Sixth Circuit Court of Appeals. And forgive me for saying so, Miss Alexander, but trying to convince me to begin a clandestine investigation of a federal prosecutor on what amounts to a hunch, or perhaps intuition, is just plain stupid. Now, if you'll excuse me I have work to do. Have a nice day."

Grace wanted to leap up and claw his eyes out. Instead, she said, "Do you have any children?"

"What? What does that have to do with anything?"

"I was just wondering. Since you don't seem to have any balls."

CHAPTER THIRTY-NINE

James Tipton had changed his security system. He used to rely on the dog, but he'd upgraded. The dog lived in the house now with him, although it went against his grain to have the animal inside. James liked his house orderly, and the dog shed and occasionally vomited, especially if James got drunk and fed it pizza or a greasy cheeseburger.

James had spent some money and hired a security company to install motion detectors around his trailer. He'd trained the dog to keep silent and wait for a command if an alarm tone sounded. The tones weren't loud. James didn't want the intruder, if one came, to run away. He wanted the intruder to come into the house. Once he breached the front door, James knew that under Tennessee law, he was fair game. A man's house was his castle in Tennessee. *Violate the sanctity of my castle, and I can use deadly force against you. I can kill you deader than dammit.*

He wasn't positive something was going to happen, that someone was going to come for him, but he couldn't shake the feeling that Ben Clancy wasn't the kind of man to leave loose ends dangling. Clancy had been in contact with James nearly every day for a month leading up to the trial. They'd met at safe houses all over Knoxville and in small restaurants and bars in the tiny mountain communities around Strawberry Plains, Pigeon Forge, and Gatlinburg. Clancy had scripted every word of James's testimony, and James had followed the script to the letter during the trial. The trial had been over for a month now, and he hadn't heard a single word from Clancy. It made him uneasy, not knowing what Clancy was doing or thinking.

On this Tuesday night, James had just come in from watching the Tennessee Smokies—the Chicago Cubs' Double-A organization in Pigeon Forge—play the Birmingham Biscuits. He had picked up a six-pack of tall boys from the BP station, a pizza from a honky tonk about two miles from his place, and had walked in the door of his trailer just before midnight. He'd let the dog out for ten minutes, retrieved him, fired up a joint, and was sitting in front of the television, half-drunk and half-stoned when an alarm tone started buzzing around one forty-five. The dog, who was lying on the floor in the kitchen, growled menacingly.

"Zeus, come," James said. The dog walked over quickly, still growling. "Quiet."

The only light in the trailer was coming from the television and James quickly flipped it off with the remote. He reached beneath the couch and pulled out a sawed-off, automatic shotgun that was loaded with five shells of double-ought buckshot. He unlocked the safety. The shotgun was ready to fire. James heard soft footfalls on the front porch. Someone was coming. James heard the doorknob jiggle. It was locked. There was silence for several seconds, then a loud *pop* and the door flew open. A second later, a bright flashlight filled the empty doorway.

"Go, Zeus!" James said, and the dog hurled itself toward the intruder. The doorway exploded with automatic rifle fire. Behind the muzzle flash, James saw what looked like the outline of a storm trooper. Bulked up in a vest. Black helmet. James knew his dog was dead. He fired one shot from the shotgun and then turned and ran as fast as he could down the narrow hallway toward his bedroom at the back of the trailer. Before he reached the bedroom, he dived through the door that led to the small backyard and the mountain beyond. He could hear the rifle fire behind him, hear the bullets blasting through the trailer's thin walls, hear the *whiz* as they passed by him.

James was across the backyard in three steps and into the woods. A thin cloud cover barely obscured the full moon, so there was enough light to enable James to see. And he knew these woods perfectly. He'd been in them since he was a small boy. He knew the trees and the roots and the paths and the caves and the creeks. He headed straight up the mountain and didn't stop for a full five minutes. His lungs were screaming and his thighs burning when he finally stopped, knelt at the base of a white oak, and listened.

At first, he could hear nothing but his own breathing and his own heart, but after a couple of minutes, he flinched as two quick rifle shots rang out from below. The flashes put the gunman in James's backyard.

"You'd better run!" a voice called from the darkness. It was, unmistakably, Ben Clancy. "You'd better run as fast and as far as you can! You'd better crawl into a deep hole, my friend, and you'd better stay there for the rest of your life! Because if you ever come out, I'll be waiting!"

James leaned heavily against the tree and slowly shook his head. He'd given in to Ben Clancy. He'd made his deal. And now life as he'd known it would never be the same.

He turned his back to Clancy and continued running up the mountain.

CHAPTER FORTY

The diesel therapy was just as the black man had described it to me. I spent between eighteen and twenty hours on buses or vans each day with the black box between my wrists and the chains tight between my handcuffs and shackles. I learned to stretch both my toes and my wrists while the marshals were hooking me up in order to give my wrists and ankles just an extra fraction of an inch. Still, both wrists and both ankles quickly became raw and bloody. I'd do my best at each stop to clean them, but there was no first aid available, no bandages. I traveled all day and most nights with desperate, angry prisoners and robotic—and sometimes sadistic—guards. For eighty-nine days, I was not offered anything but bologna sandwiches, oranges, water, and milk. I became grateful for the food after a while, although I learned to eat sparingly. I can proudly say that I did not soil myself a single time during the entire ordeal.

There's a saying in the legal profession that goes, "If you're looking for Jesus, go to jail. Everyone there finds him." I didn't find Jesus during diesel therapy and I didn't find God, but I did find peace. At some point around the halfway mark of the trip, I resolved that I wasn't going to allow these people or this system to kill me. I simply wasn't going to allow it. I resolved to survive, and I resolved to keep fighting for my freedom, no matter what it took. I would have faith in Grace. She would get my sentence reversed or get me a new trial. James Tipton would recant his testimony and tell the truth. He would tell the world why he lied, and then everyone would know that I hadn't killed Jalen Jordan. I didn't know who'd killed Jalen and I didn't know why James had said I bought a rifle from him. I suspected that Ben Clancy was responsible, but I had no idea exactly what he'd done to put that kind of pressure on James. My only hope was Grace. Grace would find out. Somehow, she would find out and I would be able to go back to my son and my mother and I'd be able to practice law and I'd rebuild my life.

Once those thoughts began to dominate my mind, I formed them into a mantra and repeated them over and over to myself. Before long, I began to believe, and once I began to believe, all of the anxiety I'd felt during the previous months suddenly melted away. I remained quiet and cautious, I didn't smile and try to engage other people, but I no longer harbored the constant fear and hatred of my captors that I had developed. I accepted them for what they were, misguided miscreants, sadistic but apparently employable, and I rode out the days in peaceful, tortuous discomfort.

Finally, the bus made its way to the United States Penitentiary at Atlanta, a foreboding hellhole more than a century old. My group was taken to the detention center that served as a pass-through point for prisoners who were either new to the federal system or being transported from one prison to another. The lighting in the hallways when we shuffled in was dim, and small cells stuffed with three or four men each lined the walls. We heard catcalls and insults, but I looked straight ahead and kept my expression neutral. After being strip-searched for at least the sixtieth time of my journey, I was eventually put in an eight-foot-by-seven-foot cell with three other men. It had a stainless steel toilet bolted to the wall but no sink. I noticed that nearly all the guards in Atlanta were black, reflecting, I supposed, the racial majority of the population near the prison. Most of the inmates were black as well, many of them with their faces covered in tattoos. I had seen my first man whose entire head and face was covered in tattoos while riding through Texas. He was a muscular white man with a shaved head, and one of the most terrifying human beings I had ever seen in my life.

An hour after we got to our cell in Atlanta, we were served a small plastic bowl of cold oatmeal and a boiled egg on a Styrofoam tray. I ate the food and, grateful to have the cuffs and shackles finally off me for an extended period of time, laid my head back against the concrete wall and passed out.

I had no idea how much time had passed when I woke up. There was a commotion of some kind, and when I opened my eyes, the other guys in my cell were walking out the door. I climbed to my feet and followed, expecting to be directed to a cell where I would again be shackled and handcuffed. Instead we were herded down the dim hallway to a large recreation room and told we had one hour to shower, use the phone, or watch television.

I desperately needed a shower. I hadn't had one in nearly three months, and not only did I smell like a wild animal, the wounds on my wrists and ankles needed to be cleaned. I got in a line of more than fifty men waiting to use one of three working shower heads. When I got to the stall, I was directed by a guard to strip out of my jumpsuit and slip on a pair of shower shoes that was on the floor. I had no underwear. My only pair had become so rancid that I'd abandoned it weeks earlier. I slipped into the shoes and was allowed approximately three minutes beneath the cold water. There were water bugs as big as my thumb on the floor and no soap. When my time was up the guard said, "Turn the water off and get the fuck out." I was told to leave the shower shoes where I'd put them on and to put my jumpsuit back on. There were no towels, so I squeezed as much water as I could out of my long hair and beard before the guard ordered me to get dressed and get out of his shower room.

I lingered for a couple of minutes at the fringe of a large group of men watching a television newscast. Radical Muslims were continuing to kill as many innocents as they could. Republicans and Democrats were sniping at each other over the economy and health care and who was to blame for the country's massive deficit. I shook my head and walked away. Nothing had changed since I'd last seen a television newscast the night before I was arrested nine months earlier.

Just a few minutes after I'd gone back to the cell and they'd closed the door, a single guard came walking up.

"Which one of you is Darren Street?" he said through the bars.

I shuddered and raised my hand as he inserted a steel key and the door swung open.

"Walk in front of me. That way."

He guided me to a room that was ten feet by ten feet. There were three steel stools. I knew immediately it was a visitor's room.

"That one," he said, pointing to the last stool.

I took three steps and looked down. On the other side of the Plexiglas was the most beautiful sight I'd ever seen.

Her name was Grace.

"Oh, Darren," she said. A slight smile crossed her lips, but I could tell immediately it was a smile of pity because a tear slipped down her right cheek. I must have looked terrible.

"Is it that bad?" I said. "I haven't seen myself in a mirror in months."

"You're so thin," she said.

"Not really by choice."

"I'm so sorry," Grace said. "It took me a few weeks of not being able to get in touch with you to realize what they were doing. Atlanta should have been a one-day trip, but I kept hearing you were 'in transit, in transit.' My boss was the one who suggested they probably had you in diesel. We started raising hell with anyone who would listen and finally got to someone in the Department of Justice who was high enough to put a stop to it, but by that time you were in Portland."

"I spent Christmas on a bus," I said. "I assume I have Clancy to thank for my tour of the United States."

"He denies it, but I have absolutely no doubt he set it in motion."

"And there's nothing anyone can do about it?"

"I'm afraid not. Are you injured? Is there anything that might be permanent?"

I showed her the open wounds on my wrists and ankles.

"These will heal. It's too early to tell about anything else," I said.

"How are you . . . mentally?"

I felt tears well in my own eyes but was able to hold them back. "They tried to break me, Grace," I said. "They tried to dehumanize me and wear me down and turn me into a malleable piece of clay that would do anything they said anytime they said it. And they did it, in a way. I'll do anything they tell me to do when they tell me to do it. To them, from the outside, it appears they've taken me over. But I learned along the way that in here, in my heart and in my mind, I'm still strong. They can't touch that."

She smiled again, and I wished I could reach through the glass and stroke her lovely face. I'd barely said a word the last time I saw her.

"I've wanted to tell you I'm sorry," I said.

"For what?"

"For not saying thank you. For not telling you what a good job you did during the trial. For being such a lousy client."

"You don't owe me an apology," she said. "I'm just glad you're safe and still in one piece."

"What's going on with the appeal?"

"I filed the notice, but I haven't filed the brief yet. I still have a couple of weeks. We've been trying to find James Tipton."

"Tipton? He's gone?"

"Seems to have disappeared off the face of the earth."

"Clancy probably killed him."

"Don't say that, Darren. Don't even think it. We're going to need James Tipton to recant to have a chance on appeal."

"I know. The trial was pretty clean."

"We'll keep looking. In the meantime, would you like to know where you're going to wind up in a few weeks?"

"Love to."

"Rosewood. Ever heard of it?"

"No. Where is it?"

"About a hundred and twenty miles east of San Francisco."

"It's a max, right?"

Grace nodded.

"Anybody famous there?"

"Probably nobody you've ever heard of. A guard was killed there by two inmates a few years ago, though. Expect it to be tough."

"I'm sure I'll love it."

"I've done a lot of asking around, Darren. I've talked to former clients who have been in and out of the system. You have something that will be of great value to you on the inside. You have a legal education. You're a real lawyer. That's going to help keep you safe until we can figure out a way to get you out."

"I'll hang a shingle outside my cell. Darren Street, Attorney at Jailhouse."

"It's good to know your sense of humor is still intact. Listen, there's one other thing I need to tell you. Your mother finally got a hearing in front of a judge. She picks up Sean and keeps him overnight every other Saturday."

My eyes filled with tears and I broke down. I was still crying when I felt a guard tug on my arm.

"Thank you, Grace," I said as the guard pulled me away. "Thank you for everything."

* * *

Late that night, I felt someone pushing on my shoulder. It was one of my cellmates, a white guy named Bobo who I'd talked with a little earlier in the evening.

"Listen up," he whispered. "Macho man's about to start up."

"What? What are you talking about?"

"See that clock over there?"

A clock on the wall above a guards' station said 2:59 a.m. I nodded.

"Three o'clock on the dot. He's done it the last three nights. The guards got really pissed off last night. Something's gonna happen."

As soon as the clock hit three, a voice in a cell across the hall and two doors down began to sing The Village People's "Macho Man" at the top of his lungs.

Two guards, both of them black and both of them large, strode by our cell and stopped in front of the macho man's.

"Shut the fuck up!"

He kept singing.

Within seconds, five more guards in cell extraction gear—Kevlar vests, knee pads, helmets, thick gloves—and carrying electronic stun shields, pepper spray, and Tasers, came running down the hall. They'd obviously geared up earlier and had been waiting for him to start singing.

"Last chance, boy. Shut your mouth, now!"

He went into the first chorus, full bore.

They opened the cell door and ordered the other two inmates who were in the cell to get out and lie facedown in the hall. As soon as the inmates were out, the guards went in. Macho man kept singing until the stun shield hit him. I saw him go down and could see the guards kicking and stomping, but I could no longer see the macho man. They dragged him out a couple of minutes later with his hands cuffed behind his back. Three guards pulled him along the floor right in front of me. Blood was bubbling from his lips, but I could hear him mumbling, "I'm the macho man, I'm the macho man." Dozens of inmates up and down the hall started yelling at them to let him go, to leave him alone, but the resistance wasn't as forceful as it might have been, and I thought I knew why. Had they become too vocal, or had someone thrown something through the bars at a guard—urine, for instance—the entire place would go on lockdown. Nobody would go to the rec room the next day. Nobody would get to use the phone or take a shower or get any commissary delivered.

There was a laundry room that I'd noticed earlier in the day about fifty feet down the hall from my cell. It was encased by Plexiglas instead of bars so the guards could see what was going on in there during the day when some of the inmates were allowed to use it. They dragged the macho man into the laundry room and turned off the lights, and for the next ten minutes, we sat there and listened to the sounds of the guards taking turns beating him. I found it so ironic— black guards beating a black man for singing a song that was written and performed originally by a black man. Eventually, they dragged him out of the laundry room and off the block, leaving a wide swath of blood in their wake.

Silence came over the cellblock then, the kind of silence caused by fear and disbelief and shock. I lay back on the concrete platform that was serving as my bed and stared through the bars. The last thing I saw that night before I dozed off was a rat scurrying down the hallway, dragging a bag of stolen potato chips.

CHAPTER FORTY-ONE

The macho man died two days after the vicious beating the guards inflicted upon him. I overheard a group of inmates talking about it during my first trip into the yard at Atlanta. It was five days after I'd arrived, and suddenly, without announcement or fanfare of any kind, the cell doors popped and we were able to wander around freely within the confines of our unit and the yard. The yard was about the size of two football fields, rectangular in shape, covered in asphalt, and surrounded by an electrified chain link fence topped with concertina wire. There were towers at the corners of the fence with stretches of catwalks between them. In the towers and on the catwalks were men who carried weapons of various sorts, from rubber grenade launchers to rifles that fired rubber bullets to shotguns to deer rifles to assault rifles. There were a couple of basketball courts on the asphalt, a weightlifting area, a track around the outside, and several areas where picnic tables served as mini casinos.

The first thing that struck me in the yard—the first place I'd been where there was actually some freedom of choice—was that the inmates separated themselves by race. Hillbilly had told me that race was important, that I shouldn't hang around with members of other races, but as I watched and listened and spoke with more and more inmates, I learned that what I was seeing was a less-than-subtle return to tribalism. Races separated into groups based on geographic commonalities. Southerners tended to gather with southerners, northerners with northerners, East Coasters with East Coasters, West Coasters with West Coasters, etc. There were further breakdowns by state and city, but race was paramount. The question that was commonly asked was: "Who you ride with?" If you were a black guy from Chicago but not a Blood or a Crip, you probably rode in the Illinois car, but that wasn't the only car from Illinois. There was a white Illinois car, a black Illinois car, and a Mexican Illinois car. If you were a Blood, you rode with the Bloods, no matter where you were from, but you tended to hang around with guys from your home state or hometown—thus, the term "homies." If you were a white, independent boy from Knoxville, Tennessee, like me, you rode in the Tennessee car, but there was a white boy car that served as an umbrella for all the white guys at the institution.

There were a lot of gangs. The Aryan Brotherhood, the Dirty White Boys, the Nazi Low Riders, the Bloods, the Crips, the Mexican Mafia—all battled to stake out their claims on various prison hustles and territories. For them, it was all about money and power, controlling the flow and price of drugs, controlling gambling or loan sharking or stores, extorting money in return for protection. The gang members were easily identified by a combination of their race, their tattoos, and the accessories they wore. But there were also a majority of inmates who didn't join gangs, who just wanted to do their time and move on, because joining a gang meant you could be ordered to commit a murder at any time and once you were ordered, you had to do it. If you didn't, the gang would murder you. The second most important reason for staying out of a gang was that once you were in, there was no getting out. Period. If you joined a gang and suddenly had a change of heart, the gang would green-light you, which meant they marked you for assassination.

Bobo, the cellmate who had awakened me the night the macho man was beaten to death, caught up to me as I walked along the track. It was a bright but blustery February morning, and I huddled inside the light jacket I'd been issued. Bobo was pleasant enough. He was a couple of years older than me, about the same height, and a little chubby around the face. His hair was buzzed and his eyes were dark brown. He had a stocking cap pulled down around his ears.

"There's something I haven't asked you, man," he said. "Which way you going, in or out?"

"In," I said.

"How long?"

"Life."

"Life? Who'd you kill?"

I turned and smiled at him. "Nobody."

He started nodding. "Yeah, boy, that's right. You keep talking that. Didn't kill nobody. Not nobody, not no how."

"I've heard that somewhere before," I said.

"*Wizard of Oz*, but you ain't Dorothy and this ain't Oz. Where they sending you?"

"Rosewood. You know it?"

"Do I know it? I just spent seven years there. Got sent to Rosewood 'cause I stabbed this boy up in Hazelton. I'm almost flat now, though. They're processing me out to a halfway house in Tallahassee. Less than a year and I'll be back home, staring at the walls, going crazy because nobody'll give me a job. But let me tell you about Rosewood. You said you don't want to bang with a gang, right?"

"Nah, I'd rather just stay independent. Keep my head down, run my appeal, and try to get out."

"What'd you do on the outside?"

"I was a lawyer, believe it or not."

"No shit? A *real* lawyer? What'd you do? Wills and stuff like that? Real estate?"

"I did criminal defense work."

Bobo stopped in his tracks. I stopped, too, and turned to look at him.

"Man, do you have any idea the kind of respect you're gonna command the second you step on the yard? A murderer *and* a lawyer? I'm assuming you didn't snitch on anybody, that right?"

"Nobody to snitch on."

"That's good. That's real good, because they're gonna want to see your paperwork as soon as you get there. You're gonna need a docket sheet, maybe a transcript of your sentencing. You have to prove you're not a snitch, because if you were a snitch, them boys at Rosewood would run you off the yard."

"What do you mean, run me off the yard?"

"It means just what it says. Convicts hate snitches. You come in with paperwork that says you got a lighter sentence because you helped the feds somehow or told on somebody, the shot caller is gonna walk you straight up to the security booth on your block and tell them you can't stay, because if you stay, you're gonna get messed up bad."

"What's a shot caller?"

"He's the guy that calls the shots for your group. He's like your congressman on the yard."

"So if they think I'm a snitch, they'll kill me?"

"They might not kill you, but they're gonna put a shank or a knife or an ice pick in you. The people who run the prison know they're serious, so what they do is, if you get run off the yard, they put you in protective custody for a few months and then they transfer you to another place. I've known dudes who did their whole bit in protective custody, moving from one federal pen to another, because they were snitches and couldn't hide it."

"So the inmates actually tell the administration who can stay and who has to go?" I said.

"Yeah, believe it or not, that's the way it works. But let's get back to Rosewood. First person you need to see is this dude named Big Pappy.

Huge guy with a ponytail, doing thirty plus for drugs. He's got more respect than anybody on the yard because of all the work he's put in on the police. He's the shot caller for the Independent White Boys and you're gonna answer to him whether you want to or not. Once you prove to him you ain't a rat and once he finds out you're a lawyer and a murderer, man, I'm telling you, you're gonna have so much respect. You'll have dudes crawling all over each other trying to be your friend and hire you for their cases. Big Pappy will watch over you. You'll get rich, man, I swear it."

"I thought we couldn't have money."

"Ain't you got anybody on the outside who can accept and bank money for you?"

"Yeah, I guess so."

Bobo shook his head and we started walking again. He was nodding his head and smiling broadly.

"Wow, man. A lawyer and a killer. I don't believe it. A lawyer and a killer. I wish I was you. I really do."

CHAPTER FORTY-TWO

The following Saturday, I stood in line for an hour in the dayroom in the detention center, waiting for one of the three phones. I'd asked around and learned how to call out. It would have to be collect, and it was exorbitantly expensive, but I hadn't talked to my mom in almost four months. I also hoped, since it was Saturday, that Sean would be there. I didn't know whether I'd be able to control myself when I heard his voice, but I'd decided I had to try. I had to stay in contact with my son. It was selfish of me to abandon him, no matter how guilty or embarrassed I felt.

My fingers were trembling when I dialed Mom's number, and I could feel droplets of perspiration running down my sides from my armpits. The phone rang once, twice, and I took a deep breath. It stopped ringing, and I knew she'd answered. A recorded voice was telling Mom she was receiving a collect call from an inmate at a federal penal institution. It was telling her what to do if she wanted to accept the call and pay the charges.

"Hello? Darren?"

"Hi, Mom."

I heard her take a deep breath, and I knew she was fighting back tears.

"Are you still in Atlanta?" she said

"Yeah, but they'll send me to California soon. The guys here say it can be anywhere from two to four weeks. Have you talked to Grace lately?"

"We spoke when she got back from visiting you. She's a wonderful girl, Darren."

"Yeah, I think a lot of her, too. Listen, Mom, I'm sorry I didn't call after the trial. I was embarrassed, you know? Depressed, I guess. I didn't want to talk to anybody. Then they put me in diesel for a couple of months. I guess Grace told you about it."

"She did, and I couldn't believe it. Are you all right?"

"Amazingly unscathed. The places on my wrists and ankles are almost healed already and I don't think there's any permanent damage of any kind. A lot has happened, but I'm still pretty tough."

"You're as tough as they come. I've always known that. I want you to know I e-mailed every representative and senator in the United States Congress and told them about what happened to you. I've been absolutely raising hell."

"Every member of the US Congress? How many is that?"

"Four hundred and thirty-five in the House and a hundred in the Senate. Took me a long time."

"You're a nut, Mom."

"Hell hath no fury like a mother scorned," she said.

We talked for a short time about how things were going at her beauty salon and about the progress of my appeal. I knew I couldn't keep the phone for long, though, because there were guys behind me waiting, and staying on the phone too long was considered a serious breach of prison inmate etiquette. Talking an extra ten minutes could get you shanked.

"Listen, Mom," I said, "there's a line behind me so I can't talk long, but Grace told me you got some visitation with Sean a couple of times a month on Saturday. Is he there?"

"He is," she said, and I felt a lump in my throat. "He's up in his room building something with Legos."

"Does he know where I am?"

"He doesn't know you're in Atlanta, but Katie told him you killed somebody and are in prison. She told him you're never coming home."

"Why doesn't that surprise me?" I said. "How did he take it?"

"I don't know. I wasn't there when she told him, but he was pretty matter-of-fact about it when he told me. You know how kids are."

"What did you say to him?"

"I told him his mother was entitled to her opinion."

"Did you tell him I'm coming home?"

"I let it go, Darren. We just don't talk about it. He's only here for a day every two weeks. I just try to make sure he has fun. I'm walking into his room now. Sean? There's someone on the phone who would like to talk to you."

I heard Sean say, "Who is it?" I heard some rattling, and then I heard breathing.

"Hello?" his little high-pitched voice said.

I bit my lip as tears burned my eyes.

"Hello?" he said again.

"Hey, little man. Do you know who this is?"

"Dad? *Dad?*"

"Yeah, yeah, it's me. It's so good to hear your voice."

I could no longer see the phone in front of me because my eyes were filled with tears. They started pouring down my cheeks, and my nose started running. I was telling myself to keep my composure, but the sound of his sweet voice triggered a longing in me that went to my core.

"Mom said you killed a man and got in a lot of trouble and they put you in jail and that you're never coming back, but Grandma says they put you in jail by mistake and that pretty soon they're going to let you out and you can come home. I told Mom you were going to come home, but she just laughed and said Grandma isn't telling me the truth, but I think I'm going to believe Grandma because I want you to come home because I miss you."

"I miss you, too, buddy."

"Are you crying, Dad?"

"I'm just really glad to hear your voice. It's been a long time since we got to talk."

"I know. Are you going to come home soon?"

"I'm going to try. Listen, Sean, the people here won't let me talk on the phone very long, but now that you're getting to see your grandma again and now that they're letting me use the phone a little, I'm going to call you every time you come to Grandma's house, okay?"

"Okay."

"I love you."

"I love you, too."

"We'll talk again soon, and I promise you I'm going to get home just as soon as I can."

"Bye, Dad."

"Bye."

I hung up the phone and my legs failed me. I was sobbing as I dropped straight to my knees. Two inmates helped me up and gave up their place in line to help me to a chair in the dayroom.

CHAPTER FORTY-THREE

I eventually made my way to the United States Penitentiary at Rosewood, California, via Con Air, also known as the Justice Prisoner and Alien Transportation System. Typical fed name—long and non-sensical. If I hadn't seen a jet in front of me when I first read the name on a shoulder patch one of the marshals was wearing, I would have thought I was about to be loaded onto a rocket and hauled off to an outer space penal colony.

When I walked onto the tarmac in Atlanta after having been given virtually no notice that I was leaving, eight US Marshals armed with assault rifles surrounded a Boeing 747. Every prisoner—there were about sixty of us—was cuffed and shackled. I, of course, was also fitted with the black box between my wrists that I'd grown to hate so much during diesel therapy. Other guys had black boxes, too, guys who, like me, were ultimately headed to a maximum security prison. I even saw a couple of guys who were wearing some kind of mesh mittens and others who had thin bags over their heads. The bags meant that at some point, those inmates had spit on a guard or a marshal. One guy—and I don't know who he was—had what looked like a hockey mask over his face.

The rumor later floated on the plane was that he was headed to the super max in Florence, Colorado.

There were another fifty or sixty inmates already on the plane when I boarded. We took off, and two and a half hours later landed at the Federal Transfer Center in Oklahoma City, which was unique in that it had its very own runway. A Jetway came out of the prison straight to the plane; our feet never touched the ground. The transfer center was a place where nearly every inmate in the federal system passes through for processing. I thought it and Atlanta were redundant, but I was quickly learning that redundancy was one of the things the feds did best. We were herded into holding cells and eventually called out, strip-searched, and processed into one of the housing units. I spent two weeks there on the third floor. It was relatively clean and the food was surprisingly good. Compared to Atlanta and most of the county jails I'd been in, the place was a paradise.

From Oklahoma City, I took another Con Air flight to San Francisco and then a bus to Rosewood, where they strip-searched me, of course, and then processed me. I went through medical and social screening, set up a commissary account, established a phone list and visitor's list, met the bureaucrats who worked in the unit—unit manager, case manager, counselor, education adviser. Finally, after a few days in holding, I was assigned a cell in one of the four housing units on the compound. It was early afternoon when I was escorted onto the block, which consisted of eighty cells on two levels, was shaped like a trapezoid, and was supposed to be my home for the next twenty years or more. My cell, number seventy-six in A block of the Jefferson unit, was on the upper level. The block, which was clean and shiny and smelled like antiseptic, was almost empty because most of the inmates were either at their jobs or out on the recreation yard. I dropped my bedroll and extra clothing (the feds outfit inmates in khakis) off at the cell, which was spotless and orderly, and went in search of Mike "Big Pappy" Donovan.

I'd been told by the unit manager that Big Pappy would be waiting for me in his cell, which was number thirty-five, almost directly below mine. I walked up to the open cell door and knocked.

"Come on in," a baritone voice with a Midwestern accent said.

Pappy was sitting at a small shelf attached to his wall that served as a desk. He stood when I walked into the cell, and I immediately understood why they called him Big Pappy. The man was massive: my guess was six feet seven inches and maybe 275 pounds of bone and muscle. He was younger than I thought he'd be, maybe thirty-eight. His khaki shirt was short-sleeved, but his tattoos ran all the way down both arms to his hands. His neck was also covered in tattoos, and I had no doubt his back and chest would look the same. His hair was shoulder-length and black, pulled into a ponytail. His eyes were a chocolate brown and, at the moment, looked genuinely friendly.

"You must be Darren Street," he said as he stuck out his hand, which I took.

"And you must be Big Pappy."

"Welcome to Rosewood."

"Thank you, I guess."

He motioned toward the chair he had vacated.

"Take a seat," he said, and he moved over and sat on the bottom bunk. "So I'm the shot caller for the Independent White Boy car here at Rosewood. I'm told you don't want to gang bang, so that puts you in my car since you're white. You cool with that?"

"Do I have a choice?"

"Yeah," he said. "Everybody's got a choice. You could refuse to get in my car, but then you're out there on the street all alone surrounded by some of the most dangerous predators you're ever going to run across. You won't last long."

"So what are my responsibilities to the . . . to the group?"

"All you really have to do is be loyal to your brothers," he said. "And when I say brothers, I mean other white guys in this prison who, like you, want to do their time with as little trouble as possible. What does loyalty include? A lot of simple things, but the most important thing is that you have to be willing to fight if it comes down to it. Our car is the biggest in this prison. About sixty percent of the inmates here are white, and most of the white guys who come here don't want to bang because the bangers are crazy. They get in little skirmishes over turf all the time, and the next thing you know the skirmish turns into a war and there's blood on the yard. If you have a beef with a banger—whether he's white, black, or Mexican—you come to me. I'll work it out. If I can't work it out, then something's going to go down and you have to be willing to be in the middle of it. If you're not willing, if we can't count on you and you pussy out, you'll answer to me personally. The bangers know we outnumber them and they know we'll spill blood if we absolutely have to. That's what keeps things peaceful most of the time. Being willing to shed blood makes us safe."

"Sounds like war propaganda to me," I said. "You should be a recruiter for the marines."

He shrugged his shoulders and smiled. "It is what it is, man," he said. "They tell me you're a lawyer."

"Yeah, well, I used to be a lawyer," I said. "What else did they tell you?"

"That you got a life sentence for murdering a dude who deserved to be murdered, but you say you didn't do it. That you got dieseled for three months because some fed doesn't like you or because you put in some work on the guards in Tennessee. How am I doing so far?"

"Pretty good, actually."

"Remember this. There are no secrets in prison. You know my background?"

"I heard you were the shot caller here when I was still in Atlanta. And my understanding of shot caller is that you represent your group in the political structure of the prison. You're the leader. You deal with shot callers from other cars, from gangs, and you negotiate with the guards and the bureaucrats occasionally. Is that basically what you do?"

"I kick some ass once in a while."

"Is that how you became a shot caller in the first place?"

He nodded. "You know that work you put in on the guards in county? I did the same thing when I first came into the federal system. It cost me two years in the hole. Two entire years, locked down twenty-three hours a day. Then I did a little work on a couple more guards about a year after they let me out of the hole. Wound up at Marion in the super max for three years."

"Did you kill them?"

"Nah, I didn't even stab them. But I hurt them all pretty bad. Broke one guy's jaw and nose and broke another guy's leg. Assholes deserved it, too. The super max was bad, though. I don't plan to mess with the guards anymore, but they don't know that. They keep their distance."

"So you're the shot caller because of what you've done in the past."

"It's a respect thing," Big Pappy said. "Respect is the most important commodity in prison, and I'm not talking about respect from the guards. Respect from other inmates is what will keep you alive."

"Yeah," I said, "that's what I keep hearing. How long have you been in?"

"I'm in my eleventh year of a thirty-five-year sentence."

"I was told drugs?"

"Coke."

"Were you guilty?"

"Absolutely not. Set up by a crooked cop, hired an idiot for a lawyer, and here I am. I've pretty much exhausted the appeals process, which is something I want to talk to you about as soon as you get settled in. Are you planning to set up shop in the law library?"

"If they'll let me."

"They'll let you," he said, "and so will I. I won't even ask for a cut, on one condition."

"Yeah? What's that?"

"Your first client has to be me."

CHAPTER FORTY-FOUR

My new cellmate was a short, skinny, acne-scarred white guy named Dino Long. All I knew about him before I walked into the cell was what I'd been told by the unit manager and the unit counselor. The feds tried to match people up as best they could so they didn't have serious problems in the cells, but they never knew for sure. They told me Dino Long was a little strange but was considered to be an "okay guy." Like more than half of the inmates at the prison, he had been convicted of a nonviolent drug offense, but he was in max because he was on the front end of a thirty-year sentence. He worked in the kitchen and had been at Rosewood for only six months. They told me his previous cellmate had suffered a massive stroke and had been transferred to another prison with a better rehab facility. Dino hadn't been in the cell when I went downstairs to talk to Big Pappy, but when I came back, he was sitting at the little desk, writing on a piece of notebook paper with a pencil. He didn't look up or acknowledge that I'd walked into the cell, so I started unrolling my bedroll.

"Don't ever touch my stuff," he said a few minutes later.

I stopped what I was doing and turned to face him. I thought I'd probably have to fight him, but he wasn't looking at me. He was still writing.

"I'm not planning to touch your stuff," I said.

"I'm a firm believer in the power of Jesus Christ, our Lord and Savior."

"Good for you."

"Are you religious?"

"No."

"Your loss," Dino said. "Are you tough? I've heard you're a tough guy."

"Yeah? Who told you that?"

"A fairy."

"I'm not a tough guy, and I'm not looking for trouble. I just want
to get the hell out of here as soon as I can."

"I thought you had a life sentence."

"Good God," I said, "this place is like a sewing circle. You guys know
more about me than I know about myself."

"And you're a lawyer, right? They told me you're a lawyer. Should I
call you counselor?"

"You should call me Darren. And I should call you?"

"Dino."

"Dino. Good. Okay. Yes, I was a lawyer on the outside, which seems
to be the first thing everybody wants to talk about, but I—"

"The psychologist here thinks I'm mentally ill," he said. "Not bad
enough to be institutionalized or anything, not bad enough to be
dangerous to other people, but he thinks I'm bipolar and I might
be a danger to myself. He says that's why I snorted so much cocaine,
to self-medicate, you know? And that's why I started selling it the
way I did. It wasn't really my fault that I lived in a big city and had
some friends in Miami who could get kilos for me and that I knew
a bunch of people who could distribute for me because I went to
college and liked to party. Do you think something like that would
be my fault?"

"Something like what?" I said.

"Like being born rich in Pittsburgh and going to Carnegie-Mellon and knowing people in Miami who could get kilos for me. Is that my fault?"

I shrugged my shoulders. I didn't want to get into a discussion about choices and responsibilities with him. He was talking fast and his voice sounded like it was cracking. Lecturing or judging him just didn't seem to be the right thing to do at the time.

"I don't know, man," I said.

"My parents are extremely disappointed in me," he said. "The feds seized every dime I had as soon as they arrested me, so my parents wound up paying a lawyer a hundred thousand dollars for my defense. Can you believe that? A hundred thousand dollars. And I was guilty as sin and I knew it, but I lied and told them I hadn't done anything and that I was being framed, and they paid this lawyer and we went to trial, and after the jury found me guilty the judge hammered me."

"I know the feeling," I said, hoping he would stop.

He spun around on the concrete stool that served as a chair and looked at me. His hair was light brown and his eyes light green and forlorn. He looked at me intensely for what seemed like forever, as though he was studying me.

"What kind of person are you?" he finally said.

I shook my head. "That's a strange question," I said. "I guess I don't really know for sure. I think I'm a good person. I try to be a good person."

"Are you hateful? Are you judgmental?"

"I don't think so. It'd be pretty difficult to be hateful and judgmental and practice criminal defense law, which is what I did for a living before I wound up here."

"My last cell mate was disgusting," he said. "He was old and big-oted and narrow-minded and I'm glad he stroked out like he did. He deserved it."

"No offense," I said. "But for somebody who's concerned about me being judgmental, you sound like a—"

"Do you know what pushed him over the edge?" Dino said. "The thing that made him have a stroke?"

"No idea."

"We were right here, talking just the way you and I are talking right now. He was standing where you're standing and I was sitting just like I am now. He was ranting and raving about his faggot son, and I said, 'Do you know that bisexual men and women are far more likely to have gay sons or lesbian daughters than straight people? Is there a chance you might be bisexual?' I have no idea whether what I said to him is true, but it absolutely freaked him out. He turned pink and took a step toward me and raised his fist. And then I said, 'And guess what, big boy? You've been rooming with a fag for the past five months.' Next thing I knew he was jerking on the floor like a chicken with its head cut off."

I stood there looking at him for a few seconds, not quite knowing how to respond. When I did say something, it was idiotic.

"So you're telling me you're gay?"

"Congratulations, genius," he said. "I just think we should be honest with each other if we're going to live together. I promise I won't try to get in your pants, and if you're really a good guy, I'd appreciate it if you'd keep my little secret to yourself."

CHAPTER FORTY-FIVE

Over the next year, I fell into the mind-numbing routine of life at Rosewood. Birthdays and holidays were just like every other day. Nothing ever changed with the exception of my marital status. Six months in, Katie was granted a divorce. They didn't go so far as to terminate my parental rights and my mother was allowed to continue her visitation with Sean, but it was a hollow victory.

The only thing that made my existence seem real was the constant fear and the violence. Guards would attack inmates. Inmates would attack guards. Inmates would attack inmates. I'll never forget the screams I heard one morning when an inmate went into another inmate's cell and poured a cup of baby oil that had been superheated in a microwave onto the sleeping man's face. I stepped out of my cell and saw the man stagger out into the middle of the common area on the first floor. He was clutching at his face. The skin came off in his hands.

The cells popped at 5:45 each morning, I rolled out of bed, and it began. Make the bed, do a hundred push-ups and a hundred crunches, shower, go to the chow hall, head for the law library and get some work done, back to the cell to stand for count, back to the law library, back to the chow hall, back to the law library, out to the rec yard for a run, to the workout room twice a week to exercise, stand for count, to the gym twice a week to play basketball, chow hall for evening meal, study law and work on cases in the evenings, stand for count, lock down at 9:30 p.m., go to sleep, get up and do it again the next day.

Dino showed me the ropes initially—what little he knew—and I gradually made acquaintances with some guys I was comfortable talking with, a couple of whom were from Tennessee. I learned from them and Big Pappy how things worked, or at least how they were supposed to work, and all about the different cars and gangs in the prison. They also told me which guards were corrupt, which ones were half-decent human beings, and which ones were straight up hard-asses who liked to either hurt people or see them get hurt.

Everybody had their hustle, including the guards. There were the card tables and the dice games, the homemade wine and liquor, the tobacco, the drugs, the protection rackets, and the stores. Most of the hustles, especially the most lucrative, were controlled by the gangs who paid the guards to turn their heads. Big Pappy controlled three card tables and about a quarter of the tobacco that was smuggled into the prison. There was a huge markup on tobacco, even though it was legal on the streets. One cigarette cost a book of stamps, which cost about six dollars. Pappy told me he could get a pouch of Bugler rolling tobacco smuggled in to him—by a guard—for about a hundred dollars. He got eighty cigarettes out of a pouch and sold them for six dollars each. Since almost everybody in the place smoked, he and his little crew sold more than a thousand cigarettes a week, which meant he was making nearly five grand a week selling cigarettes. I stayed away from all of it, though. I didn't drink, didn't touch a drug, didn't gamble, and rarely spoke to a gang banger unless it was about a legal issue. I kept my distance from the guards, too. They were at the bottom of the law enforcement food chain, men and women who were underpaid and unappreciated and who would lie, cheat, and steal for each other if it meant saving their own asses. I actually had more respect for murderers, robbers, and drug dealers than I did for many of the guards.

My hustle was law. I started taking cases about ten days after I was given a cell at Rosewood. Everything, of course, was postconviction appellate work, either direct appeals, petitions to the US Supreme Court for review, or habeas corpus petitions. I hadn't done much appellate work on the outside, but I learned the rules and procedures of the appellate courts quickly. The prison provided me access to online legal databases, so I was able to work efficiently.

The first thing I did was set up a corporation in Nevada where the privacy laws are so strong that corporate records are nearly impenetrable. My mom helped me with it. We sent the application through the mail and had the paperwork delivered to her. I was the president of our little corporation and she was the vice president. I then sent instructions to my mom to set up a corporate bank account into which I could have prisoners direct deposit money if they decided to hire me for a case. I hid those instructions to my mother in legal mail that I was sending to Grace, because the prison censors couldn't read my legal correspondence. Grace could have gotten in trouble if anyone in the legal system found out, but when I sent her a letter and asked her if I could send something to my mom through her, she wrote back and said, "Absolutely." Giving Mom access to the corporate bank account meant she could get to the money I was earning and use it for her and Sean. Katie didn't know a thing about it, which was exactly the way I wanted it.

Prisoners don't have access to the Internet, but they do have access to tightly controlled e-mail accounts. If a fellow prisoner wanted to hire me and I agreed to take the case, I would quote him a fee and give him instructions on how to deposit the money into our corporate account. Once the money was transferred, I would get an e-mail from my mother about some random subject that ended with, "P.S. Sean is doing well. I'm very proud of him."

Big Pappy Donovan was my first client. He paid me, too. I asked him for $2,000 and he didn't even flinch. It was no wonder, considering the amount of money he was making every week from the gambling and the cigarettes. It wasn't until after we'd agreed on a fee that I learned how much he was pulling down with the gambling and tobacco. I should have charged him double.

Pappy's case was interesting from the beginning, and although I didn't tell him, I thought we had a chance to get some relief. It was similar to mine, actually, although Pappy's case involved a crooked cop instead of a crooked prosecutor. The cop had a personal grudge against Pappy because, according to Pappy, Pappy had stolen a woman from him when they were all in their early twenties. They came from a small town in Georgia called Hawkinsville, just south of Macon. Pappy had played football at Mercer University and had returned to Hawkinsville, where he was in his second year as an assistant coach on the Hawkinsville High School football team and teaching biology to sophomores. He ran into a woman named Paisley Grant in a bar one Saturday night. He'd known Miss Grant in high school. She was attending a birthday party for one of her friends. She and Big Pappy started talking, hit it off, and wound up having sex in his truck in the parking lot.

"I actually liked the girl," Pappy told me. "We started dating pretty seriously after that. I saw her almost every Saturday night and would talk to her once or twice during the week. It finally fizzled out after about four months, but I enjoyed it while it lasted. She didn't tell me she'd been dating Ronnie Ray when we met at the bar and she didn't tell me she broke it off with him, not that it would have mattered. I'd known Ronnie Ray since junior high. He was a pussy."

Not just any pussy. When Ronnie Ray first learned that Big Pappy Donovan had snaked his girlfriend, he was a patrol officer for the Pulaski County Sheriff's Department, but within a year, Ray was assigned to a federal drug task force that worked southern Georgia. He apparently used that position to take revenge on Big Pappy, because he eventually arrested him for six counts of possessing and distributing crack cocaine, offenses that were punishable by up to life in prison. Ray filed the charge and, along with an informant, was the feds' star witness at trial. Pappy was convicted and sentenced to thirty-five years, and he claimed to me that every word out of Ray's mouth was a lie. He'd never seen or used crack, let alone sold it. I believed him, too. After what had happened to me and to my uncle, I knew how easy it was to railroad someone if a cop or a prosecutor really wanted it done.

Pappy had run the gamut of appeals and thought he might be finished the first time he came to see me. After we'd talked for a while, I asked him about the truck he said they had confiscated.

"I loved that truck," he said. "Hadn't had it long, but I loved it."

"Let's sue the county to get the truck back," I said. "We won't win, but we can ask for all of the investigative materials related to your case and maybe something will shake loose."

A month later, Pappy received an answer to the lawsuit, and a month after that, he received an envelope full of papers from the county's lawyers containing discovery material I'd requested. Among the papers were some of Ronnie Ray's investigative notes. Pappy brought them to me with a grin on his face the day they arrived in the mail.

"This says there was a videotape of the informant being debriefed," Pappy said to me. "That guy was a piece of garbage. I guarantee Ronnie coached him."

"Maybe," I said. "I'll try to get a judge to make them turn it over if nobody's destroyed it."

"Cops keep everything," he said. "That's one thing I've learned after all these years of appeals. But there's something better."

Pappy laid out several more sheets of paper. They were copies of Ronnie Ray's investigative notes ostensibly created during the times that Pappy was selling crack to the informant. Ray's notes said he was "observing" the buys. They listed the make, model, and license plate number of Pappy's pickup and the dates and times of the buys, along with some brief descriptions of what was allegedly going on.

"These might be it," he said. "These might be the smoking gun."

I looked at them and shook my head. They looked pretty much like every other set of investigative notes I'd ever seen.

"I don't get it," I said.

"See the dates?" Pappy said.

"Yeah. So?"

"I traded trucks. I didn't buy the truck that's listed on here until six weeks after the last time he says I sold crack. He's been lying all along and this will prove it. Can you get it in front of a judge?"

"I can try."

"Make it happen. You get me out of this place, and I'll owe you big time."

* * *

I filed Big Pappy's motion for a new trial with the trial court in Georgia, and amazingly, we got a response in less than eight weeks. Apparently, Ronnie Ray had been accused of doing some unsavory things, and the federal magistrate wanted an evidentiary hearing. He even appointed Pappy a lawyer to conduct the hearing. They set a date, and two months after that, Pappy was shipped out. He was gone for five weeks. When he came back, he came straight to my cell.

"He admitted that he lied, man," Pappy said. "The lawyer pressed him, and he didn't have an answer. And you know that tape you asked the judge for? He made them produce it. My lawyer took a look at it and said it was the worst example of witness tampering he'd ever seen in his life."

"So what are you doing back here?" I said.

"The judge said he'd issue a written opinion. Should have it before too much longer. And guess what else? I called my lawyer when I was in Oklahoma on my way back here. They fired Ronnie Ray two days after the hearing. He's gone, man. I hate to even think about it, but this could really happen. I could wind up getting out of here."

CHAPTER FORTY-SIX

Not long after Pappy got his good news, I received a letter from Grace that contained the appellate court's opinion in my own case saying my trial was clean and confirming my conviction. I read the opinion three times, and each time, I felt a little smaller, a little more insignificant. Judges are extremely careful at the trial level because they don't want an appellate court tossing a case back into their lap a year or two later. In my case, Judge Geer had been particularly deliberate in his rulings. I had no doubt that he had called friends of his, other judges, including appellate judges, prior to making rulings in my case so he had the best possible chance of getting everything right. And after reading the opinion of the Sixth Circuit Court of Appeals over and over, I realized that I was not going to get any relief based on mistakes. If I was going to get my case reversed, James Tipton would have to step forward and tell the world why he'd lied. Not only would he have to tell the world he'd lied, he would also have to do it in an extremely convincing fashion. Witnesses recanting testimony was nothing new to the appellate courts; it happened all the time. And nine times out of ten, the appellate court said, "So what?" If I was to ever get out of federal prison, James Tipton would have to come into court with something explosive. The problem with that, of course, was that we didn't have any idea where James Tipton was.

After I read the opinion and fumed for a little while, I decided to go outside for a run around the rec yard to blow off some of the frustration I was feeling. A man walked up to me just as I finished. I'd seen him around my cellblock, but I didn't know him. The tattoo on his right forearm told me he was a member of the Sons of Odin gang. The SOs were a relatively small, upstart group who said they patterned themselves after a German deity called Odin. Odin, they claimed, rode an eight-legged steed and traveled with ravens and wolves. They were known to be violent. I'd witnessed an incident in our cellblock a few weeks earlier in which an SO, after having been tipped off by a guard that a new inmate was a particularly scummy sex offender, beat the guy unconscious on the walkway that ran along the second tier of cells on our block, then dragged him down the steps by his feet onto the floor below, and then mounted him and started beating his head against the floor. The sex offender apparently lived, but I don't know how. The beating was almost as brutal as the one the guards in Atlanta had dished out to the macho man. The gang member got three months in the hole. He didn't even catch a formal charge.

The guy who approached me looked like a juicer, a steroid user. A lot of guys in prison juiced. Bringing in steroids like Dianabol and Winstrol and Deca Durabolin and human growth hormone was one of the medium-size hustles, and from what I'd been told, there was decent money in it. He was about three inches taller and thirty or forty pounds heavier than me, and he had a puffy face and looked like someone had injected helium into his muscles. His neck was thick beneath his shaved head, both arms were sleeved in tattoos, and he had fierce-looking, aquamarine-blue eyes.

"You the lawyer man?" he said as he folded his arms in front of his chest.

"Yeah," I said. I noticed immediately that something about him wasn't quite right. His left eye wandered a tiny bit and he had a slight speech impediment. "Lawyer" was very close to "wahyer."

"You need to file an appeal for me."

"Really?" I said, sensing danger in his tone. "How far along are you in the process?"

"What are you talking about?"

"The process. How long have you been in prison? How many appeals have you filed? I need to know where you are before I can make a decision on whether we can file."

"I said you need to file an appeal for me, and that's what you need to do."

"Do you have money?" I said. "I don't work for free."

"You'll work for free for me."

I looked over his shoulder and saw a few of his boys, fellow gang members, sitting at a picnic table they occupied every day on the yard. They were looking at us and laughing. One of them was pointing. Less than a hundred feet away was the table where Big Pappy was sitting with his usual crew. I noticed he was watching, too.

"Mind if we walk while I cool down?" I said. I was still breathing pretty heavily from the run and I wanted to get closer to Pappy and his Independent White Boys in case something happened.

"We stay right here," he said.

"You got a name, asshole?" I said belligerently, deliberately insulting him. He'd already disrespected me, and I couldn't just let it go.

"Of course I got a fucking name," he said. "Everybody got a fucking name."

"Mine's Darren," I said. "What's yours?"

"Robert Edward Lee Frazier," he said. "My boys call me Bobby Lee. You can call me Sir Robert."

"Okay," I said. "Go fuck yourself, Sir Robert."

I brushed past him and started walking away from the fence toward Big Pappy and his group. I needed to get away from Sir Robert. I didn't want to get trapped against the fence. I could feel adrenaline kicking in as I anticipated a fight. It had been a while since I'd been in a physical altercation, but I'd stayed in excellent physical condition and I wasn't afraid. I took three or four steps and turned to look at him to see where he was. He'd hesitated, probably because I'd surprised him. He was such an intimidating figure that I was sure he was used to people cowing to him. The hesitation didn't last long, though. I heard him curse under his breath and the next thing I knew he was charging me like an enraged bull. I sidestepped him and managed to punch him in the ear with my right fist as he went past. I could hear and sense commotion to my left, but I had to stay focused on Sir Robert, who regained his balance, turned toward me, and put his fists up in a boxing stance. Around this time I heard amplified voices from the guard towers. I reacted to Sir Robert's boxing stance by kicking him squarely in the scrotum. He bent over and I kicked him in the face. He staggered forward and I kicked him in the face again, which sent him to his knees.

Strong hands began pulling on my shirt and strong arms wrapped around me, restraining me. I became aware of a voice in my ear.

"Easy, dude. Easy now." The voice belonged to Big Pappy.

I then became aware of yelling and cursing and people surging around me. There was another amplified sound, this one of a shotgun round being pumped into the chamber. It was a recording the guards played over the loud speakers when trouble was brewing. Then there was gunfire from a guard tower, and everyone was on his stomach on the ground.

The last thing I heard before two guards dragged me off to the hole was Sir Robert's voice.

"You're dead, motherfucker!" he yelled. "You're a dead man!"

CHAPTER FORTY-SEVEN

They walked me out of the Special Housing Unit, also known as the hole, a month after I kicked Bobby Lee Frazier in the nuts. It didn't matter that Bobby had started the fight. All that mattered was that I had been involved in a fight with another inmate, and the institution, by its own rules, had to punish me for it. The punishment was being locked down in the darkness for twenty-three hours a day, one hour of rec, no phone privileges, one short shower a week, and no contact with anyone other than the guards who brought cold food, usually bologna sandwiches, which were slid through the pie hole twice a day. It was back to the existence I'd lived early on during my incarceration, the existence of an animal. It also put all of my legal cases on hold, but I was fortunate in that I didn't miss any deadlines. The system worked excruciatingly slowly, especially when it came to prisoners who are representing themselves or using a jailhouse lawyer, but the system would have been more than happy to spit a case out and bar it forever because the jailhouse lawyer was cooling his jets in the hole and missed a filing deadline.

But the institution and my legal work were the least of my problems. I had attacked a gang member, a Son of Odin. I didn't kill him, but I'd knocked him down in front of everybody. I'd embarrassed him. The fact that he deserved it didn't matter. The SOs would be looking for me as soon as I walked back out onto the yard. They had to back up their boy. I didn't know how they'd come at me, whether it would be one guy or two or five or whether they'd bring knives or shanks or clubs or maybe even a gun, but I knew as certain as the sun would rise and set that they were coming. The thought entered my mind a couple of times that all I had to do was put up no resistance, just let them kill me, and I would be free of the nightmare I'd been living, but I knew when they came, I'd fight them with everything I had.

As I walked through the metal detector and into the cellblock, I was keenly aware of my surroundings. Frazier lived on the same block, although he lived downstairs and several cells over. It was late afternoon and a lot of the inmates had come into the block from the rec yard or the chow hall. Guys were moving in and out of the cells and the workout rooms or sitting at the card tables. I didn't see Frazier or any of his gang brothers. I walked up the steps, went into my cell, and was relieved to see Dino sitting there. The place was spotless. Dino smiled, stood, and put out his hand.

"Welcome back, Darren," he said.

"Thanks."

"And how was the hole?"

"Dark and smelly, much like you'd expect."

"Was there a toilet there or do they make you use a bucket?"

"Toilet, Dino."

"Good, good. I was envisioning you having to squat—"

"Dino, please. Didn't you have anything better to think about?"

I noticed a shadow behind me and turned quickly. I was relieved to see Big Pappy's wide frame filling the doorway.

"Mind if I come in?" he said, as if we had a choice. Still, he was polite about it, which was important in the etiquette-conscious world of the convicted felon.

"It looks like you made it in one piece," Pappy said.

"Yeah," I said, "I think I'll live."

"That's what I came to talk to you about," Pappy said. "Mind if I take a seat?"

"Suit yourself," I said.

As Pappy moved toward the concrete stool, Dino began to wiggle by him.

"I'll just go downstairs until you're finished," Dino said.

"Might as well stay," Pappy said "You're his cellie. You need to hear this, too."

I leaned against the corner of the top bunk while Dino sat on the bottom bunk.

"Bobby Lee's still in the hole," Big Pappy said. "They gave him two weeks more than you because he was the aggressor, even though you whipped him. It's a problem, though, Darren. It's a problem for you, for Bobby Lee, for his car, my car, for everybody. I mean, this could potentially blow up big, you know what I mean?"

"Not really," I said.

"It could turn into a riot, or at least a huge fight, which would mean lockdown for everybody for a couple of months minimum. But I met up with Midas. You know Midas, right?"

"Shot caller for the Sons of Odin. Big, nasty-looking guy."

"He's an okay dude, you know? Just doing what everybody else is doing, which is time. Trying to get his hustle on while he's doing his time. But he got into this little Odin thing a few years back and now he's the man and there isn't any going back for him. They all look up to him and he has to do right by his people. I can totally respect that. One of those people is this dim-witted cracker Bobby Lee. Bobby Lee's got some mental problems, some shit caused by him getting pounded on by a stepfather that tried to kill him when he was three or four years old. So Midas looks at Bobby Lee kind of like a son; he says he's got this father complex for him. But he realizes that Bobby Lee did wrong.

I mean you don't just go jump a man the way he did to you out on the yard without somebody's prior approval, without letting somebody know what was going to happen. He didn't ask permission from Midas or anything."

"I don't believe that," I said. "With all due respect, of course. Midas and his friends were watching the whole thing. They were laughing."

"Maybe they knew, maybe they didn't," Pappy said. "The point is, though, that he says he didn't know. Now we have to go forward without the yard going up in smoke. You understand that's why the feds allow the whole gang thing to go on, don't you? They could stop it if they wanted, but they let it go on. Do you understand why?"

"I suppose it has something to do with discipline."

"Exactly," Pappy said. "Discipline and control. The gangs command discipline, they have rules. Gang members have to live within those rules. When they break the rules, they're disciplined by their own. Otherwise this place would get out of hand in a heartbeat. There would be constant fights, constant riots, and constant killings."

"So you're saying Bobby Lee broke the rules when he came after me on the yard without getting permission from his shot caller?"

"Right, and now he's going to pay the price."

"Which is?"

"He's lost his back up. He's on his own."

I shook my head, still not quite understanding. "I don't get it," I said.

"I told Midas that I'd keep my boys out of it if he'd keep his out of it," Pappy said. "But he's still gonna come, Darren. He's gonna come alone, and he has to keep it private."

"Private? You mean—"

"He'll come here. He'll come to the cell, and he'll be armed. Do you have a weapon?"

I shook my head.

"Get one. He'll be out in fourteen days. If you handle him, it'll be over. Even if you kill him. Midas says it's between the two of you now."

"And if he kills me?"

"I guess you'll be dead and the rest of us will keep on living. That's just the way it has to be."

CHAPTER FORTY-EIGHT

He came the same day he got out of the hole.

I was in my cell, lying in my bunk reading a legal brief I'd printed out in the library. Dino was there, sitting at the desk writing a letter to his mother. It was eight thirty or so, about an hour before we'd be locked down for the night. I'd looked for Bobby Lee Frazier all day because I knew he was scheduled to get out of the hole, but I hadn't seen him. I found myself hoping he'd done something in the hole to get his stay extended, or maybe the powers that be had decided to transfer him to another max.

It started with a warning from below. Someone down at one of the card tables saw Bobby Lee walk into the block, stop by his cell for a few seconds, and then head straight for the staircase. Bobby Lee's cell was downstairs. Mine was upstairs.

"Trouble comin' your way, Darren Street!" a voice called out.

By the time I jumped down off the bunk and chased Dino out of the cell, Bobby Lee was in the doorway. I saw him lift his shirt and pull out an ice pick that was at least a foot long. And then it was just Bobby Lee and me, in the small cell together. He was so big he seemed to fill the entire space. I hadn't gotten a weapon as Big Pappy had suggested. I just couldn't make myself do it, I couldn't picture myself as a knife fighter, but as I stood there looking at that pointed steel, I wished I had something to even things up a little.

He came at me slowly this time, remembering, I suppose, what I'd done to him when he bull rushed me on the yard. I was focused so intently on the ice pick that I didn't react quickly enough when he punched me with his left fist, his empty hand. The punch caught me in the right temple and sent me staggering back against the wall, and then he was on me. I felt the ice pick slip into my belly the first time and remember thinking it didn't hurt as badly as I'd thought it would. I started punching Bobby Lee in the face with everything I had, but he stayed right in front of me. He wouldn't go down, and I didn't have room to maneuver and grapple with him. In the meantime, I kept feeling the ice pick, again and again. I remember my vision starting to blur, then I started to get cold.

At some point, I had what I believed to be a dream of someone cutting Bobby Lee's throat. A large knife appeared out of nowhere and slid across his neck from under his left ear all the way across to beneath his right ear. I was showered in warm blood.

I began to slide down the wall. Warm blood was also running down my lower body; it was almost pleasant. My head became lighter and lighter. I looked up and thought I saw Dino standing over Bobby Lee, holding a knife. Big Pappy walked into the cell and took the knife from Dino's hand. I think.

And then I left my body and floated to the ceiling, where I watched the guards come in first and then the medical people. I wanted to float outside the cell, through the roof, out of the prison and off to a different and better place, but I couldn't. Something was making me stay.

I later found out what it was. Life. Life made me stay. Bobby Lee Frazier had stabbed me eleven times with that ice pick, but he didn't kill me. The human body can withstand an incredible amount of abuse and still survive.

Unfortunately, I was living proof.

CHAPTER FORTY-NINE

Prison infirmaries are almost as good as the military when it comes to trauma care. They see a lot of stab wounds, and they're well trained when it comes to reacting to life and death situations. The staff at Rosewood, I was told, was as good as it gets. I didn't know whether I should regard that as a blessing or a curse.

I lost a lot of blood, but a transfusion had taken care of that. The stab wounds had punctured various organs and had perforated my bowel in a couple of places, but the doctors had worked their surgical magic and seemed to think I'd be fine in a few months. They had done all they could with the wounds and were managing the pain with medications. Now all I had to do was heal.

On my fourth day in the infirmary, a female officer came to see me. She was a green-eyed, pale-skinned redhead of around forty, tall and slim with rounded shoulders. She smelled of soap in her starched uniform and had a businesslike, matter-of-fact air about her. Her name tag said Gibbons. She didn't ask me how I was feeling or whether I was comfortable talking to her. She just walked into the room and stood next to the bed.

"I'm investigating the stabbing that took place in your cell," she said without introducing herself.

I nodded.

"Are you willing to talk about it?" she asked.

"Not really."

"Why not? You were almost killed."

"You know how it is," I said. "If I talk to you, all I do is cause problems for myself. Either you'll charge me with something or you'll charge somebody else with something and want me to be witness. I wind up with a charge or labeled as a snitch. It's lose-lose for me."

"I'm not going to charge you with anything," she said. "All I'm looking for is confirmation of some things we already know."

"If you already know, then you don't need confirmation."

"Mr. Frazier came to your cell armed with an ice pick, is that correct?" she said.

"Somebody was obviously armed with an ice pick. I have the holes in me to prove it."

"And it was Mr. Frazier?"

"I didn't say that. Didn't you find an ice pick on whoever was in my cell?"

She shook her head. "The weapons had been removed from the cell by the time our people were able to get in and secure the scene."

"Weapons? As in more than one? I didn't have a weapon."

"There were two weapons used in the altercation, Mr. Street. An icepick and a knife. A butcher knife had been stolen from the kitchen, where your cellmate, Mr. Long, happened to work. We think that was the second weapon."

"Dino didn't give me a knife," I said. "Wait just a second. What happened to the guy who stabbed me? You say his name is Frazier? Where is he?"

"He's dead. You didn't see someone nearly cut his head off?"

I lifted my arm and covered my eyes. "I dreamed it," I said. "At least I thought I was dreaming it."

"Must have been a pretty vivid dream. You had blood all over you. I've never seen so much blood in a cell, and I've seen a lot. So in this dream of yours, who was holding the knife? Was it your cellmate, Mr. Long?"

"I have no idea. I'd been stabbed a bunch of times. I was going down, fading out, and I had this dream where I thought I saw a knife cutting a throat."

"What you saw was your cellmate, Mr. Long, cutting Bobby Lee Frazier's throat. Mr. Long was covered in blood, too, when we got in there. But while you and Mr. Frazier were bleeding all over the place, somebody took the weapons. We've searched for them, but we're probably not going to find them. Weapons tend to disappear when something like this happens; it's certainly nothing new. Inmates get rid of as much evidence as they can and then clam up. Nobody saw anything. As far as we're concerned, anything you did was in self-defense, so you're not looking at another charge. They're not even going to send you back to the Special Housing Unit for fighting after you get out of here. But just for administrative purposes, I'd like to know whether you saw Mr. Long kill Mr. Frazier."

"Administrative purposes? That's what you call pinning a murder charge on Dino Long, who may very well have saved my life? And you want me to be a witness? Forget it, lady. Not a snowball's chance in hell."

"From the evidence I've seen, Mr. Long used deadly force and killed Mr. Frazier in defense of another, which, as I'm sure you know since you were a lawyer on the outside, is a recognized legal defense to a charge of murder. But even if I wanted to charge Mr. Long with murder and have him take his chances with a jury, I couldn't do it."

"Why not?" I said. "Does the warden have you guys on a short leash?"

"Mr. Long is dead," she said. "He hanged himself in a holding cell while we were conducting our investigation. So even if I wanted to, there's nobody left to charge."

Dino was dead? I closed my eyes and opened them again, hoping, once again, that I was somehow dreaming and not living this nightmare that wouldn't seem to end. Dino had never struck me as the kind of guy who would do violence. He was quiet, almost meek, most of the time. And she was probably right. He must have gotten the knife he used from the kitchen, but he hadn't said a word to me about it and he knew—just as I did—that Bobby Lee would come to our cell. That meant he intended all along to fight with me, to fight for me. He'd killed a man for me, and the weight of the act had apparently crushed his already fragile psyche. I turned my head toward the wall as my body howled for more pain medication.

"Get out," I said to the guard.

"So you don't want—"

"Get the fuck out of here!" I yelled, and she turned and strutted out of the room.

CHAPTER FIFTY

I was sitting in the chow hall eating lunch when Big Pappy came hurrying in. I'd been out of the infirmary for only a week and had finally gotten through the withdrawal symptoms from the narcotic painkillers I'd taken. It had also taken a few days to get used to Dino not being there. All of his things had been cleared out and, I assumed, shipped to his parents. I'd thought of him often while I was in the infirmary, but each time I did, the last image in my mind was of him hanging from a belt. I spent a lot of time blaming myself, telling myself that if I hadn't reacted violently on the yard with Bobby Lee, none of this would have happened and Dino would still be alive. It was sad and painful, but I realized during that time that I'd been through so much sorrow and pain over the past eighteen months that I was becoming numb to it. It was as though my heart had become calloused, and I wondered whether I would ever be able to feel anything meaningful again.

Pappy stood over me, smiling. He was carrying a sheaf of papers in his right hand.

"You did it," he said. "You did it, Darren. Check this out."

He handed me a forty-page opinion written by the federal magistrate who had heard the evidence that was presented when he'd gone back to Georgia a couple of months earlier. The judge had found that Ronnie Ray, the police officer, had perjured himself during the trial and that the video of the informant being debriefed revealed dozens of inconsistencies that could have been used by Pappy's lawyer at trial to impeach the informant. The judge wrote that Pappy had been denied a fair trial and ordered a new trial in the federal district court.

"You know what this means, don't you?" I said. "It means you're out of here. There's no way they're going to retry you on something like this. They could appeal, but they'd be beating a dead horse. Your ticket is punched, big guy. You're as good as gone."

"That's what I was hoping you'd say, man. I can't believe it."

He sat down across from me and took a deep breath. I'd come in late and was one of only four guys in the chow hall. Pappy made five. The other three were sitting together across the room.

"I wonder how long it will take them to process you out of here and get you back to Georgia," I said.

"You'd think they'd move pretty quick, right? I mean, this judge practically says I was railroaded and shouldn't be here. I'll bet I'm gone inside a month."

"Congratulations, Pappy," I said. "I'm happy for you."

"And I owe you," he said. "I mean it. I owe you. What can I do?"

I'd actually thought about having this conversation many times since Pappy had told me what happened at the hearing when he went back to Georgia. The cop had admitted to perjury, so I knew the opinion would come fairly soon, and I knew it would be favorable. I'd also been thinking about my own situation. Finding James Tipton was the only hope I had of getting out of prison, and nobody on the outside was having any luck. Grace was trying. She wrote to me often, so I knew she'd been talking to agents from the FBI and DEA and that she'd tried to locate Tipton on her own, but her resources and her time were limited. If Tipton was going to be found, someone would have to make it their mission, and I knew I was the only person who would do it. I placed my hands on the table, leaned forward, and lowered my voice.

"Can you get me out?" I said.

He blinked slowly a few times before he responded.

"You mean get you out of here, I assume. You're talking about helping you escape."

"I don't belong in here," I said. "I'm not going to make it much longer."

"You'll make it as long as you want to," he said, "because you're smart and you're tough, but you're right when you say you don't belong in here. You don't."

"Do you think it could be done?" I said.

"Yeah, it could be done. As a matter of fact, I've had something in mind for a few years now. Never tried it, but I think it could work. It'd cost some money. Ten, maybe twenty grand."

"I have money," I said, "which is ironic because I didn't have any when I was a lawyer on the outside. But I've been saving pretty much every dime I've earned in here."

"What would you do if you got out?" Pappy said. "I mean if you got out and got away from the prison clean. Where would you go?"

"Back to Tennessee. I need to find a guy who testified against me at my trial. I'm not sure where he is, but I'd start in Tennessee."

"So you'll need to get outside the walls and then get a ride back to Tennessee. You'll need clothes and traveling money, a vehicle, a prepaid cell phone or two and some sort of fake identification in case you get stopped by a cop. You know that's the first place they're going to look for you. You're from Knoxville, right?"

"Yeah."

"Knoxville will be crawling with feds looking for you. They'll be all over your mom and your boy. You won't be able to go near them. And they'll pop you with an escape charge if they catch you."

"And do what? Give me life plus ten years?"

"They'll probably diesel you for a year and then throw you in the hole for another year."

"If you help me get out, I'm not coming back," I said. "I'll shoot myself before I'll come back here."

I'd spent so much time alone that I felt I knew myself better than ever before, and I knew that if I got out, I would never willingly come back. After being a part of and seeing so much brutality and cruelty and injustice, I knew that if I got away and was about to be caught, I would put a bullet in my brain before I allowed them to subject me to the kind of mental and physical abuse I'd endured for the past two years. I wouldn't let them do it to me for the rest of my life.

"Speaking of, will you need a gun?"

"Yeah, if you can do it."

"I can do anything, Darren. I'm the shot caller on this yard, and I've made enough money to buy an island."

"Why haven't you escaped, then?"

"I'm not really sure, except I've always had a feeling that Ronnie Ray would eventually be exposed for the lying piece of shit he really is and I'd get out. I believed in the system."

"That's a load of crap, Pappy."

"You're right. Sue me."

"So how would it work?"

"Pretty simple, really, if my guy is willing to do it."

"Your guy? Who's that?"

"A cowboy I know. Crazy as hell. Not afraid of anything. We did three years together at Lewisburg when I first came in. He can get you past the gates if everything goes well. Then I'll hook you up with a cow*girl* I know. She's crazier than the cowboy. I guess she's my woman now. She also works for me on the outside."

"Works for you? Doing what?"

"I run a legit trucking company on the outside. Got two eighteen-wheelers. She drives one of them. We'll get you from him to her and put you in the sleeper of her truck. She can drive you across the country."

"How is your cowboy going to get me past the gates?"

"It'll be a hoot, Darren. You'll love it. Timing will be everything."

"How long will it take you to set it up?"

"Not long. If I know the cowboy like I think I do, he'll drop everything and come as soon as we want him to. I'll get in touch with the woman, too, and have her head this way. Maybe a week. When do you want to go?"

"The sooner the better. What happens if you get transferred back to Georgia in the meantime?"

"I could make it happen from the outside, but I'd rather be here when it goes down. I want to watch."

"You'd really do all this for me?"

"Yeah, man. You realize you're already a legend in this place, don't you?"

"You're crazy. Ninety-nine percent of the guys in here don't even know I'm alive."

"You're wrong. Guys talk about you all the time. Think about it. You're a lawyer who went down on a charge of killing a child-molesting murderer. You put in a bunch of work on the guards and got dieseled for months. That's legendary stuff right there, but then you come in here and start taking up cases for people, doing good work, and you kicked that redneck's ass in front of God and everybody on the yard. Then you take him on again in your cell, get popped eleven times with twelve inches of steel, live through it, and won't talk to the police about it. That's powerful, man, and it gets around. Plus you don't have any vices, which shows everybody you're mentally strong. You have as much respect as any man on this yard, including me."

"And here I sit talking about leaving all of it. How selfish of me."

"And now you're going to escape? I'm getting chills thinking about it. You'll be like a god. If you ever get caught—which you probably will—and you don't shoot yourself—which you probably won't—you'll go straight to the top of the class when you come back inside. You'll be a shot caller as soon as you walk on a yard."

"That's great, Pappy," I said. "It gives me great comfort knowing I have so much to look forward to if I don't manage to kill myself and get sent back here."

"You won't get sent back here, Darren, now that I think about it. Prison administrators hate guys like you, guys that gain so much respect. They'll think you have too much power, so they'll neutralize you. They'll send you to Marion or Florence for at least three years, probably five. If you escape and then get caught, you're going straight to super max."

CHAPTER FIFTY-ONE

Just the thought of getting out of Rosewood and getting back to the world made me feel weightless over the next week. I was terrified, too, because I had no idea what would happen during the escape attempt and because I wasn't sure what I'd do even if I made it out and got back to Tennessee. I knew where I was going to start, but I didn't know where it would lead. Still, the worst thing that could happen, as far as I was concerned, was being captured and returned to prison. The thought of getting killed—which was entirely possible—didn't really bother me.

Big Pappy set everything up. We had several conversations, usually in his cell. We kept them short so we wouldn't arouse undue suspicion, but by that time Pappy and I had become close enough friends that it wasn't unusual for us to be seen talking to each other. During one of the conversations, I learned how Pappy communicated so easily with the outside world. He bought prepaid cell phones that one of the guards smuggled in. They cost him $1,000 apiece, but he was able to use them to run the various businesses he'd set up during his prison tenure. He told me he'd made $4 million during his eleven years in prison off tobacco and gambling and he'd been able to turn it into $10 million.

The woman who would be driving me back to Tennessee, whom Pappy described as a hellcat named Linda Lacy, was responsible for running the day-to-day operations of Pappy's trucking company. She had been his girlfriend when he was arrested and had stayed loyal to him throughout his incarceration.

He wouldn't tell me much about the cowboy other than he was "the craziest son of a bitch I've ever met." Two days before I was supposed to go, I said, "You haven't even told me how I'm getting past the walls."

"You're going to fly," Pappy said. "All you have to do is be where I tell you to be when I tell you to be there. The cowboy was a drug mule back in the day. The army taught him to fly helicopters, and as soon as he got out, he started moving cocaine for some dudes in Philadelphia. He wound up getting popped and served three years. That's how we met. He got his pilot's license back a year after he got out and wound up starting a charter service in Phoenix."

"And he's willing to risk everything to help me get out of here?"

"He isn't doing it for free," Pappy said, "but I think he might have if I'd asked him. This is just something that appeals to his flair for the outrageous and dramatic. Besides, he says he's bored. We're going to set the exact time tomorrow. It looks like the weather is going to be good. He's going to come screaming in here, scoop you up, and get out. There won't be any ID numbers on the helo, and it'll be painted a different color within twenty-four hours of the escape. If everything goes right, it shouldn't take more than ten, fifteen seconds to get in and out. The guards might get off a shot or two, but they might not. Nobody's ever tried to escape from this place by helicopter, so it'll take them by surprise. Maybe they'll think the director of the Bureau of Prisons has come to visit. Once you're out, he's going to fly you to meet Linda on Highway 41 about forty-five miles from here. He'll drop you off and then fly straight to a cabin in the Sierra Nevadas. Then he's flying straight back to Phoenix the next morning. It's risky, but if anybody can pull it off, it's Cowboy."

Forty-eight hours later, I was on the yard at 6:45 p.m. It was mid-April, almost two years to the day since I'd been arrested for Jalen Jordan's murder. The sky had been clear all day. I'd said thank you one last time to Big Pappy Donovan and told him I'd see him again someday—on the outside. I hoped I was right. I'd jogged around the perimeter fence for a while like I always did, but at 6:49 p.m. I walked to the middle of the soccer field and looked to the west.

Thirty seconds later, I thought I heard the *whop-whop-whop* of heli-copter blades. I looked to the west again but was blinded by the setting sun. Suddenly, I saw it, and within seconds I was engulfed in a cloud of dust and deafening noise as the helicopter came out of the sun, cleared the outer wall, and appeared to stand on its legs like a rearing horse. It touched down thirty feet from where I was standing and I made a break for it. The door opened, and I dived inside onto one of two seats in the cockpit. The pilot was wearing a ski mask. He reached over me and pulled the door shut, pulled the stick, and we were off the ground and over the concertina-wire-topped wall. I looked at the guard tower in the center of the prison yard and could see two guards scrambling onto the catwalk with weapons. We were gone before they could get off a shot.

The man in the seat next to me pulled the ski mask off his head. He looked to be in his early thirties and had light-brown hair cut like a marine's. He was grinning widely and turned and winked at me. He motioned toward a pair of headphones that were hanging over the seat behind me. I picked them up and put them on.

"Hot damn!" he said. "What a rush! I'm Cowboy. You must be Darren."

"Yeah, I'm Darren. I appreciate the ride."

"You did great," he said. "You were on board less than five seconds after I hit the deck. I was afraid we might end up with a straggler or two, but you got on so fast nobody could react quick enough to cause us a problem."

"So what now?" I said.

"I'm going to head north for another two minutes so they think that's the direction we're heading in then I'm going to head east and double back to the south. We're going into the Sierra Nevada Mountains. Pappy's woman is driving an eighteen-wheeler on Highway 41. I know exactly where she's supposed to be. It's a curvy mountain road, and there isn't much traffic. As soon as it's clear, we're gonna do the same thing we did back at the prison, only this time you're getting out of the helicopter instead of into it. You jump out of the chopper and into the truck. I'll fly away, and she'll take it from there."

"Every cop in this part of the country is going to be looking for you," I said.

"Yeah, ain't it cool as hell? Don't worry about it. It's desert and mountains around here. Very few people, very few cops. Besides, I've got a pretty good plan. I'll make it back home tomorrow, and nobody'll know a thing."

He was right about the terrain. It was barren and rugged. The sun was still up, barely, and we were close to the ground.

"How fast are we going?" I said.

"A little over a hundred knots. About a hundred and twenty miles an hour."

We flew for another thirty seconds before he turned the helicopter to the east and then to the south. We flew for about ten minutes before he turned east again and started into the mountains. About three minutes later, he pointed down and I spotted a truck snaking through a switchback.

"That's gonna be her," Cowboy said.

He flipped a switch on a radio and said some things I couldn't hear. The next thing I knew the earth was coming up quickly. I saw the truck slow to a stop and Cowboy landed the helicopter in the middle of the road about fifty yards away.

"Good luck, brother man," Cowboy yelled.

He reached across me, opened the door, and gave me a shove. I hit the ground running and climbed into the cab of the truck.

PART III

CHAPTER FIFTY-TWO

I climbed into the cab of Linda Lacy's eighteen-wheeler and watched Cowboy climb away in his helicopter just as darkness was beginning to fall.

"Hey, baby, you made it!" she said as I looked at her stupidly. She was a striking woman, with long sandy-blonde hair that fell out from beneath a straw cowboy hat. Her face was pretty, dominated by cool-blue eyes and a sharp nose, and she seemed to dwarf me in the cab. Unfolded, I'd have bet she was well over six feet tall. I supposed it was one of the attractions to Big Pappy, who was one of the largest human beings I'd ever met in my life.

"What's the matter? Did they numb your brain in prison?" she said as the truck rolled forward. There hadn't been a single vehicle in sight when Cowboy set the helicopter down on the road. I had to give them credit. They'd planned my escape thoroughly, although we still had a long way to go.

"Sorry," I said. "I guess I'm still in shock a little. I was in a maximum security federal penitentiary fifteen minutes ago."

"And now you're out," Linda said. "On the road to sweet freedom. And before we go any further, I just want to say thank you for what you've done for Michael. He was beginning to lose hope."

"Michael?" I said.

"My Michael. His big-shot name in prison is Big Pappy, but to me he's just plain ol' Michael. Listen, you need to crawl up into this sleeper here behind me and change clothes. I think they'll fit."

She pulled a curtain back and I climbed through an opening and onto a bed. Sitting on the bed was a small pile of neatly folded clothes—black jeans, a white T-shirt, and a light-blue denim work shirt, a belt, a pair of underwear, a pair of white socks, and a pair of Nike running shoes.

"There's a false wall back there," Linda said when I was finished. "If you'll just reach down behind the mattress toward where the pillow is. No, sweetie, on the other wall, yeah, there, feel it? Pull that latch. Now just push the back wall up. See? If we get stopped, you crawl back in there and stay quiet. For now, put your jail clothes in there. We'll burn them first chance we get."

"How long before we get back to Tennessee?" I said.

"What? You've been in my truck for five minutes and you already want to know how long before you get out? That's a bit ungrateful, don't you think?"

"I'm sorry . . . Linda? Your name is Linda, right? I'm grateful for everything you've done and for everything you're going to do. I'll ride around with you for as long as you like. I was just curious."

She turned around and leered at me.

"Now you're patronizing me," she said. "Why is it that men always think they can patronize women just by being polite?"

"I wasn't trying to . . . I didn't mean to—"

"You think women aren't as smart as men, don't you?"

"Of course not."

"Name one woman that you think is as smart as men, not including your mother. Be quick about it."

"Marie Curie."

"Who?"

"Marie Curie. She was a physicist and chemist, lived in the late eighteen, early nineteen hundreds. She was Polish but wound up moving to France. She was the first woman to win a Nobel Prize. She was as smart as any man who's ever lived."

"Right," Linda said. "What about somebody more recent?"

"Hillary Clinton's pretty smart. First lady, US senator, secretary of state."

"That doesn't mean she's smart." Linda's voice moved up in pitch. "She's just conniving."

"So you're a Republican, then?"

"Yes, I'm a Republican, and I'm proud to be a Republican. It doesn't make me hateful and it doesn't make me stupid. What about you? I guess you're one of those blue dog Democrats."

"Right now I'm a convicted felon and an escapee. I don't think anybody's going to care about my personal political preferences."

She was quiet for a while after that. I lay in the sleeper cab and watched road signs go by. We headed south on Interstate 5. In the meantime, Linda was listening to the radio for news about the escape. The first story came about an hour after I got into the truck. The reporters were saying that I was last seen heading north from Rosewood in a helicopter. *So far, so good,* I thought. But within ten minutes of hearing that story, I saw flashing lights ahead at the side of the road.

"Better get on back behind the false wall," Linda said.

I pulled the latch, lifted the wall, rolled back, and pushed it down. My heart was beating so hard I could feel it against my chest. I could feel my hands shaking, my breath coming in short gasps. I'd been out for only an hour. *Would Linda screw up? Would they have dogs? Would they catch me and have me back in the hole at Rosewood by morning?*

The truck slowed agonizingly, then it stopped.

"Evening, ma'am," I heard a male voice say. "License and registration, please? Where you headed?"

"Georgia by way of Nashville," Linda said.

"Long trip. What are you hauling?"

"Hardwood flooring."

"Had anything to drink tonight?"

"No, sir. I don't drink alcohol."

"My wife wishes I could say the same. Have you heard about the escape?"

"As a matter of fact, I heard something on the radio about an escape just before I saw your lights."

"A man was plucked out of a federal penitentiary by helicopter. He might switch to some other form of transportation, though. It happened just a short time ago, but we've managed to get some flyers out. Would you mind taking a few and spreading them around the next time you pull into a truck stop?"

"I wouldn't mind at all, sir."

"Mind if I take a quick look around inside your cab?"

"Go right ahead."

I shuddered as I lay in the complete darkness, the utter stillness of the false compartment. My heart kept pounding: *Th-thump! Th-thump! Th-thump!*

An endless thirty seconds passed.

"Okay, ma'am, you have a safe night."

I heard the truck's engine roar and felt the rig pull back onto the road and get up to speed.

"Hey, Darren," I heard Linda say. "You can come out now."

I pulled the inside latch, lifted the door, and crawled out. Linda tossed a small stack of papers over her shoulder at me.

"The good thing is, you take a nice photograph," she said. "The bad thing is, they look just like you."

CHAPTER FIFTY-THREE

For five days, I'd ridden across the United States in Linda Lacy's sleeper. She drove nine hours a day, and at night we shared a motel room. On the first night, she colored my hair blond, took a picture of me on her cell phone, and texted it to someone.

"For your ID," she said.

The next morning, rather than follow I-40 straight across the middle of the country, she drove north into Colorado and drove across Kansas and Missouri. It added some extra miles and a day to the trip, but she thought it was prudent, and who was I to argue?

Linda acted like a cross between a mother and a frustrated nymphomaniac. Her man had been in prison for eleven years, and she had apparently been loyal to him with the exception of the various sexual toys she'd used and which she described to me in painful detail. The poor woman was as horny as any I'd ever seen. She talked nonstop and blared country and western music through the cab's speakers. If I never hear another Merle Haggard song again, it'll be just fine with me.

She didn't try to seduce me, though, not that I would have allowed it. Big Pappy had gotten me out of prison. I wouldn't have repaid him by surreptitiously having sex with his woman. But as much as I hate to, I have to admit I thought about it. She was a lanky, big-breasted Amazon who looked fantastic in a pair of blue jeans and who I'm certain would have given me the ride of my life. Besides, I was fresh out of prison and was as frustrated as she was. I hadn't touched a woman in two years. I found myself imagining what she'd look like naked on more than one occasion.

We finally made it to Knoxville on the fifth night. I felt a surge of adrenaline as we passed by the University of Tennessee campus and the World's Fair tower around ten at night. Linda had told me we would be meeting up with a friend of hers at the Strawberry Plains exit. When we got there, she pulled off the road into a parking lot adjacent to a liquor store. Sitting in the lot with its lights on was a Hyundai Elantra that was silver and maybe five years old.

"This is it, baby doll," Linda said. "You're on your own from here."

I slid into the seat next to her.

"Everything you need will be in the car," she said. "A driver's license, registration, insurance papers, everything. If you get stopped and the cops run the tag, it'll come back registered to the name on the license. It's a clean car. You'll find money, three prepaid cell phones, more clothes, and a gun in the trunk."

"I don't know how to thank you," I said.

She reached over, grabbed me by the neck, pulled me toward her, and gave me a long kiss on the lips. At the same time, she reached between my legs and gave me a nice little rub.

"Good luck, desperado," she said. "Maybe Michael and I will see you again sometime."

"I hope so," I said, and I turned and climbed down out of the cab and took a deep breath. It was spring in the mountains of East Tennessee. There was a chill in the air, but the sky was clear and the place smelled like heaven. I couldn't believe I was back. I walked over to the Elantra, which was running, and opened the door. Just then, I noticed a man walk quickly between the car and the cab of the truck. He opened the door and climbed into the same seat I had just vacated. I didn't get a look at his face.

I got into the Elantra and started driving east on Interstate 40. I got off the interstate at the Gatlinburg/Pigeon Forge exit and turned south. Forty-five minutes later, I drove past James Tipton's driveway. I went back and forth a couple of times before I finally pulled in. It was one of the eeriest sights I'd ever seen. The skulls remained, but James's trailer was gone. I pulled up close to the spot and could see a pile of black ashes on the ground and the skeleton of his former home. Grace had told me only that James had disappeared. She hadn't told me his trailer was burned.

I turned the car around and pulled back onto the road, heading up the mountain. After another half mile, I turned the car off the road into a chat driveway that was nearly a half-mile long and led into a hollow at the base of a steep mountain ridge. At the end of the driveway was a small wooden house, neatly kept and painted white, flanked by two cabins. It was the same house where I'd watched the Tipton family dance in the yard. It was the same house where I'd shared their food and their drink and listened to their music and their stories. It was Granny Tipton's house.

I got out of the car, walked around to the back, and opened the trunk. There was a black duffel bag sitting there, and I began to feel around inside of it. I felt the clothing, the phones, a couple of stacks of money, and, finally, the cold steel of a pistol.

Before I was able to pull the pistol out of the bag, I heard two clicks behind me. They sounded like hammers being pulled back on shotguns.

"What the hell you doin' up here, boy?" a voice said, and I felt a gun barrel being pressed to the back of my neck.

I saw a flash of bright light, and then there was nothing.

CHAPTER FIFTY-FOUR

Grace walked into Boots Little Honky Tonk on Northside Drive in Knoxville just after eight at night. The cigarette smoke rolling out of the place nearly choked her. A fat, male karaoke singer in a brown cowboy hat was butchering Tim McGraw's "Live Like You Were Dying" on a makeshift stage, and the music was *loud*. As she looked around, a bit stunned, she felt someone take her arm from behind. She turned and found herself standing face to face with Gary DuBose, a DEA agent whom she knew casually and who had called earlier in the day and asked to meet at this most unusual spot.

"I've got a booth in the back," DuBose hollered over the din.

Grace followed him past a red car hood that was hanging on a wall with a huge-breasted image of Dolly Parton painted on it. The place was full and loud and smelled of fried bar food, stale beer, and, of course, cigarettes. As DuBose walked in front of her, Grace took note of his wide shoulders and thick neck. He was wearing blue jeans and a black-and-red flannel shirt along with a pair of boots. His head was covered by a black baseball cap with an orange *T* above the bill. They settled into the booth. Grace's back was to the front door and the majority of the crowd, which made her immediately uncomfortable, but her only alternative would have been to slide across and sit next to DuBose, and that wasn't going to happen.

She noticed DuBose had a Budweiser sitting in front of him. His reputation was that he was honest and hardworking, the son of the former sheriff of Knox County. He had testified during two hearings in which Grace had been involved, and he had given what she believed to be truthful and unexaggerated testimony.

"Beer?" DuBose said as a waitress approached.

Grace nodded. "Sure. Same as yours."

DuBose pointed at his bottle, held up two fingers, and the waitress went away.

"Okay, I'm intrigued," Grace said. "What can I do for you?"

DuBose took a sip from his beer.

"What do you hear from Darren Street?"

It had been five days since Darren's unbelievable escape from the federal penitentiary in California. Every US Marshal and FBI agent within fifty miles had called and asked her the same question.

"Are you kidding me?" Grace said. "You asked me down here to try to drag information about my client out of me?"

Grace started to get up to leave, but DuBose placed a hand on her forearm.

"Please, don't go," he said. "It was just a joke. I want to talk to you about something important. It might help you and it might help your client."

Grace sat back down and folded her arms.

"I'll listen, but not for long," she said.

"You have to understand this is hard for me, Miss Alexander," DuBose said. "I'm a law enforcement guy. I'm part of a fraternity. My father was a sheriff. He and Ben Clancy were friends for a long time, although I have to admit toward the end, before my father fell off the roof and was killed, he'd told me he was starting to worry about some of the things Clancy was doing and had done in the past. I think his conscience was starting to bother him."

"Why are you telling me all this?" Grace said.

"Because my conscience has been bothering me, too," DuBose said. "Especially since your client has been back in the news, back in everyone's faces. I've thought about it and prayed about it and thought about it and prayed about it some more. My father always taught me to try to do the right thing, even when it was difficult. Well, like I said, this is really difficult."

The waitress arrived with two beers. DuBose gave her a ten-dollar bill and told her to keep the change.

"Did you call me the night before the trial?" Grace said.

"Beg your pardon?"

"Somebody called me the night before the trial started and told me Darren was innocent. Was it you?"

"No, it wasn't."

Grace studied his face, trying to read whether he was lying. His expression didn't change a bit, and she decided he was telling the truth.

"And you say this has something to do with Darren Street?"

DuBose nodded. "James Tipton lied at the trial, Miss Alexander. I don't know everything he lied about and I don't know exactly why, but he lied. And Ben Clancy knew he was lying and let him do it. He may even have put him up to it."

Grace felt her back stiffen and her pulse quicken. She told herself to stay calm, go slowly, think clearly. This could be nothing, or this could be everything. Think like a lawyer. Don't be emotional. Be analytical.

"What specifically did he lie about at trial and how do you know it?" Grace said.

"He lied when you asked him if he'd been offered anything by the government in return for his testimony. I wasn't at the trial, but I read it in the paper. The paper said you made a big deal out of him being offered something, but he kept saying the only reason he was there was because they'd found that gun and traced it back to him and were trying to pin the murder on him. That they weren't offering him anything."

"Do you know exactly what James Tipton had been offered?"

"I know his drug case disappeared completely. I was working the case myself. We were close to indicting him. If we'd done it and he'd been convicted, he would have gone away for thirty years."

"What else can you tell me?" Grace said, ignoring the beer.

"This is how it happened, Miss Alexander, to the best of my knowledge. I'm sure your client has told you he initially tried to hire James Tipton to kill Jalen Jordan, since he testified to it publicly at the trial. I'd been to see Tipton not too long before that to tell him we were about to indict him and to find out whether I could squeeze information about his suppliers in Florida out of him. Initially, he wouldn't help me so I just kept working the case like normal. But then one night, out of the blue, Tipton calls me and tells me about this encounter with Darren Street. He says Street came to his house and tried to hire him, that a child killer might possibly be involved, and asked whether I would be willing to make a deal for that kind of information. I tell him I might, and I immediately call Ben Clancy because of Clancy's longtime relationship with my father and because Darren Street had said some pretty nasty things about my father before he died. Thinking back on it, I probably shouldn't have gone to Clancy, but then again, who else would I go to? If I'd gone to my boss, he'd have gone to Clancy. If I'd gone to the FBI, they'd have gone to Clancy. If I'd gone to Clancy's boss, he would've turned it over to Clancy.

"So anyway, I meet Clancy the next morning and tell him that Street has tried to hire a hit man and has already paid fifty thousand in cash. Clancy doesn't set up stings or start assigning agents as you would expect. He tells me he wants to handle the whole thing himself, and because of the bad blood between him and Street, I can sort of understand it. He has me set up a meet with Tipton at a safe house, and from then on, I don't see Tipton again. Clancy does come to my boss later on, about a month after Jalen Jordan was shot, and asks him to bury the drug case on Tipton so he can get a conviction on Darren. He convinces my boss Darren is guilty of murder and that Tipton is his best witness, and my boss agrees to lose the paperwork and the computer files. Poof! No more drug case."

"You realize that this is enough to get Darren a new trial, maybe even a dismissal?" Grace said.

"I do, and I'm sorry I didn't tell you about it sooner. Like I said, I worried about it and prayed about it so much that I thought I'd lose my mind. I finally was able to block it out, but lately, now that Street has escaped and has been all over the news, it's been on my mind again. And I'll tell you something else, Miss Alexander. I don't think Darren Street killed Jalen Jordan at all. I think Tipton did it, and I think Ben Clancy put him up to it so he could frame Street."

"Can you prove that?"

"No, ma'am. I can't. But that's what I think, for what it's worth."

"Would you be willing to sign a sworn statement repeating what you've just told me?"

"At this point, yes, ma'am, I would. It'll probably cost me my job, but I can't live with this kind of guilt any more. My daddy would be ashamed of me."

"Would you be willing to come into court and testify under oath?"

"Yes, ma'am."

"Do you have any idea where James Tipton is?"

"No, ma'am."

"Clancy and your boss are both going to call you a liar."

"Clancy asked me for a paper copy of my investigative files. I kept one for myself."

Grace had to restrain herself from yelling out loud. She wanted to get on the table and break into a dance. She wanted to wrap her arms around DuBose's neck and give him a huge hug. Instead, she picked her beer up off the table and held it up.

"To the truth," she said, and she clinked the bottle against DuBose's. "May it set Darren Street free."

CHAPTER FIFTY-FIVE

I awoke in a barn, tied to a chair, surrounded by three men, who all were wielding shotguns. My head was splitting. They came into focus slowly, like ships emerging from a fog. Mountain men. Rugged looking. Beards on two of them. All wearing billed caps. One wearing bib overalls. I thought I recognized him but wasn't sure.

We were in the middle of the barn with stalls on two sides of us. The place reeked of dung, and I could hear the snorts of some kind of animal nearby. More than one animal, actually, several animals. The light flickered, and as I looked around I saw oil lanterns hanging from support posts in three corners.

"He's awake," I heard a deep voice say.

The man in the overalls stepped in front of me, feet spread. I looked at his boots and gazed up until I met his eyes.

"Give me one reason I shouldn't blow a hole in you right now and bury you back in the woods," he said.

"I'm Darren Street," I said.

"Who?"

"Darren Street. I was James's lawyer a couple of years ago. I've seen you . . . at the party after his trial. I know who you are, but I'm sorry, I can't remember your name."

"That ain't what the driver's license and paperwork we found in the trunk of your car says. It says your name is William Hickman. And Darren Street didn't have no blond hair."

"I'm him. I'm Darren Street; I swear it," I said.

"What are you doing coming up here at night with a gun?"

"I escaped from a prison in California five days ago. You've probably heard about it. Hell, everybody's heard about it by now. I just got back to Knoxville. The people who helped me get out of prison left me the car, the gun, the clothes, the money, the identification, everything. They left it for me in the trunk of the car so I could—"

"So you could what? Come up here and kill James because he testified against you?"

"No. No, I don't want to kill him. I just want to talk to him. I was hoping . . . I was hoping Granny might tell me where he is. I went by his house, but I saw it had burned down. So I came up here hoping to talk to Granny."

The other two men walked over and squatted in front of me. Both of them stared at me for a long time. One spit a stream of tobacco juice onto my pant leg.

"He's lying," the tobacco spitter said. "It might be him. It might be the lawyer, but I say he came here to kill James and anybody else he could get to."

"I didn't come here to kill anyone," I said. "Listen, the last thing I want is for James to be dead. I need him to clear my name. I need him to tell me why he came to court and lied about me. I need him to—"

"Shut your mouth," the man in the bib overalls said. "It's him. Now that I can see his eyes good I know it's him. Ronnie, walk down to the house and get Granny. Bring her on up here and we'll figure out what to do with him."

Ronnie snorted like one of the pigs and stalked out of the barn. The other man backed off into the shadows. I racked my brain trying to remember bib overalls's name, and finally, it came to me.

"You're Eugene," I said. "I remember now, at the party, you called yourself Eugene the dancing machine. Had a nice wife named . . . let's see . . . Sherry, right? And a pretty little dark-haired girl named Dorothy, but you called her Dot."

"You ain't sweet-talking your way out of nothing, Counselor," Eugene said. "Might as well shut it until Granny gets here. She'll be the one to decide what happens to you."

"So Granny's the shot caller on this yard?"

"What's that?"

"Never mind."

We sat in silence for nearly ten minutes. It was unnerving, sitting bound to an old wooden chair that was probably used to milk cows, the light flickering, the hogs rooting and snorting, and two men—one who was James's brother and another I didn't know—lurking ominously. Finally, I heard footsteps and looked toward the door that Ronnie had exited through earlier. Granny walked in first, wearing a pair of black sweat pants and an oversize, light-blue denim shirt. She had a white cotton scarf wrapped around her head in a Windsor style that covered her hair. She walked into the barn and stood a few feet in front of me. The brown eyes that had looked upon me fondly in the past were now hard and emotionless. There was no compassion. Her face gave away nothing. She reminded me of so many of the judges I'd seen in the past, about to pass sentence.

"I'm sorry to see you here like this, Darren," she said.

"It's good to see you again, Granny Tipton," I said. "I apologize for the circumstances."

"Ronnie tells me you came here to see James."

"Yes, ma'am. I need his help."

"You realize you're the one who is ultimately responsible for everything, don't you? If you hadn't come to James's house and asked him to commit a killing for you and then bought a gun from him, none of this would have happened."

I shook my head. "I didn't buy a gun from him, Granny Tipton. I admit I asked him to kill Jalen Jordan and that was wrong. I've thought about it a million times over the past two years. I wish I could change it. I wish I could—"

"And now you bring more trouble to my home. You escape from prison, and you come here."

"I didn't know where else to go. I didn't know what else to do. I thought if . . . I thought if—"

"You thought if James would just tell you he killed that boy, then you could run to the judge and tell him who really did it and James could go on to prison in your place. Is that what you thought? Are you really that naïve?"

"Is that what happened? Did James kill him?"

"James didn't kill anybody," she said. "Eugene, maybe we should just call the sheriff and tell him we have an escaped prisoner on our property."

"No!" I yelled. I began to strain against the ropes. "No! Just kill me, please! Shoot me in the head, but don't send me back. Don't send me back. I'd rather be dead."

"I don't want your death on my conscience," Granny said. "You've already caused me enough pain."

"What have I done to you?"

"You put my grandson in harm's way."

"I called it off the next morning, and if James has told you the truth, you already know that. I admit I made a mistake by going to him in the first place, but my son's life had been threatened twice, I was terrified, and he was the first person I thought of to ask for help. But I realized I made a mistake and I went back. I told him not to do it and I let him keep the money. I'm sorry for that. I'm sorry for it every day of my life. But everything he said in court was a lie. I didn't buy a gun from him. I didn't stalk Jalen Jordan and shoot him down on a trail in the woods.

I didn't do it. And now I'm supposed to spend the rest of my life in prison? I'll tell you what. You don't want my death on your conscience? You don't want to kill me? Fine. Just lay the gun that was in the trunk of my car down right over there. Cut these ropes and walk out the door. I'll walk over to that pig stall, climb in, and shoot myself. The pigs will clean me up. You won't have to do a damned thing."

Just then, I heard the sound of a vehicle, probably a four-wheeler, pulling up outside. A few seconds later, a man wearing a hoodie walked in. He took a few steps inside the door and pulled the hood off his head.

It was James, or at least I thought it was James. He'd gained at least thirty pounds since the last time I'd seen him and was now nearly bald on top of his head. He stood there looking at me with his hands in the pockets of his hoodie. Finally, after all that time, there he was, in the flesh. There were a million things I wanted to say to him, but only one word came out.

"Why?" I said.

He didn't answer. He was looking at the floor.

"Please," I said. "Was it Clancy?"

At the sound of the name, he looked me in the eye, and I knew I was right.

"What did he do? Tell me, James. Tell me why I've been in hell for the past two years."

He looked unsure of himself. His eyes began to dart around the room from his granny to his brothers and back to me.

"I didn't buy a rifle from you and you know it, and I came and called the whole thing off," I said. "You know I'm telling the truth, James. I've been in prison for almost two years for something I didn't do, and I think I deserve an explanation. If you want to kill me after you tell me why you did this to me, then go ahead. But tell me why you lied."

"I let myself get deep into the drugs," he said quietly. "I'm off now, but back then, I'd let it get away from me. Granny, Eugene, Ronnie . . . I ain't ever told y'all any of this. I lied about everything. But Darren's been doing time for something I was forced to do by Clancy."

He took a couple of steps closer to me and drew a deep breath.

"When Darren came and asked me to kill that boy, I'd already been freelancing. I don't know why, exactly. I guess I just got greedy. I was buying up extra oxycodone out of Florida and paying some boys to haul it up to Eastern Kentucky where I'd found a distributor I could count on. Somebody up there got caught and eventually ratted me out to the feds. This agent named DuBose came to see me one night and told me they were about to indict me. Wanted me to give up our operation here, my suppliers in Florida, plus what I was doing in Kentucky. I told him to go straight to hell, but I was scared shitless. He said I was looking at thirty years and eventually he'd get to all of y'all. I didn't think he'd really get to any of you because he didn't offer any details, and I knew how we'd been doing business all this time, but I wasn't sure. And I was afraid he might be telling the truth about me. I was afraid he might really be able to get to me because of the rats in Kentucky."

James went on to recount the tale of the night I went to see him and how I hired him and then came back and called it off. He said he betrayed me because he was high and because he was frightened, and then he told a long tale of how Clancy had used him to set me up. As he was speaking, I thought back about the time leading up to the killing, about my conversation with Jordan, about the underwear in the van. About Clancy. The devious son of a bitch. I'd been right all along. It was him.

"Jalen Jordan had been stopped by the Knoxville police four days before he was shot," I said when James finally broke for a second. "They found a bag in the van he was driving that had two pairs of underwear in it. The underwear belonged to those two little boys who were found dead out at The Sinks. The FBI was probably watching every move he made. They would have been talking to Clancy."

"He mentioned that Jordan was a child killer, same as you did," James said. "But it wasn't until after I did it, after I killed Jordan, that

I found out exactly what Clancy was up to. I mean, I knew he hated you and he'd mentioned he wanted to get back at you, but he hadn't really spelled it out. We met that night and he told me the whole plan, how we were going to pin the whole thing on you. The story about me buying the gun, the deer stand in your garage, the fingerprints on the money, the whole thing. And he did it, too."

He looked at me and shook his head.

"You damned sure made it easy enough for him," he said. "Running around doing all that crazy shit you did."

"Fuck you, James," I said. "Like you said a minute ago, I've been doing your time. I'VE BEEN DOING YOUR TIME! IN A FUCKING FEDERAL MAX PRISON!"

I yelled so loudly that Eugene, who was closest to me, flinched and raised his shotgun.

"I'm sorry, Darren," James said. "I didn't mean for it to turn out the way it did."

"FUCK YOU AND YOUR APOLOGY! TAKE IT AND SHOVE IT UP YOUR ASS! GO AND TELL MY LITTLE BOY HOW SORRY YOU ARE! GO TELL MY MOTHER, YOU FUCKING COWARD!"

I started leaning from side to side in the chair, pulling it forward a bit at a time in an effort to get at him. He started backing away, and I spit at him. The next thing I knew, a boot caught me flush across the mouth and I went over onto my back. I lay there stunned for a second, but then I rolled onto my side and was trying to get to my feet when the butt of a shotgun cracked me in the jaw and I went down again. I laid there on the dirt floor of the barn for a couple of minutes, maybe more, and gradually, from deep inside me, a pitiful moan began to rise. The moan crescendoed into a primordial scream, and I writhed on the floor and screamed until my lungs failed me. Finally, I managed to get back to my knees. I'd loosened the ropes that were holding me enough to be able to semistraighten my back, and I looked up at James again.

"Do you know what the most important thing a man can gain in prison is?" I said through the blood that was oozing from the cut inside my mouth. "Respect. Without respect, you're either dead or somebody's bitch. I have no respect for you, James, and your family shouldn't, either. Because you're nothing but Clancy's bitch, and if you don't do something about him, that's all you're ever going to be."

"I've heard about enough of this boy's bullshit," one of the brothers growled, and suddenly all three of the men in the barn were pointing their shotguns at me. I heard the hammers cock and waited for the glorious death that was about to come.

"Wait," James said. "Wait. Don't kill him."

"Appears to me like it's him or you," Eugene said. "You want to go to prison?"

I looked alternately from the brothers to Granny, wondering what was to come next, hoping they would just go ahead and end it. These were mountain people, bound by blood. If a choice was to be made between one of their own and me, I knew I didn't stand a chance, but I honestly didn't care at that point. Granny, who had stood silently for a long time, finally spoke.

"Cut him loose," she said to Eugene.

The shotguns were lowered, Eugene produced a knife from his pocket, popped open the blade, and a second later I was free. I stood uneasily, my head still aching, my nose and jaw throbbing from the blows I'd received earlier.

"You need to be on your way, Darren," Granny said.

"What? On my way? To where?"

"You're on the run. Keep running."

"I'm not running, Granny. We're back to square one. Just leave me a gun and walk outside. It'll be over in just a minute."

"I can't abide sending James off to prison," she said, "even after hearing what he did."

"The only other option is to go to court," I said. "I have a good lawyer. I'll help James find a lawyer of his own. Maybe we can make a deal. If we can prove what Clancy did, James might still be able to walk away from this."

"We don't rely on the law," she said. "We rely on ourselves."

"You relied on it once. You relied on me. You trusted me. I'm not even sure I can ask you this in good conscience after what I've been through, but would you be willing to trust in the law one more time? The system can be skewed by people like Ben Clancy, but for the most part, it works."

"You can't promise anything," Granny said. "You can't guarantee one single thing."

"That's true. I can't guarantee anything, but—"

"Like I said a while ago, I was high through a lot of what happened back then, but I did manage to do something that might help," James said.

"Please," I said hopefully. "Tell me you have recordings."

"I've got something better in a safety deposit box," he said.

"What is it?"

"A pair of shoes."

CHAPTER FIFTY-SIX

I got Grace on the phone by telling the secretary I was a legendary professor from the University of Tennessee Law School named Payne. Grace and I had both attended UT, and anyone who went through that place had heard of Dale Payne. She picked up immediately.

"Professor Payne? It's Grace Alexander. So nice to hear from you."

"Hello, Miss Alexander," I said.

Silence.

"Miss Alexander?"

"Just a moment, professor."

I heard the phone drop onto a desk, heard the sound of heels on hardwood, and heard a door close. More footsteps.

"Darren?" she said in a high-pitched whisper. "Oh my God, Darren? What are you . . . where are you . . . are you *all right*?"

"I'm fine, Grace. I'm not going to tell you exactly where I am, but I'm close."

"You broke out of a federal prison! In a helicopter! You've embarrassed the United States Bureau of Prisons and the Department of Justice. Every US Marshal and FBI agent in the country is looking for you, not to mention every state trooper, city cop, sheriff's deputy, and wannabe cop with a carry permit. Do you know the president of the United States mentioned you at a press conference the other day?"

"Really? The president? I'm flattered."

"Flattered? Are you crazy? Have you gone completely insane? They're going to shoot you on sight. Your face has been flashed so many times in Knoxville, it's burned into the memory of every man, woman, and child in the city. They're saying you should be considered armed and dangerous. If you come anywhere near here, you're going to wind up dead, and there won't be a thing I or anyone else can do about it."

"I found James Tipton."

There was a pause as Grace processed the tidbit.

"You found him? Where?"

"They don't record your phone calls there, do they?"

"No," Grace said. "We're defense lawyers. I mean, we have a way to record if we want to, but as far as some Big Brother thing, no. I would be incredibly surprised."

"That's comforting."

"Is he alive?" she said.

"Tipton? Yes, and he has something you need to see. I know it's a lot to ask, but you need to come out and meet me, Grace. What Tipton has could change everything for me."

"Where?"

"Give me your cell number."

It occurred to me that I'd known Grace for more than two years, had had dozens of conversations with her, felt genuinely close to her—in fact, I was fairly certain I was in love with her—and I didn't even know her cell phone number. How rare was that in the twenty-first century?

"You're on a secure phone, I assume," she said.

"As secure as it gets in this day and age. This is the only time I'm going to use it. As soon as I hang up, I'm destroying it."

She gave me the number, and I wrote it down on a pad Granny had given me.

"So I have your number," I said. "Does this mean we're official? How does it work now? Are we talking? Dating? In a relationship?"

"I can't believe you're being so flippant. My chest is about to explode."

"Drive to Gatlinburg and make sure you aren't followed. When can you be there?"

"I have a couple of things to do here. Give me two hours."

"Eleven o'clock, then?"

"Will I be breaking a bunch of federal laws by meeting you? Shit, never mind. I don't even care. Eleven o'clock will work."

"What will you be driving?"

"A blue Ford Fusion hybrid."

"Figures. I'm going to call you again at eleven. Be in the parking lot at the Space Needle."

"I'll be there."

* * *

Grace's cell phone rang at precisely eleven o'clock. She looked down at the caller ID and it was blocked. It had to be him. Her heart started racing again and her finger trembled as she pushed the button to answer. What could he possibly have discovered? And why did the prospect of seeing Darren making her tremble?

"Hello?"

"Don't freak out." It was Darren's voice. "In about thirty seconds, an old black Jeep is going to pull up right next to your door. Driving that Jeep is going to be a very scary looking guy named Eugene. As soon as he pulls up, just get out of your car and get in the Jeep."

"Are you with him?"

"No, but I'm not far away. One of Eugene's brothers and I are in another vehicle. We're going to—"

"Oh my God, he's here."

"Get in the Jeep. Don't be afraid."

"Don't be afraid? I'm about to pee on myself, Darren."

"Are you getting in the Jeep?"

"Yes."

Grace climbed into the Jeep and found herself staring into the gleaming blue eyes of one of the fiercest-looking men she'd ever seen. He nodded at her, gunned the accelerator, and they pulled out of the parking lot.

"We're on the road," Grace said.

"You're about to go into the mountains. It's about a half-hour drive to where you're going. I'm behind you. Like I started to say a second ago, we're going to make sure nobody is following you."

"Okay."

"I'll see you soon, Grace. I can't believe I'm really saying that, but I'll see you soon."

The idea of seeing Darren outside a jail cell or courtroom was almost unnerving. She'd come to admire his strength and courage during the time they'd known each other and she'd developed a strong affection for him, but she hadn't really given a real relationship any thought because of Darren's situation. He'd been in prison every day since she'd known him, and she hadn't allowed herself to believe he'd ever get out. Now he was a fugitive, a wanted man on the run. Grace wondered again what Tipton would have to offer. It would have to be something explosive, something that would practically knock the socks off a federal judge. Otherwise, Darren would be headed straight back to prison, if they didn't kill him first.

The man named Eugene was silent as they wound through forest and mountain laurels, beside creeks and up steep inclines. The road was full of switchbacks. After twenty minutes of steady climbing, the asphalt ended and the road became gravel. Eventually, the road ended and they pulled onto what appeared to be a driveway of clay and chat.

"Are we close?" Grace said uncertainly, wondering whether the driver would answer.

"This is our land," Eugene said. "Two hundred acres. Been in our family for a hundred years. My granny owns the biggest share of it now. Me and my two brothers own equal shares of the rest."

"What about your parents?"

"Gone. Both of them."

"I'm sorry," Grace said as the Jeep bumped along. "Are you farmers?"

Grace saw Eugene's head turn toward her out of the corner of her eye, and she looked at him. He turned his face back toward the road again and smiled.

"Among other things," he said.

At the end of the driveway was a clearing, and in the clearing were three homes arranged in a triangle. Two of them were large log cabins and the other was a white-frame house. There was a large barn behind the house, a split-rail fence, and a couple of outbuildings, one of which Grace recognized as a smokehouse. Grace had expected redneck poverty, but this place was actually quite beautiful.

As Eugene parked the Jeep and shut off the engine, she looked up to see a white-haired woman standing on the front porch of the house.

"Is that your grandmother?" she said.

"That's her. C'mon."

"Where's Darren?"

"He'll be along directly."

Grace and Eugene walked onto the porch. The woman nodded and said, "I'm Luanne Tipton. Welcome to my home."

"Grace Alexander. Thank you. I assume you're related to James Tipton?"

"He's my grandson."

"Is he here?"

"He's inside. You'll meet him in a minute."

Grace had never felt quite like she did in that moment. There was incredible anticipation, both in seeing Darren and in finding out what

Tipton had to say. Was he ready to recant? Would he be able to provide some kind of corroboration if he was?

Grace heard an engine and looked down the driveway. A red pickup was coming. It pulled up next to the Jeep and Darren climbed out of the passenger side. Before she realized what she was doing, Grace was down the steps and running across the front yard. She jumped into Darren's arms, buried her face in his neck, and felt his arms wrap around her.

"I can't believe you're here," she said. "I was afraid I might never see you again."

His arms tightened even more, and he lifted her from the ground.

"You're the most beautiful thing I've ever seen in my life," Darren said.

They held each other for a full minute before Darren set her back on the ground and loosened his grip. She stepped back and looked at him.

"You're blond," she said.

"Yeah, like it?"

"Not really." She looked at his swollen nose and jaw. "What happened to your face? What is it with you? Every time I see you, you look like somebody's beaten the crap out of you."

"Doesn't matter," he said. "Come on, let's go inside. James is in there, and he has a hell of a story to tell you."

CHAPTER FIFTY-SEVEN

Grace had been through mock trials in law school, plea negotiations in the real world, and jury trials in federal court, but she'd never been through anything like this. She'd called and insisted on a meeting with United States Attorney Stephen Blackburn and, after a half hour of wrangling, had finally been granted an audience.

But she hadn't expected Ben Clancy to be there.

It was the morning after she'd gone to the Tipton farm and talked with James and Darren. What she'd seen and heard had made her stomach turn. To think that a man of Ben Clancy's power and position would use it for such evil purposes shook her faith in the justice system, a system she had believed in fervently when she first came out of law school. She had a copy of the file Gary DuBose had given to her sitting on her lap, along with a copy of a flash drive James Tipton had provided.

James had told Grace that after he'd killed Jalen Jordan, he knew he was doomed. Yet even in his drug-addled state, he had tried desperately to figure out some way to get some leverage over Clancy on the slim chance he would ever be able to actually use it. Clancy had contacted him immediately after Darren Street was arrested, and the coaching had begun. Clancy always patted him down carefully and inspected him closely, but James had noticed early that Clancy never looked at his shoes. He'd gone online and found a $300 pair of shoes that looked, for all the world, like an ordinary pair of running shoes. He wore them every time he met Clancy. In the tongue of one of the shoes was a digital camera with audio capability, and in the tongue of the other was a tiny transmitter that sent a signal through a Bluetooth connection to a receiver in James's laptop in the trunk of his Dodge Charger, which was always nearby since Clancy always wanted to meet in some hastily arranged fashion.

The quality of the video was poor because the angles were always odd and the audio wasn't great, but the shoes had served their purpose. Each time he met Clancy, immediately following the visit, James would check to make sure he'd captured the meeting, then he would burn copies onto flash drives and compact discs and take them to his bank, where he had a safety deposit box. He'd also buried copies of the drives and discs in the barrels where his cash was hidden.

Grace had given backup copies to her boss in the federal defender's office, an intelligent but timid fifty-year-old bureaucrat named Roy Seaton. Seaton had listened to what she had to say, briefly glanced at the paper evidence she'd gathered, shaken his head when she asked whether he wanted to watch the video, and politely declined her invitation to accompany her to the US Attorney's Office.

"Let me know how it turns out," Seaton had said.

Now Grace sat alone in a room with two men thirty years her senior, men she knew to be close friends, both veterans of legal and political wars. Blackburn was behind his massive desk and Clancy was sitting to her left. They looked like clones in their navy-blue suits, white shirts, and red-white-and-blue-striped ties. When she'd first walked into the room she'd been intimidated. She'd felt her hands begin to tremble slightly and had briefly considered telling Blackburn she was feeling ill and would like to reschedule, but then she'd forced herself to look hard

Scott Pratt

at Ben Clancy and the slow burn had begun. She was a lawyer. Her job
was to stand up to people like Clancy. She thought about Darren and
the innumerable humiliations he'd faced, the beatings he'd taken, the
immeasurable losses he'd endured.

"I was hoping we could speak privately," Grace said to Blackburn.

"You said this was about Darren Street," Blackburn said. "Anything
that concerns Darren Street concerns Ben. Do you know where he is?"

"No," Grace said. She turned her head toward Clancy. "But I know
where James Tipton is."

Clancy's flinch was barely perceptible.

"Who?" Blackburn said. "James Tipton? Who is James Tipton?"

"He was Mr. Clancy's star witness against Darren Street."

"So you know where he is," Blackburn said. "Is that supposed to
mean something? How is that important?"

"Mr. Clancy blackmailed him into killing Jalen Jordan, the man
Darren was convicted of killing, and then lying at the trial. Every bit
of Tipton's testimony was a lie, and every bit of it was coached by Mr.
Clancy. But that wasn't enough. After the trial was over and Darren
had been convicted, Mr. Clancy had him sent on a long diesel therapy
session. You're familiar with diesel therapy, I assume?"

"My understanding is that diesel therapy is more of a legend than
anything else," Blackburn said.

"Oh, no, it's very real," Grace said. "Isn't it, Mr. Clancy?"

"I have no idea," Clancy said.

"He didn't stop there," Grace said. "According to James Tipton, Mr.
Clancy tried to kill him, I suppose to clean up loose ends. Then he
burned Tipton's home to the ground."

Blackburn's eyebrows raised, but a burst of laughter came from Clancy.

"These are the most outrageous things I've ever heard," Clancy
said. "I've been accused of a lot during my years as a prosecutor, Miss
Alexander, but this takes the cake. I'm hearing conspiracy to commit
murder, subornation of perjury, attempted murder, and arson. Please

tell me you haven't come in here making these accusations without some kind of proof."

Grace refused to respond to him.

"Mr. Clancy also made a drug case against Mr. Tipton disappear," Grace said to Blackburn. "My understanding is that all of the digital records of the case have been deleted, but I have this."

Grace leaned forward and set the file Gary DuBose had given her in front of Blackburn. He picked it up, thumbed through it for a couple of minutes, and closed it. He looked at Clancy.

"Well?" he said.

"Where did you allegedly get whatever it is you just gave to Stephen?" Clancy said to Grace, who again refused to respond directly to him.

"The file was provided to me by a DEA agent who is as appalled as I am, and as everyone else will be, by what Mr. Clancy did," Grace said to Blackburn. "When I asked Mr. Clancy's witness in court whether he had been offered anything by the government in exchange for his testimony, the witness said no. That in itself is enough to get Darren Street a new trial. Mr. Clancy, of course, knew he was committing perjury. As a matter of fact, Mr. Clancy was the one who went to the DEA supervisor and convinced him to make Mr. Tipton's drug case disappear from the computer."

"Who is the agent?" Clancy said.

"Be quiet, Ben," Blackburn said. "Do you have anything else, Miss Alexander?"

Grace reached into the pocket of the jacket she was wearing and produced a flash drive. She opened her briefcase and removed her laptop, turned it on, and inserted the device.

"I'm just going to show you a few examples," she said. "There are hours and hours of video and audio on this drive. I'll leave it with you. I have plenty of copies."

Grace began showing snippets—a sort of highlight film she'd put together the previous night—of the video and audio for Blackburn and

Clancy. She would hear the occasional snort and chuckle from Clancy, but Blackburn watched intently and without comment. After about twenty minutes, Blackburn raised his hand and said, "That's enough." He looked at Clancy and said, "Ben, thank you for your time. Miss Alexander and I will take it from here."

"But she's making unsubstantiated allegations against me," Clancy said. "She's assassinating my character. I'm entitled to defend myself."

"She isn't the first person to come to me with concerns about the way you conducted yourself on this case," Blackburn said. "Now, for the last time, get up and leave the room."

Grace breathed a sigh of relief as Clancy closed the door behind him.

"What do you want, Miss Alexander?" Blackburn said.

Grace looked at him curiously. "What do I want? I'm not sure what you mean."

"You've obviously come here to make some kind of deal," Blackburn said. "I'm asking you what you want. What are your terms, your objectives?"

"I think it's pretty obvious," Grace said. "He needs to go straight to prison."

"Not going to happen," Blackburn said.

"I beg your pardon?"

"Ben Clancy isn't going to prison. You can remove that from your list before we go another step."

"But why? How can you . . . after what I've just shown you, how could you possibly—"

"What you just showed me were some papers that could easily and simply have been made up. They don't prove a thing, and I can promise you won't get any corroboration from anyone in the DEA."

"But they made a case disappear. There will be a supervisor, other agents."

"No, Miss Alexander, there won't. Do you know what happens to whistle-blowers in the federal system? Especially in law enforcement? They're turned into outcasts, they're sent to Boise and assigned to minutiae, or they're investigated closely and charged with crimes themselves.

They don't become heroes. The agent who decided to provide you with this file made a mistake in judgment. I don't know who he is, but I could find out very easily. I'm willing to forgive his indiscretion, however, provided you're willing to be reasonable."

"I'll go straight to the press," Grace said.

"Ah, yes, take it to the tattletales. The whiny voyeurs. All you'd accomplish would be to embarrass yourself. This paper file? Forged. Made up by a troubled agent looking for some kind of validation. Not a scrap of corroboration. At best, you might get some congressional committee to appoint a former FBI assistant director or a retired US attorney to conduct an independent investigation, which will ultimately, two or three years down the road, conclude that there isn't enough proof to take any meaningful action. In the meantime, your client, Mr. Street, will most likely be caught or killed. And your video? You have nothing that was taped prior to Jalen Jordan's murder. You have images and recordings of very poor quality that may or may not be Ben Clancy talking about a case he is prosecuting. Even if I was willing to agree that it's Ben on those recordings—and I'm not—prosecutors talk to their witnesses all the time, just like defense lawyers talk to their witnesses all the time."

Grace began to pack up her things. The smugness, the arrogance that was being displayed was making her angrier by the second.

"You still haven't answered my question, Miss Alexander," Blackburn said.

"What question?" Grace said through clenched teeth.

"What . . . do . . . you . . . want? Within reason, and without Mr. Clancy going to prison. I'm the United States attorney for the Eastern District of Tennessee. I was appointed to this office by the president of the Unites States. I simply will not allow you to bring disgrace upon me and everyone else in this office. I will not allow you to make us all look like fools by agreeing to sacrifice one of my assistants, especially one who has been a friend for most of my life."

"I can't believe you'd allow him to continue to—"

"He won't be continuing. Today will be his last day on the job if you and I can come to some kind of agreement. He will retire. Ben Clancy has been, for the most part, an effective and passionate prosecutor, although I admit he has, on occasion, become overzealous."

"Overzealous? He orchestrated a murder and pinned it on Darren Street. That's a bit beyond overzealous, don't you think?"

"Again, what do you want?"

"I want the jury's verdict vacated in Darren Street's case immediately and I want him declared not guilty. I'm sure an escape charge has been filed against him in the district court in California, and I want that dropped. I want Darren to be able to get his life back, the life Ben Clancy took from him. I want a guarantee, in writing, that James Tipton will not face any criminal charges for killing Jalen Jordan, or for anything else. He gets blanket immunity."

"I can't put it in writing, but I'll give you my word," Blackburn said. "Tipton won't be bothered."

"And Darren Street?"

"Done," Blackburn said.

Grace felt her jaw drop.

"Done? Just like that?"

"Just like that."

"How can you do it?" Grace said. "I mean, without the press knowing. Can you sell it to a judge?"

"Like Ben Clancy, Judge Geer happens to be an old and dear friend. I'll stop by his house this evening. When we go into open court, after the judgment is entered and Mr. Street is officially declared not guilty, I'll request the files be sealed due to the sensitive nature of the ongoing investigation. Nobody will really care that Jalen Jordan's killer might still be walking around, so I don't expect there to be a huge uproar, and even if there is, I'll refuse to talk to anyone in the press. It will blow over quickly."

"And you'll call off the dogs at the Marshals' and the FBI so Darren doesn't get killed before we get it done?"

Blackburn nodded.

"So do we have a deal, Miss Alexander?" Blackburn said. "Your client goes free and James Tipton gets a free pass on a murder that he may or may not have committed."

"And Clancy never sets foot in a courtroom again," Grace said.

"And Ben retires, effective immediately. He'll still have a law license. Nothing I can do to keep him from practicing if he wants to. I'm assuming you can produce Mr. Street?"

"I know how to get in touch with him."

"Have him in Judge Geer's courtroom at eight thirty in the morning, and if anyone from the press shows up, I'll know it was you who called them."

"I won't talk to them," Grace said, "and I'm sure Darren will feel the same way."

"If he doesn't, it will definitely be a problem, and now that I think about it, I'm going to protect myself just a bit. I'll ask the court to vacate the jury verdict and dismiss the murder charge with prejudice, but I'm going to keep my options open on the escape. I'll get the US attorney in California to ask the court there to dismiss the case, but not with prejudice. That way, if your client decides to start popping off to the press, he'll suddenly find himself doing ten years."

"I'm not going to let you hold him hostage," Grace said.

"Take it or leave it. You already know how I feel about taking a case against Ben to the grand jury. If you want to rely on the press to be your knight in shining armor, be my guest."

Grace looked at Blackburn closely, trying to read his face. She hadn't heard anything about Blackburn in her three years in the federal defender's office that would cause her to distrust him, but the compromise he was proposing was almost untenable. Clancy walk away scot free? From a murder? And besides, could she trust him?

On the other hand, she'd accomplished her primary goal, which was to set Darren free and get the escape charge dismissed. He could walk out of court tomorrow a free man. *To hell with Clancy,* she thought. *I'll take it.*

She set her briefcase on the floor, stood, took a step toward Blackburn's desk, and, as much as she hated the thought of touching him, stuck out her hand. Blackburn also stood. Their hands clasped.

"I don't know how you live with yourself," Grace said.

"I sleep quite well, Miss Alexander," Blackburn said. "I'll see you in the morning."

CHAPTER FIFTY-EIGHT

As soon as Ben Clancy saw Grace Alexander walk past his office, he was on his feet. He strode past Stephen Blackburn's secretary and burst into Blackburn's office without knocking.

"I've never been so humiliated in my life," Clancy said as he stood in front of Blackburn's desk. His heart was pounding, and he could feel heat in his cheeks.

"It could have been worse," Blackburn said calmly. "Sit down, Ben, and keep your mouth shut."

"How dare you speak to me in such a—"

"I said SIT DOWN AND SHUT YOUR MOUTH!"

Clancy was stunned by the tone. In all of the years he'd known Blackburn, he'd never heard him speak so harshly. Clancy slid slowly into the chair, wondering what was to come next.

"Dan Reid came to me the day after Jalen Jordan was shot—and after you'd accused him and his people of being involved—and told me he thought you were responsible. He couldn't prove it, of course, but he made a far more compelling argument than you did at the time. I let it go because I thought both of you were simply overreacting to the stress of the situation and because I couldn't allow myself to believe that I'd misjudged your character so badly."

"You haven't misjudged my—"

"I told you to be quiet, and I meant it. You're this close to being arrested for murder."

Clancy folded his arms and began rocking back and forth in the seat. He rolled his eyes, scoffing at the idea he might be arrested.

"After having seen and heard what I did a little while ago, I've come to the conclusion that you were directly responsible for the death of Jalen Jordan and that you knowingly and intentionally framed Darren Street. You conspired with James Tipton to commit murder, you instructed him to plant and manipulate evidence, you obstructed justice, you committed perjury, and you suborned perjury. You initiated and perpetrated a blatant fraud on the United States District Court, and you did it purely out of spite, because you hate Darren Street. And why do you hate Darren Street? Because he exposed you for doing the same kind of thing to his uncle. I've been a fool, Ben. You've played all of us for fools, but that stops today. I made a deal with Miss Alexander. Darren Street gets out, and so do you. You're out of here, Ben, as of this minute. I was thinking about allowing you to retire, but I've decided I'm not going to ask the taxpayers of the United States to keep you up after what you've done."

Clancy started to say something as Blackburn picked up his phone and punched in a few numbers, but Blackburn held up his hand.

"Marshal Cole?" Blackburn said. "Would you please send three of your people to Ben Clancy's office immediately to escort him out of the building? He's been fired."

Clancy leaned forward and extended his hands, palms up, as Blackburn set the phone down.

"Stephen, please," Clancy said. "We're old friends."

"Not anymore."

"But this will ruin me. My reputation . . . how will I make a living?"

"I don't care. Now get out before I change my mind and have you arrested."

Clancy stood. He could feel his cheeks warming, and his hands had involuntarily clenched into fists.

"You haven't heard the last of me," Clancy said. "I'll sue. I'll drag you into court."

"Be my guest," Blackburn said, just as the marshals walked through the door.

CHAPTER FIFTY-NINE

Ben Clancy looked over as his wife, Rose, finished her morning coffee, rinsed the cup in the kitchen sink, and loaded it into the dishwasher. He'd grown to hate the woman over the years, but right now he had other people to hate, primarily Stephen Blackburn.

"Ben," Rose said, "this is really bothering me. Why won't you tell me what happened at the office?"

"Nothing happened," Ben snapped.

"I tried to call Stephen Blackburn yesterday after you got home and he wouldn't speak to me. Maybe he was out of the office, but I didn't—"

Ben was in her face immediately.

"Don't ever call there again!" he yelled. "How dare you? I've never struck you, Rose, but I swear, if you continue to push me and nag me, I don't know what I might do."

"Go ahead and hit me," Rose said. "You'll very quickly find yourself in one of those jails you loved to fill with other people."

Clancy spun around and walked toward the garage. He was soon in his car, which he drove down the road a short ways. He turned left onto a dead end called Charlie's Cove, parked the car, got out, locked the door, and stuck the keys in his pocket. Charlie's Cove was about a half mile from his home on the Tennessee River. The morning was brisk and windy because a cold front had rolled in. The sun was not quite over the ridge to the east, and Clancy had dressed quickly and warmly in a jacket and a stocking cap. He carried a stick of hickory in his right hand and began walking.

The shock of what had happened the previous day was still fresh in his mind. The nerve of James Tipton. Shoes? Clancy had never remotely considered that Tipton might have the brains or ingenuity to pull off something so clever. But the videos had been of poor quality and the audio really didn't prove much. And Tipton was the real killer. So why was he, Clancy, being persecuted?

His tenure in the US Attorney's Office might be over, but Clancy wasn't finished. Not by a long shot. He would take a brief vacation and leave his carping wife at home. The South Carolina coast was always beautiful. He'd go there and think, consider his options.

Congress, he thought suddenly. *I'll run for a seat in the United States Congress and I'll win. The guy in office now is an idiot.*

Charlie's Cove dead-ended at a circular cul-de-sac, and it was just as he'd gone around the circle and was heading back in the opposite direction that Clancy first noticed the SUV coming slowly toward him. He encountered traffic on Charlie's Cove occasionally, but he could go days without seeing a vehicle. The vehicle rolled slowly by. It was black with windows tinted so darkly that Clancy couldn't see inside.

Clancy kept walking. The rush of the wind drowned out the sound of the van's engine, and within seconds, Clancy's mind had moved on to the organization he would have to build in order to make an effective run for Congress. Many of the pieces were already in place from the last campaign he ran when he was defeated by Mike Smith in the Knox County district attorney general's race. There were a few people he wouldn't ask to return, people he thought were ineffective and who had reacted slowly and stupidly to Darren Street's smear campaign.

The thought of Street made his blood pressure rise even more. Street, whom he'd convicted of murder, had escaped from a federal penitentiary and now he would be walking the streets a free man. Clancy shook his head. He should have found ways to kill both Street and Tipton.

But he'd be back. He had to make it back. Living well was the best revenge, and Clancy intended to live well. He'd served the taxpayers of the district his entire adult life. He saw no reason to stop now. Being elected to the US Congress would pay him nearly $200,000 a year, more than he made as a district attorney general and more than he made as an assistant US attorney. He snickered at the thought of being run out of governmental service only to return triumphantly with more power and at a higher salary.

Clancy saw a flash to his left and realized the SUV had pulled up next to him and stopped. The doors popped open and men with guns quickly surrounded him. Dan Reid, the special agent in charge of the Knoxville office, walked around the front of the car. He was smiling.

"You're under arrest, you miserable son of a bitch," Reid said as Clancy felt cold steel wrap around his wrists.

CHAPTER SIXTY

I'd barely slept in two nights. The first night, I was up with James and Grace all night while he was showing her his video and audio evidence. It was the second time I'd seen and heard Clancy scheming to frame me for murder, and it made my blood boil. The next night, after Grace had her meeting with Stephen Blackburn, I was so full of conflict I could barely close my eyes. On the one hand, the realization that my nightmare might be over was creeping into my consciousness, causing me to feel a cautious excitement. *Would I really be allowed to start over? Would I practice law again? Would I sleep in a regular bed and eat real food again? Would I hold my son in my arms?*

Or would I be locked up again as soon as I showed my face in court?

Granny had allowed me to stay in a small, spare bedroom at her house that was usually reserved for when one or more of her grandchildren wanted to sleep over. She'd fed me a breakfast of eggs, bacon, sausage, hash browns, and biscuits and gravy with coffee. It was the best food I'd tasted in years, but I'd eaten very little. At 7:00 a.m., I dialed my mother's number on the second of my three burn phones.

"Hello?" she said.

"It's me."

I heard her inhale and exhale deeply.

"I thought you . . . I thought you might be . . ."

"I'm fine, Mom. I'm not all that far away from you. Can you be at the federal courthouse at eight thirty?"

"I . . . I . . . why, Darren?"

"I'm going to turn myself in."

"Turn yourself in? Why did you escape in the first place? What the hell was going through your mind? Did you really think you could get away with it? Did you think you'd ride off into the sunset? Did you think you'd somehow miraculously prove yourself innocent and they'd let you go? Or were you hoping they'd kill you?"

"Calm down, Mom."

"Calm down? They're going to squash you again, Darren, and if you think I'm going to come to the courthouse and watch them do it, you've got another think coming!"

"They're going to let me go."

There was a long silence. I could envision her, standing or sitting in her kitchen with her forehead resting on her long fingers.

"What did you say?"

"They're going to let me go, Mom, at least that's what I think. Grace did it. I'll explain it to you afterward because what you're going to see and hear in the courtroom won't be the whole truth. Will you come? Please? I'm going to need a place to stay for a while."

She broke down. I could hear her crying at the other end of the phone and desperately wanted to wrap my arms around her.

"I'm sorry for everything I've put you through, Mom," I said.

She continued to cry, apparently unable to speak. Eventually she was able to squeak something that sounded like, "I'll be there," and the phone went dead.

* * *

Eugene gave me a ride down the mountain and dropped me off in downtown Knoxville, about five blocks from the courthouse. I was still wearing the bruises from the beating he'd given me, but I felt absolutely no animosity toward him.

"Thank you," I said as I climbed out of the Jeep.

"Good luck to you, Counselor," Eugene said, and he pulled away from the curb and drove off.

Grace and I met a block away and walked in the front door at 8:00 a.m. The two marshals who manned the metal detectors recognized me immediately. Both of them walked toward me as one produced a set of handcuffs. Both were pressing the buttons on their ear sets and talking quietly. I felt an urge to turn and run.

"Wait," Grace said as she stepped between them and me. "This is prearranged. The charges against him are going to be dismissed."

"But as of this moment, they're still pending and he's a fugitive," the taller of the two marshals said. "He's going to holding."

"Stop it!" Grace said. They were pulling my hands behind my back. She reached out and tried to pull one of them away. He held her off while they finished locking the cuffs.

"We didn't shoot him," the marshal said, "and we could have. We're just following orders. He walks in the door; he gets cuffed; he goes to lockup until the judge is ready for him. After that, we'll see."

They were pulling me away from the door by the elbows as two other marshals showed up and took their places on the door.

"It'll be fine, Darren," Grace was saying behind me. "Everything will be okay."

"You're one lucky sonofabitch," the marshal to my left said into my ear as we walked down the hall to an elevator.

"Yeah? How's that?"

"Break out of Rosewood in a helicopter and you're still alive a week later? Up until this morning, we've all had orders to shoot you on sight."

"Your idea of luck and mine are entirely different," I said. "Maybe someday you'll be fortunate enough to share in some of the luck I've experienced during the past two years."

We entered an elevator, and the guy on my left pushed a button.

"Are you busting my balls, inmate?" he said.

I decided to take a calculated risk. I didn't think they'd want to take me into the courtroom with any fresh bruises.

"Go fuck yourself, robot," I said.

The kidney punch drove me to my knees, and I decided to shut my mouth. His final gesture was to kick me in the ass so hard as I walked into the holding cell that I couldn't feel my left leg for twenty minutes. They left the cuffs on me.

When it came time for me to go into the courtroom, two different marshals accompanied me. Neither of them said a word during the walk. I didn't, either. When I walked into the courtroom, Grace was sitting at the defense table. She got up immediately and stepped to the lectern where the marshals led me. A man I recognized as US Attorney Stephen Blackburn was standing next to the prosecution table. There was a clerk sitting next to the judge's bench, my mother sitting in the gallery, and that was it. There was no one else. No lawyers milling around. No reporters. The two marshals who brought me in were standing against the wall, seemingly camouflaged by the woodwork. Grace put her hand on my forearm and patted it.

"Almost there," she said.

One of the marshals came off the wall long enough to announce that court was in session as Judge Donnie Geer walked in. Geer took his seat and peered down over his nose at me like I was an insect, an unsavory pest.

"Well, Mr. Street, you're back," he said.

"Yes, sir."

"Unusual circumstances this time."

"Pretty unusual circumstances last time, too," I said, and I felt Grace kick me in the ankle. She obviously wanted me to shut up.

"I understand the government has a motion in this case," the judge said.

"Yes, Your Honor," Blackburn said from my left. "New evidence has come to light in Mr. Street's case, evidence that leads me to believe beyond any doubt that Mr. Street did not commit the crime for which he was convicted. I cannot, unfortunately, comment on the exact nature of the evidence at this time because to do so would impede or, at the worst, entirely compromise an ongoing investigation. However, given the evidence, I also cannot, in good conscience, allow Mr. Street to remain in prison. Therefore, the government moves the court to vacate the jury's verdict against Mr. Street and enter a judgment of not guilty."

"I understand an escape charge was filed against him in the district court in California," the judge said "Is he to be remanded to custody to deal with that charge?"

"No, sir. I have here a copy of an order signed by a judge in the eastern district of California yesterday afternoon. The case is dismissed."

Blackburn passed a copy of the order to the clerk, who handed it to the judge.

"Very well, then," Judge Geer said. "Miss Alexander, do you have anything to say?"

"I thought the file was going to be sealed," Grace said.

"There really isn't any need," Blackburn said. "We arrested Ben Clancy this morning."

Grace's head jerked toward Blackburn, who looked at her and said, "I changed my mind. We'll let a jury sort it out."

"Thank you," Grace said. I could tell she was as stunned as I was. The first thing that went through my mind was Clancy having to squat and cough during a strip search. The bastard. He'd finally get a little of what he deserved.

"Mr. Street?" the judge said. "Anything you'd like to say?"

"No, sir."

"All right. Then upon motion of the government and there being no opposition from the defense, the court hereby vacates the jury's verdict in *The United States of America versus Darren Street.*"

"Would you please ask the marshals to remove his handcuffs?" Grace said.

The judge nodded toward the marshals, and one of them walked over and removed the cuffs. I rubbed my wrists and looked up at Geer, and a feeling of relief enveloped me like a lagoon of warm seawater. My vision suddenly became clearer, and Grace's perfume filled my nostrils. I felt light, like rice paper. If a gentle breeze had blown at that moment, it would have lifted me up and floated me out of the courtroom.

"I presided over your trial, as you know, Mr. Street," the judge said. "I heard all of the evidence, and from what I heard, the jury was justified in returning the verdict it did, so I don't think this court owes you an apology. I admit that signing Mr. Clancy's arrest warrant troubled me greatly, but seeing you released like this reaffirms my faith in what I believe to be the most effective system of criminal justice in the world. In the meantime, I wish you the best in your return to society. Do you plan to return to practicing law?"

"I'm not really sure," I said. "Maybe. Probably."

"Perhaps I'll see you again sometime, then. Mr. Street, you're free to go. Court is adjourned."

Suddenly, Grace, Mom, and I were the only people in the courtroom. We wrapped our arms around each other and stood near the bar. Tears were streaming freely and I was unashamed.

None of us could say a word.

CHAPTER SIXTY-ONE

I walked out of the courtroom that day a free man, but my life as I knew it had still been obliterated. It was as though I'd woken up from a coma that had lasted for more than two years; I had to start over from scratch. I had a little money stashed in the corporation my mother had helped me form when I was in prison, but I'd paid a substantial amount to Big Pappy Donovan and what I had left was barely enough to get by on. I had no job, no car, no house or apartment, so I immediately moved in with my mom, who was genuinely glad to have me but who had grown accustomed to living on her own. We worked it out, but not without some tense moments.

As soon as Katie read in the paper that I'd been released from prison, she had her lawyer file a petition in court to revoke my mother's visitation privileges with Sean. I filed my own petition asking for visitation rights. I represented myself and it took months, but I was finally able to get in front of a judge and Katie was forced to let me see my son. The visits for the first month were supervised by a worker from the Tennessee Department of Children's Services, but she very quickly figured out how much I loved Sean and how much he loved me, and the supervision ended. I get him every other weekend right now.

Katie demanded child support, of course, which I was more than happy to pay. I'm paying 21 percent of the approximately $500 a week I'm making as a freelance paralegal for several different lawyers in Knoxville. She gets $420 a month. I'm hoping to get joint custody of Sean as soon as I can afford my own place. I'm sure Katie knows it's coming, and I'm sure she'll fight me tooth and nail. She still lives in the nice home we bought when we were married, and from what I understand, her parents are helping her out a great deal. She's also still seeing her sugar daddy from Lexington. I hope he has a heart attack in the sack.

Initially, I sent an e-mail to the Tennessee Board of Professional Responsibility and asked them to reinstate me as an attorney since the jury's verdict had been vacated in my case. I was very quickly informed by those miserable, bureaucratic bastards that I had been disbarred because I was a "danger to the community," and the only way to have my license reinstated was to go through a long, drawn-out hearing process, during which a heavy burden of proof would be placed upon me to prove I was no longer dangerous. I told them to schedule the hearing. They said it would be six months, which is two months from now.

Grace and I are taking it slow, which, I believe, is a sign that I'm not as impetuous as I may have been in the past. She's a remarkable woman, and I remain convinced that I'm in love with her, but we went through such a turbulent time together that I want to be sure we can stick together without a war to fight, without a cause to champion. If it works out, and I have no reason to think it won't, then I could see us having a future together, maybe even working together. I'd like nothing better than to build a firm that would usurp Richie Fels's firm as the top group of criminal defense lawyers in the state of Tennessee.

Two weeks ago, Grace, my mom, and I made a trip up the mountain to spend an afternoon with the Tipton clan to celebrate Granny's seventy-fifth birthday. It wasn't my weekend with Sean, and even if it had been, I wouldn't have taken him. The Tiptons were, after all, alleged drug dealers. But those folks knew how to throw a party. They'd smoked chicken and ribs and had slow roasted a small pig and pulled the meat from it. There was also a large picnic table covered entirely in side dishes and desserts. The barbecue sauce they'd made for the meat was the best I'd ever tasted. All three grandsons were there along with wives and children and several close friends who I suspected were employees of the family drug business. A bluegrass band consisting of a guitarist, an upright bass player, a fiddler, and a banjo picker was set up on Granny's front porch. About fifteen minutes into their first set, they broke into a song called "Rollin' in my Sweet Baby's Arms," and I felt a tug on my arm.

"Let's dance," Grace said.

I'd never danced to mountain music, but I'd had a couple of beers and was feeling pretty good, so I said, "Okay."

I took her right hand in my left and wrapped my other hand around her waist, and we started gliding across the grass.

"You're a natural," Grace said. She was smiling widely, which I loved.

"My partner ain't bad, either," I said.

We danced around the yard for a few minutes with the sun on our faces and Grace's beautiful hair flying like a golden web. When the music stopped, she leaned in and kissed me on the cheek.

"Thank you," she said.

She did those sorts of things all the time. Simple things. A smile here, a wink and a nod there, a kiss on the cheek. And every time she did something like that, it gave me goose bumps.

We spent the afternoon eating, drinking, dancing, and playing. Along about seven thirty, as the sun was starting to drop behind the mountain ridges to the west, Granny, who had a white shawl wrapped around her shoulders, came up and placed her hand on my elbow.

"Do you have a minute for an old lady?" she said.

"I have all the time you need," I said.

"Walk with me."

She wrapped her right arm in my left and we wandered away from the others. Before I knew it, we were standing in back of the barn. Four hogs were on the other side of a stout wooden fence. When they saw Granny, they came over and began snorting and rooting.

"I wanted to tell you we're out of the business we used to be in," she said. "It was just too much trouble, too dangerous."

"That's good to hear, Granny. What are you guys going to do?"

She chuckled and her eyes flickered.

"We're going to make moonshine, but we're going to do it legal. Eugene has already gotten things pretty much set up. We're having a still shipped in from Canada, of all places. It should be here in a couple of weeks."

"Good luck with it," I said. "I hope it works out well."

"Can I ask your honest opinion about something?" Granny said.

"Absolutely."

"Do you think they'll be able to convict Ben Clancy?"

I'd given that a lot of thought, and I didn't like the government's prospects.

"It'll be tough," I said. "James has already testified in my trial, and you can believe Richie Fels will have the transcript. He's going to hammer James. It'll be, 'are you lying now or were you lying then?' James will have to admit he committed perjury during my trial, and Fels will use the admission to plant doubt in the jury's mind. Plus, James will have to admit that he pulled the trigger and that he isn't going to serve any time. I don't see the jury convicting him."

She was nodding slowly as I talked.

"That's what I thought," she said. "But the man tried to ruin James's life. I don't think he'll ever quite get over it. Forced him to kill a man, forced him to lie about it and help send you to prison, burned his home, and tried to kill him. That's an evil man."

"I agree with you about that. He's evil."

"Do you believe in karma?"

I pondered the question for a few seconds. "I'm not sure if I'd call it that, exactly, but I think there might be some kind of moral force in the universe that eventually balances things out. It takes a while sometimes, but eventually people seem to get what they deserve."

"I believe a person ought to get what he or she deserves," Granny said. "Sometimes it happens naturally, and sometimes . . . well, sometimes somebody has to help things along."

She moved closer to the fence and nodded toward the pigs.

"How much do you know about hogs?" she said.

"Not much. I'm a city boy."

"I'll tell you why I ask. You remember that night you came here after you got out of prison?"

"I don't know how I could ever forget it."

"You said something that night that made me curious. You asked us to leave you a gun. You said you'd climb in with the hogs and shoot yourself. You said they'd clean up the mess. What made you think a hog would eat a human?"

"I'm not really sure. I guess I've probably read it somewhere sometime. Maybe it's just some kind of urban legend."

She nodded and was quiet for a minute. "I've been around hogs all my life," she said. "I've helped butcher hundreds of them, maybe a thousand or more. They'll eat most anything, including a human. And if the jury doesn't convict him and they let him go, I might just see to it that Clancy winds up in this pig pen."

"I'm going to pretend I didn't hear that,' I said, and she gave me a coy smile. I had no doubt she was capable of killing Clancy, or having him killed. If Clancy wound up being acquitted and suddenly disappeared . . . I put the thought out of my mind.

We turned and walked back toward the party as the sun continued to drop behind the ridge to the west. The mountains were shimmering in the soft light, and I suddenly felt a sense of deep contentment. I'd made it through false accusation, humiliation, indignity, government-sponsored isolation and torture, beatings, and stab wounds. It had taken years, but the wheels of justice, which had nearly ground me to dust, had somehow been reversed and were trying, at least, to make things right. Clancy probably wouldn't be convicted, but he might. And in the meantime, he'd been denied bond and was sitting in the same county jail on the same max block where I'd awaited trial.

The fact that Clancy was in jail and I was out gave me a satisfying sense of redemption, but the contentment came from something much deeper. As I walked along with Granny and I spotted Grace and my mother standing together among the small crowd of people, it dawned on me how fortunate I was to have them and Sean and how much I wanted to serve them, to protect them, to help make their lives meaningful and enjoyable. When we got close to the group, I broke away from Granny and walked straight up to Grace. I wrapped my arms around her waist, lifted her off the ground, and began to turn slowly in a circle.

"Have I thanked you for everything you did for me, Grace?" I said. "I'm here today because of you."

She lifted her hands to my face and kissed me softly on the lips.

"You're here today because you're a survivor," she said. "And I'm glad to be along for the rest of the ride."

The rest of the ride. I had no idea what it would entail, but if it was to be anything like the ride I'd been on for the past couple of years, one thing was certain.

At least it wouldn't be boring.

ACKNOWLEDGMENTS

Thank you to Kjersti Egerdahl and the team at Thomas & Mercer for giving me this opportunity and helping me along the way. And thank you to Charlotte Herscher and Ivan Kenneally, who reminded me of the importance of top-notch editors.

ABOUT THE AUTHOR

Photo © 2015 Dwain Rowe

Scott Pratt's first novel, *An Innocent Client*—the first book in his Joe Dillard series—was chosen as a finalist for the Mystery Readers International's Macavity Award. Born in Michigan and raised in Tennessee, he earned a bachelor of arts degree in English from East Tennessee State University and a doctor of jurisprudence degree from the University of Tennessee. He is a veteran of the United States Air Force. He resides in northeast Tennessee with his wife, two dogs, and a parrot.